MOTHER'S MILK

A NOVEL BY
EDWARD ST. AUBYN

 OPEN CITY BOOKS

NEW YORK

Printed in the United States of America

Design by Nick Stone

Library of Congress Cataloging-in-Publication Data
St. Aubyn, Edward, 1960–
Mother's milk : a novel / by Edward St. Aubyn.
p.   cm.
ISBN 1-890447-40-4
1. Parent and adult child—Fiction. 2. Marital conflict—Fiction.
3. New Age movement—Fiction. 4. Mothers and sons—Fiction.
5. Disinheritance—Fiction. 6. Motherhood—Fiction.
7. England—Fiction. I. Title.
PR6069.T134M68 2006
813'.54   2005020312

OPEN CITY BOOKS
270 Lafayette Street
New York, NY 10012
www.opencity.org

First Edition
05 06 07 08 09   10 9 8 7 6 5 4 3 2 1

For Lucian

AUGUST 2000

1

Why had they pretended to kill him when he was born? Keeping him awake for days, banging his head again and again against a closed cervix; twisting the cord around his throat and throttling him; chomping through his mother's abdomen with cold shears; clamping his head and wrenching his neck from side to side; dragging him out of his home and hitting him; shining lights in his eyes and doing experiments; taking him away from his mother while she lay on the table, half-dead. Maybe the idea was to destroy his nostalgia for the old world. First the confinement to make him hungry for space, then pretending to kill him so that he would be grateful for the space when he got it, even this loud desert, with only the bandages of his mother's arms to wrap around him, never the whole thing again, the whole warm thing all around him, being everything.

The curtains were breathing light into their hospital room. Swelling from the hot afternoon, and then flopping back against the French windows, easing the glare outside.

Someone opened the door and the curtains leaped up and rippled their edges; loose paper rustled, the room whitened, and the shudder of the road works grew a little louder. Then the door clunked and the curtains sighed and the room dimmed.

"Oh, no, not more flowers," said his mother.

He could see everything through the transparent walls of his fish tank crib. He was looked over by the sticky eye of a splayed lily. Sometimes the breeze blew the peppery smell of freesias over him and he wanted to sneeze it away. On his mother's nightgown spots of blood mingled with streaks of dark-orange pollen.

"It's so nice of people…" she was laughing from weakness and frustration. "I mean, is there any room in the bath?"

"Not really, you've got the roses in there already and the other things."

"Oh, God, I can't bear it. Hundreds of flowers have been cut down and squeezed into these white vases, just to make us happy." She couldn't stop laughing. There were tears running down her face. "They should have been left where they were, in a garden somewhere."

The nurse looked at the chart.

"It's time for you to take your Voltarol," she said. "You've got to control the pain before it takes over."

Then the nurse looked at Robert and he locked on to her blue eyes in the heaving dimness.

"He's very alert. He's really checking me out."

"He is going to be all right, isn't he?" said his mother, suddenly terrified.

Suddenly Robert was terrified too. They were not together in the way they used to be, but they still had their helplessness in common. They had been washed up on a wild shore. Too tired to crawl up the beach, they could only loll in the roar and the dazzle of being there. He had to face facts though: they had been separated. He understood now that his mother had already been on the outside. For her this wild shore was a new role, for him it was a new world.

The strange thing was that he felt as if he had been there before. He had known there was an outside all along. He used to think it was a muffled watery world out there and that he lived at the heart of things. Now the walls had tumbled down and he could see what a muddle he had been in. How could he avoid getting in a new muddle in this hammeringly bright place? How could he kick and spin like he used to in this heavy atmosphere where the air stung his skin?

Yesterday he had thought he was dying. Perhaps he was right and this was what happened. Everything was open to question, except the fact that he was separated from his mother. Now that he realized there was a difference between them, he loved his mother with a new sharpness. He used to be close to her. Now he longed to be close to her. The first taste of longing was the saddest thing in the world.

"Oh, dear, what's wrong?" said the nurse. "Are we hungry, or do we just want a cuddle?"

The nurse lifted him out of the fish-tank crib, over the crevasse that separated it from the bed and delivered him into his mother's bruised arms.

"Try giving him a little time on the breast and then try to get some rest. You've both been through a lot in the last couple of days."

He was an inconsolable wreck. He couldn't live with so much doubt and so much intensity. He vomited colostrum over his mother and then in the hazy moment of emptiness that followed, he caught sight of the curtains bulging with light. They held his attention. That's how it worked here. They fascinated you with things to make you forget about the separation.

Still, he didn't want to exaggerate his decline. Things had been getting cramped in the old world. Toward the end he was desperate to get out, but he had imagined himself expanding back into the boundless ocean of his youth, not exiled in this harsh land. Perhaps he could revisit the ocean in his dreams, if it weren't for the veil of violence that hung between him and the past.

He was drifting into the syrupy borders of sleep, not knowing whether it would take him into the floating world, or back to the butchery of the birth room.

"Poor Baba, he was probably having a bad dream," said his mother, stroking him. His crying started to break up and fade.

She kissed him on the forehead and he realized that although they didn't share a body anymore, they still had the same thoughts and the same feelings. He shuddered with relief and stared at the curtains, watching the light flow.

He must have been asleep for a while, because his father had arrived and was already locked on to something. He couldn't stop talking.

"I looked at some more flats today and I can tell you, it's really depressing. London property is completely out of control. I'm leaning back toward plan C."

"What's plan C? I've forgotten."

"Stay where we are and squeeze another bedroom out of the kitchen. If we divide it in half, the broom cupboard becomes his toy cupboard and the bed goes where the fridge is."

"Where do the brooms go?"

"I don't know—somewhere."

"And the fridge?"

"It could go in the cupboard next to the washing machine."

"It won't fit."

"How do you know?"

"I just know."

"Anyway . . . we'll work it out. I'm just trying to be practical. Everything changes when you have a baby."

His father leaned closer, whispering "There's always Scotland."

He had come to be practical. He knew that his wife and son were drowning in a puddle of confusion and sensitivity and he was going to save them. Robert could feel what he was feeling.

"God, his hands are so tiny," said his father. "Just as well, really."

He raised Robert's hand with his little finger and kissed it. "Can I hold him?"

She lifted him toward his father. "Watch out for his neck, it's very floppy. You have to support it."

They all felt nervous.

"Like this?" His father's hand edged up his spine, took over from his mother, and slipped under Robert's head. Robert tried to keep calm. He didn't want his parents to get upset.

"Sort of. I don't really know either."

"Ahh . . . how come we're allowed to do this without a license? You can't have a dog or a television without a license. Maybe we can learn from the maternity nurse—what's her name?"

"Margaret."

"By the way, where is Margaret going to sleep on the night before we go to my mother's?"

"She says she's perfectly happy on the sofa."

"I wonder if the sofa feels the same way."

"Don't be mean, she's on a 'chemical diet.'"

"How exciting. I hadn't seen her in that light."

"She's had a lot of experience."

"Haven't we all?"

"With babies."

"Oh, babies." His father scraped Robert's cheek with his stubble and made a kissing sound in his ear.

"But we adore him," said his mother, her eyes swimming with tears. "Isn't that enough?"

"Being adored by two trainee parents with inadequate housing? Thank goodness he's got the backup of one grandmother who's on permanent holiday, and another who's too busy saving the planet to be entirely pleased by this additional strain on its resources. My mother's house is already too full of shamanic rattles and 'power animals' and 'inner children' to accommodate anything as grown-up as a child."

"We'll be all right," said his mother. "We're not children anymore, we're parents."

"We're both," said his father, "that's the trouble. Do you know what my mother told me the other day? A child born in a developed nation will consume two hundred and forty times the resources consumed by a child born in Bangladesh. If we'd had the self-restraint to have two hundred and thirty nine Bangladeshi children, she would have given us a warmer welcome, but this gargantuan westerner, who is going to take up acres of landfill with his disposable nappies, and will soon be clamoring for a personal computer powerful enough to launch a Mars flight while playing tic-tac-toe with a virtual buddy in Dubrovnik, is not likely to win her approval." His father paused. "Are you all right?" he asked.

"I've never been happier," said his mother, wiping her glistening cheeks with the back of her hand. "I just feel so empty."

She guided the baby's head toward her nipple and he started to suck. A thin stream from his old home flooded his mouth and they were together again. He could sense her heartbeat. Peace shrouded them like a new womb. Perhaps this was a good place to be after all, just difficult to get into.

That was about all that Robert could remember from the first few days of his life. The memories had come back to him last month when his brother Thomas was born. He couldn't be sure that some of the things hadn't been said last month, but even if they had been, they reminded him of when he was in hospital; so the memories really belonged to him.

Robert was obsessed with his past. He was five years old now. He could feel his infancy disintegrating, and among the bellows of congratulation that accompanied each little step toward full citizenship, he heard the whisper of loss. Something had started to happen as he became dominated by talk. His early memories were breaking off, like slabs from those orange cliffs behind him, and crashing into an all-consuming sea which only glared back at him when he tried to look into it. His infancy was being obliterated by his childhood. He wanted it back, otherwise Thomas would have the whole thing.

Robert had left his parents, his little brother, and Margaret behind, and he was wobbling his way across the rocks toward the clattering stones of the lower beach, holding in one of his outstretched hands a scuffed plastic bucket decorated with vaulting dolphins. Brilliant pebbles, fading as he ran back to show them off, no longer tricked him. What he was looking for now were those jellybeans of blunted glass buried under the fine rush of black and gold gravel on the shore. Even when they were dry they had a bruised glow. His father told him that glass was made of sand, so they were halfway back to where they came from.

Robert had arrived at the shoreline now. He left his bucket on a high rock and started the hunt for wave-licked glass. The water foamed around his ankles and as it rushed down the beach he scanned the bubbling sand. To his astonishment he could see something under the first wave, not one of the pale green or cloudy white beads, but a rare yellow gem. He pulled it out of the sand, washed the grit from it with the next wave and held it up to the light, a little amber kidney between his finger and thumb. He looked up the beach to share his excitement, but his parents were huddled around the baby, while Margaret rummaged in a bag.

He could remember Margaret very well now that she was back. She had looked after him when he was a baby. It was different then because he had been his mother's only child.

9

Margaret liked to say that she was a "general chatterbox" but in fact her only subject was herself. His father said that she was an expert on "the theory of dieting." He was not sure what that was but it seemed to have made her very fat. To save money his parents weren't planning to have a maternity nurse this time but they had changed their minds just before coming to France. They almost changed them back when the agency said that Margaret was the only one available at such short notice. "I suppose she'll be an extra pair of hands," his mother had said. "If only they didn't come with the extra mouth," said his father.

He had first met Margaret when he came back from the hospital after being born. He woke up in his parents' kitchen, jiggling up and down in her arms.

"I've changed his majesty's nappy so he'll have a nice dry botty," she said.

"Oh," said his mother, "thank you."

He immediately felt that Margaret was different from his mother. Words drained out of her like an unplugged bath. His mother didn't really like talking but when she did talk it was like being held.

"Does he like his little crib?" asked Margaret.

"I don't really know, he was with us in the bed last night."

A quiet growl came out of Margaret. "Hmmm," she said, "bad habits."

"He wouldn't settle in his crib."

"They never will if you take them into your bed."

"'Never' is a long time. He was inside me until Wednesday evening; my instinct is to have him next to me for a while—do things gradually."

"Well, I don't like to question your instincts, dear," said Margaret, spitting the word out the moment it formed in her mouth, "but in my forty years of *experience* I've had mothers thank me again and again for putting the baby down and leaving it in the crib. I had one mother, she's an Arab lady, actually, nice enough, rang me only the other day in Botley and said, 'I wish I'd listened to you, Margaret, and not taken Yasmin into the bed with me. I can't do anything with her now.' She wanted me back, but I said, 'I'm sorry, dear, but I'm starting a new job next week, and I shall be going to the south of France for July to stay with the baby's grandmother.'"

Margaret tossed her head and strutted about the kitchen, a downpour of crumbs tickling Robert's face. His mother said nothing, but Margaret rumbled on.

"I don't think it's fair on the baby apart from anything else— they like to have their own little crib. Of course, I'm used to having sole charge. It's usually *me* has them during the night."

His father came into the room and kissed Robert on the forehead.

"Good morning, Margaret," he said. "I hope you got some sleep, because none of the rest of us did."

"Yes, thank you, your sofa's quite comfortable, actually; not that I shall be complaining when I have a room of my own at your mother's."

"I should hope not," said his father. "Are you all packed and ready to go? Our taxi is coming any minute now."

"Well, I haven't exactly had time to *un*pack, have I? Except for my sun hat. I got that out in case it's blazing at the other end."

"It's always blazing at the other end. My mother wouldn't stand for anything less than catastrophic global warming."

"Hmmm, we could do with a bit of global warming in Botley."

"I wouldn't make that sort of remark if you want a good room at the Foundation."

"What's that, dear?"

"Oh, my mother's made a 'Transpersonal Foundation.'"

"Is the house not going to be yours then?"

"No."

"Do you hear that?" said Margaret, her waxen pallor looming over Robert and spraying shortbread in his face with renewed vigor.

Robert could sense his father's irritation.

"He's far too cool to be worried about all that," said his mother.

Everyone started to move about at the same time. Margaret, wearing her sun hat, took the lead, Robert's parents struggling behind with the luggage. They were taking him outside, where the light came from. He was amazed. The world was a birth room screaming with ambitious life. Branches climbing, leaves flickering, cumulo-nimbus mountains drifting, their melting edges curling in the light-flooded sky. He could feel his mother's thoughts, he could feel his father's thoughts, he could feel Margaret's thoughts.

"He loves the clouds," said his mother.

"He can't see the clouds, dear," said Margaret. "They can't focus at his age."

"He might still be looking at them without seeing them as we do," said his father.

Margaret grunted as she got into the humming taxi.

He was lying still in his mother's lap, but the land and sky were slipping by outside the window. If he got involved in the moving scene he thought he was moving too. Light flashed on the window panes of passing houses, vibrations washed over him from all directions, and then the canyon of buildings broke open and a wedge of sunlight drifted across his face, turning his eyelids orange pink.

They were on their way to his grandmother's house, the same house they were staying in now, a week after his brother's birth.

2

Robert was sitting in the windowsill of his bedroom, playing with the beads he had collected on the beach. He had been arranging them in every possible combination. Beyond his mosquito net (with its bandaged cut) was a mass of ripe leaves belonging to the big plane tree on the terrace. When the wind moved through the leaves it made a sound like lips smacking. If a fire broke out, he could climb out of the window and down those convenient branches. On the other hand, a kidnapper could climb up them. He never used to think about the other hand, now he thought about it all the time. His mother had told him that when he was a baby he loved lying under that plane tree in his crib. Thomas was lying there now, bracketed by his parents.

Margaret was leaving the next day—thank God, as his father said. His parents had given her an extra day off, but she was already back from the village, bearing down on them with a deadly bulletin. Robert waddled across the room pretending to be Margaret and circled back to the window. Everyone said he did amazing imitations; his headmaster went further and said that it was a "thoroughly sinister talent, which I hope he will learn to channel constructively." It was true that once he was intrigued by a situation, as he was by Margaret being back with his family, he could absorb everything he wanted. He pressed against the mosquito net to get a better view.

"Ooh, it's that hot," said Margaret, fanning herself with a knitting magazine. "I couldn't find any of the cottage cheese in Bandol. They didn't speak a word of English in the supermarket. 'Cottage cheese,' I said, pointing to the house on the other side of the street, 'Cottage, you know, as in house, only smaller,' but they still couldn't make head or tail of what I was saying."

"They sound incredibly stupid," said his father, "with so many helpful clues."

"Hmm. I had to get some of the French cheeses in the end," said Margaret, sitting down on the low wall with a sigh. "How's the baby?"

"He seems very tired," said his mother.

"I'm not surprised in this heat," said Margaret. "I think I must have got sunstroke on that boat, frankly. I'm done to a crisp. Give him plenty of water, dear. It's the only way to cool them down. They can't sweat at that age."

"Another amazing oversight," said his father. "Can't sweat, can't walk, can't talk, can't read, can't drive, can't sign a check. Foals are standing a few hours after they're born. If horses went in for banking, they'd have a credit line by the end of the week."

"Horses don't have any use for banking," said Margaret.

"No," said his father, exhausted.

In a moment of ecstatic song the cicadas drowned out Margaret's voice, and Robert felt he could remember exactly what it was like being in that crib, lying under the plane trees in a cool green shade, listening to the wall of cicada song collapse to a solitary call and escalate again to a dry frenzy. He let things rest where they fell, the sounds, the sights, the impressions. Things resolved themselves in that cool green shade, not because he knew how they worked, but because he knew his own thoughts and feelings without needing to explain them. And if he wanted to play with his thoughts nobody could stop him. Just lying there in his crib, they couldn't tell whether he was doing anything dangerous. Sometimes he imagined he was the thing he was looking at, sometimes he imagined he was in the space in between, but the best was when he was just looking, without being anyone in particular or looking at anything in particular, and then he floated in the looking, like the breeze blowing without needing cheeks to blow or having anywhere particular to go.

His brother was probably floating right now in Robert's old crib. The grown-ups didn't know what to make of floating. That was the trouble with grown-ups: they always wanted to be the center of attention, with their battering rams of food, and their sleep routines, and their obsession with making you learn what they knew and forget what they had forgotten. Robert dreaded sleep. He might miss something: a beach of yellow beads, or grasshopper wings like sparks flying from his feet as he crunched through the dry grass.

He loved it down here at his grandmother's house. His family only came once a year, but they had been every year since he was born. Her house was a Transpersonal Foundation. He didn't really know what that was, and nobody else seemed to know either, even Seamus Dourke who ran it.

"Your grandmother is a wonderful woman," he had told Robert, looking at him with his dim twinkly eyes. "She's helped a lot of people to connect."

"With what?" asked Robert.

"With the other reality."

Sometimes he didn't ask grown-ups what they meant because he thought it would make him seem stupid; sometimes it was because he knew they were being stupid. This time it was both. He thought about what Seamus had said and he didn't see how there could be more than one reality. There could only be different states of mind with reality housing all of them. That's what he had told his mother, and she said, "You're so brilliant, darling," but she wasn't really paying attention to his theories like she used to. She was always too busy now. What they didn't understand was that he really wanted to know the answer.

Back under the plane tree, his brother had started screaming. Robert wished someone would make him stop. He could feel his brother's infancy exploding like a depth charge in his memory. Thomas's screams reminded Robert of his own helplessness: the ache of his toothless gums, the involuntary twitching of his limbs, the softness of the fontanelle, only a thumb's thrust away from his growing brain. He felt that he could remember objects without names and names without objects pelting down on him all day long, but there was something he could only dimly sense: a world before the wild banality of childhood, before he had to be the first to rush out and spoil the snow, before he had even assembled himself into a viewer gazing at the white landscape through a bedroom window, when his mind had been level with the fields of silent crystal, still waiting for the dent of a fallen berry.

He had seen Thomas's eyes expressing states of mind which he couldn't have invented for himself. They reared up from the scrawny desert of his experience like brief pyramids. Where did they come from? Sometimes he was a snuffling little animal and then, seconds later, he was radiating an ancient calm, at ease with everything. Robert felt that he was definitely not making up these complex states of mind, and neither was Thomas. It was just that Thomas wouldn't know what he knew until he started to tell himself a story about what was happening to him. The trouble was that he was a baby, and he didn't have the attention span to tell himself a story yet. Robert was just going to have to do it for him. What was an older brother for? Robert was already caught in a narrative loop, so he might as well take his little brother along with him. After all, in his way, Thomas was help-ing Robert to piece his own story together.

Outside, he could hear Margaret again, taking on the cicadas and getting the upper hand.

"With the breast feeding you've got to build yourself up," she started out reasonably enough. "Have you not got any digestive biscuits? Or Rich Tea biscuits? We could have a few of those right away, actually. And then you want to have a nice big lunch, with lots of carbohydrates. Not too many vegetables, they'll give him wind. Nice bit of roast beef and Yorkshire pudding is good, with some roast potatoes, and then a slice or two of sponge cake at tea time."

"Good God, I don't think I can manage all that. In my book it says grilled fish and grilled vegetables," said his tired, thin, ele-gant mother.

"*Some* vegetables are all right," grumbled Margaret. "Not onions or garlic though, or anything too spicy. I had one mother had a curry on my day off! The baby was howling its head off when I got back. 'Save me, Margaret! Mummy's set my little digestive system on fire!' Personally, I always say, 'I'll have the meat and two veg, but don't worry too much about the veg.'"

Robert had stuffed a cushion under his T-shirt and was tot-tering around the room pretending to be Margaret. Once his head was jammed full of someone's words he had to get them out. He was so involved in his performance that he didn't notice his father coming into the room.

"What are you doing?" asked his father, half knowing already.

"I was just being Margaret."

"That's all we need—another Margaret. Come down and have some tea."

"I'm that stuffed already," said Robert, patting his cushion. "Daddy, when Margaret leaves, I'll still be here to give Mummy bad advice about how to look after babies. And I won't charge you anything."

"Things are looking up," said his father, holding out his hand to pull Robert up. Robert groaned and staggered across the floor and the two of them headed downstairs, sharing their secret joke.

After tea Robert refused to join the others outside. All they did was talk about his brother and speculate about his state of mind. Walking up the stairs, his decision grew heavier with each step, and by the time he reached the landing he was in two minds. Eventually, he sank to the floor and looked down through the banisters, wondering if his parents would notice his sad and wounded departure.

In the hall, angular blocks of evening light slanted across the floor and stretched up the walls. One piece of light, reflected in the mirror, had broken away and trembled on the ceiling. Thomas was trying to comment. His mother, who understood his thoughts, took him over to the mirror and showed him where the light bounced off the glass.

His father came into the hall and handed a bright-red drink to Margaret.

"Ooh, thank you very much," said Margaret. "I shouldn't really get tipsy on top of my sunstroke. Frankly, this is more of a holiday for me than a job, with you being so involved and that. Oh, look, Baby's admiring himself in the mirror." She leaned the pink shine of her face toward Thomas.

"You can't tell whether you're over here or over there, can you?"

"I think he knows that he's in his body rather than stuck to a piece of glass," said Robert's father. "He hasn't read Lacan's essay on the mirror stage yet, that's when the real confusion sets in."

"Ooh, well, you'd better stick to Peter Rabbit then," chuckled Margaret, taking a gulp of the red liquid.

"Much as I'd love to join you outside," said his father, "I have a million important letters to answer."

"Ooh, Daddy's going to be answering his important letters," said Margaret, breathing the red smell into Thomas's face. "You'll just have to content yourself with Margaret and Mummy."

She swung her way toward the front door. The lozenge of light disappeared from the ceiling and then flickered back. Robert's parents stared at each other silently.

As they stepped outside, he imagined his brother feeling the vast space around him.

He stole halfway down the stairs and looked through the doorway. A golden light was claiming the tops of the pines and the bone-white stones of the olive grove. His mother, still barefoot, walked over the grass and sat under their favorite pepper tree. Crossing her legs and raising her knees slightly, she placed his brother in the hammock formed by her skirt, still holding him with one hand and stroking his side with the other. Her face was dappled by the shadow of the small bright leaves that dangled around them.

Robert wandered hesitantly outside, not sure where he belonged. Nobody called him and so he turned around the corner of the house as if he had always meant to go down to the second pond and look at the goldfish. Glancing back, he saw the stick with sparkly wheels that Margaret had bought his brother at the little carousel in Lacoste. The stub of the stick had been planted in the ground near the pepper tree. The wheels spun in the wind, gold and pink and blue and green. "It's the color and the movement," said Margaret when she bought it, "they love that." He had snatched it from the corner of his brother's pram and run around the carousel, making the wheels turn. When he was swishing it through the air he somehow broke the stick and everyone got upset on his brother's behalf because he never really got the chance to enjoy his sparkly windmill before it was broken. Robert's father had asked him a lot of questions, or rather the same question in a lot of different ways, as if it would do him good to admit that he had broken it on purpose. Do you think you're jealous? Do you think you're angry that he's getting all the attention and the new toys? Do you? Do you? Do you? Well, he had just said it was an accident and wouldn't budge. And it really was an accident, but it so happened that he did hate his brother, and he wished that he didn't. Couldn't his parents remember what it was like when it was just the three of them? They loved each other so much that it hurt when one of them left the room. What had been wrong with having just him on his own? Wasn't he enough? They used to sit on the lawn, where his brother was now, and throw each other the red ball (he had hidden it; Thomas wasn't going to get that as well) and whether he caught it or dropped it, they had all laughed and everything was perfect. How could they want to spoil that?

Maybe he was too old. Maybe babies were better. Babies were impressed by pretty well anything. Take the fish pond he was throwing pebbles into. He had seen his mother carrying Thomas to the edge of the pond and pointing to the fish saying, "Fish." It was no use trying that sort of thing with Robert. What he couldn't help wondering was how his brother was supposed to know whether she meant the pond, the water, the weeds, the clouds reflected on the water, or the fish, if he could see them. How did he even know that "fish" was a thing rather than a color or something that you do? Sometimes, come to think of it, it was something to do.

Once you got words you thought the world was everything that could be described, but it was also what couldn't be described. In a way things were more perfect when you couldn't describe anything. Having a brother made Robert wonder what it had been like when he only had his own thoughts to guide him. Once you locked into language, all you could do was shuffle the greasy pack of a few thousand words that millions of

people had used before. There might be little moments of fresh-
ness, not because the life of the world has been successfully
translated but because a new life has been made out of this
thought stuff. But before the thoughts got mixed up with the
words, it wasn't as if the dazzle of the world hadn't been exploding in the sky of his attention.

Suddenly, he heard his mother scream.

"What have you done to him?" she shouted.

He sprinted around the corner of the terrace and met his
father running out of the front door. Margaret was lying on the
lawn, holding Thomas sprawled on her bosom.

"It's all right, dear, it's all right," said Margaret. "Look, he's
even stopped crying. I took the fall, you see, on my bottom. It's
my training. I think I may have broken my finger, but there's no
need to worry about silly old Margaret as long as no harm has
come to the baby."

"That's the first sensible thing I've ever heard you say," said
his mother, who never said anything unkind. She lifted Thomas
out of Margaret's arms and kissed his head again and again. She
was taut with anger but as she kissed him tenderness started to
drown it out.

"Is he all right?" asked Robert.

"I think so," said his mother.

"I don't want him to be hurt," Robert said, and they walked
back into the house together, leaving Margaret talking on the
ground.

The next morning, they were all hiding from Margaret in his
parents' bedroom. Robert's father had to drive Margaret to the
airport that afternoon.

"I suppose we ought to go down," said his mother, closing
the snaps of Thomas's jumpsuit, and lifting him into her arms.

"No," howled his father, throwing himself onto the bed.

"Don't be such a baby."

"Having a baby makes you more childish, haven't you noticed?"

"I haven't got time to be more childish, that's a privilege reserved for fathers."

"You would have time if you were getting any competent help."

"Come on," said Robert's mother, reaching out to his father with her spare hand.

He clasped it lightly but didn't move.

"I can't decide which is worse," he said, "talking to Margaret, or listening to her."

"Listening to her," Robert voted. "That's why I'm going to do my Margaret imitation all the time after she's gone."

"Thanks a lot," said his mother. "Look, even Thomas is smiling at such a mad idea."

"That's not smiling, dear," grumbled Robert, "that's wind tormenting his little insides."

They all started laughing and then his mother said, "Shhh, she might hear us," but it was too late, Robert was determined to entertain them. Swinging his body sideways to lubricate the forward motion, he rocked over to his mother's side.

"It's no use trying to blind me with science, dear," he said, "I can tell he doesn't like that formula you're giving him, even if it is made by organic goats. When I was in Saudi Arabia—she was a princess, actually—I said to them, 'I can't work with this formula, I have to have the Cow and Gate Gold Standard,' and they said to me, 'With all your experience, Margaret, we trust you completely,' and they had some flown out from England in their private jet."

"How do you remember all this?" asked his mother. "It's terrifying. I told her that we didn't have a private jet."

"Oh, money was no object to them," Robert went on, with a proud little toss of his head. "One day I remarked, you know, quite *casually*, on how nice the princess's slippers were, and the next thing I knew there was a pair waiting for me in my bedroom. The same thing happened with the prince's camera. It was quite embarrassing, actually. Every time I did it, I'd say to myself, 'Margaret, you must learn to keep your mouth shut.'"

Robert wagged his finger in the air, and then sat down on the bed next to his father and carried on with a sad sigh.

"But then it would just pop out, you know: 'Ooh, that's a lovely shawl, dear; lovely soft fabric,' and sure enough I'd find one spread out on my bed that evening. I had to get a new suitcase in the end."

His parents were trying not to make too much noise but they had hopeless giggles. As long as he was performing they hardly paid any attention to Thomas at all.

"Now it's even harder for us to go down," said his mother, joining them on the bed.

"It's impossible," said his father. "There's a force field around the door."

Robert ran up to the door and pretended to bounce back. "Ah," he shouted, "it's the Margaret field. There's no way through, Captain."

He rolled around on the floor for a while and then climbed back onto the bed with his parents.

"We're like the dinner guests in *The Exterminating Angel*," said his father. "We might be here for days. We might have to be rescued by the army."

"We've got to pull ourselves together," said his mother. "We must try to end her visit on a kind note."

None of them moved.

"Why do you think it's so hard for us to leave?" asked his father. "Do you think we're using Margaret as a scapegoat? We feel guilty that we can't protect Thomas from the basic suffering of life, so we pretend that Margaret is the cause—something like that."

"Let's not complicate it, darling," said his mother. "She's the most boring person we've ever met and she's no good at looking after Thomas. That's why we don't want to see her."

Silence. Thomas had fallen asleep, and so there was a general agreement to keep quiet. They all settled comfortably on the bed. Robert stretched out and rested his head on his folded hands, scanning the beams of the ceiling. Familiar patterns of stains and knots emerged from the woodwork. At first he could take or leave the profile of the man with the pointed nose and the helmet, but soon the figure refused to be dissolved back into the grain, acquiring wild eyes and hollow cheeks. He knew the ceiling well, because he used to lie underneath it when it was his grandmother's bedroom. His parents had moved in after his grandmother was taken to the nursing home. He still remembered the old silver-framed photograph that used to be on her desk. He had been curious about it because it was taken when his grandmother had been only a few days old. The baby in the picture was smothered in pelts and satin and lace, her head bound in a beaded turban. Her eyes had a fanatical intensity that looked to him like panic at being buried in the immensity of her mother's shopping.

"I keep it here," his grandmother had told him, "to remind me of when I had just come into the world and I was closer to the source."

"What source?" he asked.

"Closer to God," she said shyly.

"But you don't look very happy," he said.

"I think I look as if I haven't forgotten yet. But in a way you're right, I don't think I've ever really got used to being on the material plane."

"What material plane?"

"The Earth," she said.

"Would you rather live on the Moon?" he had asked.

She smiled and stroked his cheek and said, "You'll understand one day."

Instead of the photograph, there was a changing mat on the desk now, with a stack of nappies next to it and a bowl of water.

He still loved his grandmother, even if she was not leaving them the house. Her face was a cobweb of creases earned from trying so hard to be good, from worrying about really huge things like the planet, or the universe, or the millions of suffering people she had never met, or God's opinion of what she should do next. He knew his father didn't think she was good, and discounted how badly she wanted to be. He kept telling Robert that they must love his grandmother "despite everything." That was how Robert knew that his father didn't love her anymore.

"Will he remember that fall for the rest of his life?" Robert asked, staring at the ceiling.

"Of course not," said his father. "You can't remember what happened to you when you were a few weeks old."

"Yes I can," said Robert.

"We must all reassure him," said his mother, changing the subject as if she didn't want to point out that Robert was lying. But he wasn't lying.

"He doesn't need reassuring," said his father. "He wasn't actually hurt, and so he can't tell that he shouldn't be bouncing off Margaret's floundering body. We're the ones who are freaked out because we know how dangerous it was."

"That's why he needs reassuring," said his mother, "because he can tell that we're upset."

"Yes, at that level," his father agreed, "but in general babies live in a democracy of strangeness. Things happen for the first time all the time—what's surprising is things happening again."

Babies are great, thought Robert. You can invent more or less anything about them because they never answer back.

"It's twelve o'clock," his father sighed.

They all struggled with their reluctance but the effort to escape seemed to drag them deeper into the quicksand of the mattress. He wanted to delay his parents just a little longer.

"Sometimes," he began dreamily in his Margaret voice, "when I'm stopped at home for a couple of weeks between jobs, I get itchy fingers. I'm that keen to lay my hands on another baby." He grabbed hold of Thomas's feet and made a devouring sound.

"Gently," said Robert's mother.

"He's right, though," said his father, 'she's got a baby habit. She needs them more than they need her. Babies are allowed to be unconscious and greedy, so she uses them for camouflage."

After all the moral effort they had put in to conceding another hour of their lives to Margaret, they felt cheated when they found that she wasn't waiting for them downstairs. His mother went off to the kitchen and he sat with his father on the sofa with Thomas between them. Thomas fell silent and became absorbed in staring at the picture on the wall immediately above the sofa. Robert moved his head down beside Thomas's and as he looked up he could tell from the angle that Thomas couldn't see the picture itself, because of the glass that protected it. He remembered being fascinated by the same thing when he was a baby. As he looked at the image reflected in the glass, it drew him deeper into the space behind him. In the reflection was the doorway, a brilliant and perfect miniature, and through the doorway the still smaller, but in fact larger, oleander bush outside, its flowers tiny pink lights on the surface of the glass. His attention was funneled toward the vanishing point of sky between the oleander branches, and then his imagination expanded into the real sky beyond it, so that his mind was like two cones tip to tip. He was there with Thomas, or rather, Thomas was there with him, riding to infinity on that little patch of light. Then he noticed that the flowers had disappeared and a new image filled the doorway.

"Margaret's here," he said.

His father turned around while Robert watched her plaintive bulk roll toward them. She came to a halt a few feet away from them.

"No harm done," she said, half asking.

"He seems okay," said his father.

"This won't affect my reference, will it?"

"What reference?" asked his father.

"Oh, I see," said Margaret, half wounded, half angry, all dignified.

"Shall we have lunch?" said his father.

"I shan't be needing any lunch, thank you very much," said Margaret.

She turned toward the staircase and began her laborious climb.

Suddenly, Robert couldn't bear it any longer.

"Poor Margaret," he said.

"Poor Margaret," said his father. "What will we do without her?"

3

Robert was watching an ant disappear behind the sweating bottle of white wine on the stone table. The condensation suddenly streaked down the side of the bottle, smoothing the beaded surface in its wake. The ant reappeared, magnified through the pale green glass, its legs knitting frantically as it sampled a glittering grain of sugar spilled by Julia when she had sweetened her coffee after lunch. The sound of the cicadas billowed around them in and out of time with the limp flapping of the canvas awning over their heads. His mother was having a siesta with Thomas, and Lucy was watching a video, but he had stayed behind, despite Julia almost forcing him to join Lucy.

"Most people wait for their parents to die with a mixture of tremendous sadness and plans for a new swimming pool," his father was saying to Julia. "Since I'm going to have to renounce the swimming pool, I thought I might ditch the sadness as well."

"But couldn't you pretend to be a shaman and keep this place?" said Julia.

"Alas, I'm one of the few people on the planet with absolutely no healing powers. I know that everyone else has just discovered their inner shaman, but I remain trapped in my materialistic conception of the universe."

"There's such a thing as hypocrisy, you know," said Julia. "There's a shop around the corner from me called The Rainbow Path, I could get you a drum and some feathers."

"I can already feel the power surging into my fingertips," said his father, yawning. "I, too, have a special gift to offer the tribe. I didn't realize until now that I have incredible psychic powers."

"There you go," said Julia encouragingly, "you'll be running the place in no time."

"I have enough trouble looking after my family without saving the world."

"Looking after children can be a subtle way of giving up," said Julia, smiling at Robert sternly. "They become the whole ones, the well ones, the postponement of happiness, the ones who won't drink too much, give up, get divorced, become mentally ill. The part of oneself that's fighting against decay and depression is transferred to guarding them from decay and depression. In the meantime one decays and gets depressed."

"I disagree," said his father, "when you're just fighting for yourself it's defensive and grim."

"Very useful qualities," Julia interrupted him. "That's why it's important not to treat children too well—they won't be able to compete in the real world. If you want your children to become television producers, for instance, or chief executives, it's no use filling their little heads with ideas of trust and truth-telling and reliability. They'll just end up being somebody's secretary."

Robert decided to ask his mother whether this was true, or whether Julia was being—well, like Julia. She came to stay every year with Lucy, her quite stuck-up daughter, who was a year older than Robert. He knew his mother wasn't wild about Julia, because she was an old girlfriend of his father. She felt a little bit jealous of her, but also a little bit bored. Julia didn't know how to stop wanting people to think she was clever. "Really clever people are just thinking aloud," his mother had told him, "Julia is thinking about what she sounds like."

Julia was always trying to throw Robert and Lucy together. The day before, Lucy had tried to kiss him. That was why he didn't want to watch a video with her. He doubted that his front teeth would survive another collision like that. The theory that it was good for him to spend time with children of his own age, even if he didn't like them, ground on. Would his father ask a woman to tea just because she was forty-two?

Julia was playing with the sugar again, spooning it back and forth in the bowl.

"Since divorcing Richard," she said, "I get these horrible moments of vertigo. I suddenly feel as if I don't exist."

"I get that!" said Robert, excited that they had chosen a subject he knew something about.

"At your age," said Julia, "I think that's very pretentious. Are you sure you haven't just heard grown-ups talking about it?"

"No," he said, in his dazed by injustice voice, "I get it all on my own."

"I think you're being unfair," said his father to Julia. "Robert has always had a capacity for horror well beyond his years. It doesn't interfere with his being a happy child."

"Well, it does, actually," he corrected his father, "when it's going on."

"Ah, when it's going on," his father conceded with a gentle smile.

"I see," said Julia, resting her hand on Robert's. "In that case, welcome to the club, darling."

He didn't want to be a member of Julia's club. He felt prickly all over his body because he wanted to take his hand away but didn't want to be rude.

"I always thought children were simpler than us," said Julia, removing her hand and placing it on his father's forearm. "We're like ice-breakers crashing our way toward the next object of desire."

"What could be simpler than crashing one's way toward the next object of desire?" asked his father.

"*Not* crashing one's way toward it."

"That's renunciation—not as simple as it looks."

"It's only renunciation if you have the desire in the first place," said Julia.

"Children have plenty of desire in the first place," said his father, "but I think you're right, it's essentially one desire: to be close to the people they love."

"The normal ones want to watch *Raiders of the Lost Ark* as well," said Julia.

"We're more easily distracted," said his father, ignoring her last remark, "more used to a culture of substitution, more easily confused about exactly who we do love."

"Are we?" said Julia, smiling. "That's nice."

"Up to a point," said his father.

He didn't really know what they were talking about now, but Julia seemed to have cheered up. Substitution must be something pretty wonderful. Before he got the chance to ask what it meant, a voice, a caring Irish voice, called out.

"Hello? Hello?"

"Oh, Christ," muttered his father, "it's the boss."

"Patrick!" said Seamus warmly, walking toward them in a shirt covered in palm trees and rainbows. "Robert," he greeted him, ruffling his hair vigorously. "Pleased to meet you," he said to Julia, fixing her with his candid blue eyes and his firm hand-shake. Nobody could accuse him of not being friendly.

"Oh, it's a lovely spot here," he said, "lovely. We often sit out here after a session, with everyone laughing or crying, or just being with themselves, you know. This is definitely a power point, a place of tremendous release. That's right," he sighed, as if agreeing with someone else's wise insight, "I've seen people let go of a lot of stuff here."

"Talking of 'letting go of a lot of stuff,'" his father handed the phrase back to Seamus, held by the corner like someone else's used handkerchief, "when I opened the drawer of my bedside table I found it so full of Healing Drum brochures that there was no room for my passport. There are also several hundred copies of 'The Way of the Shaman' in my wardrobe, which are getting in the way of the shoes."

"The Way of the Shoes," said Seamus, letting out a great roar of healthy laughter, "now that would be a good title for a book about, you know, staying grounded."

"Do you think that these signs of institutional life," continued his father coldly, rapidly, "could be removed before we come down here on holiday? After all, my mother does want the house to return each August to its incarnation as a family home."

"Of course, of course," said Seamus. "I apologize, Patrick. That'll be Kevin and Anette. They were going through a very powerful personal process, you know, before going back to Ireland on holiday, and they obviously weren't thorough enough in getting things ready for you."

"Are you also going back to Ireland?" his father asked.

"No, I'll be in the cottage through August," said Seamus. "The Pegasus Press has asked me to write a short book about the shamanic work."

"Oh, really," said Julia, "how fascinating. Are you a shaman yourself?"

"I had a look at the book that was in the way of my shoes," said his father, "and some obvious questions sprung to mind. Have you spent twenty years being the disciple of a Siberian witch doctor? Have you gathered rare plants under the full moon during the brief summer? Have you been buried alive and died to the world? Have your eyes watered in the smoke of campfires while you muttered prayers to the spirits who might help you to save a dying man? Have you drunk the urine of caribou who have grazed on outcrops of *amanita mascara* and journeyed into other worlds to solve the mystery of a difficult diagnosis? Or did you study in Brazil with the *ayahuasqueros* of the Amazon basin?"

"Well," said Seamus, "I trained as a nurse with the Irish National Health."

"I'm sure that was an adequate substitute for being buried alive," said his father.

"I worked in a nursing home for many years, doing the basics, you know: washing patients who were covered in their own feces and urine; spoon-feeding old people who couldn't feed themselves anymore."

"Please," said Julia, "we've only just finished our lunch."

"That was my reality at the time," said Seamus. "I sometimes wondered why I hadn't gone on to university and got the medical qualifications, but looking back I'm grateful for those years in the nursing home—they've helped to keep me grounded. When I discovered the Holotropic Breathwork and went to California to study with Stan Grof, I met some pretty out-there people, you know. I remember one particular lady, wearing a sunset-colored dress, and she stood up and said, 'I am Tamara from the Vega system, and I have come to the Earth to heal and to teach.' Well, at that point, I thought about the old people in the home in Ireland and I was grateful to them for keeping my feet firmly planted on the ground."

"Is holo . . . whatever you called it, a shamanic thing?" asked Julia.

"No, not really. That's what I was doing before I got into the shamanic work, but it all ties in, you know. It gets people in touch with that something beyond, that other dimension. When people touch that, it can trigger a radical change in their lives."

"But I don't understand why this counts as a charity. People pay to come here, don't they?" said Julia.

"They do, they do," said Seamus, "but we recycle the profits, you see, so as to give scholarships to students like Kevin and Anette who are learning the shamanic work. And they've started to bring groups of inner-city kids from the estates in Dublin. We let them attend the courses for free, you know, and it's a wonderful thing to see the transformations. They love the trance music and the drumming. They come up to me and say, "Seamus, this is incredible, it's like tripping without the drugs," and they take that message back to the inner city and start up shamanic groups of their own."

"Do we need a charity for tripping?" asked his father. "Of all the ills in the world the fact that there are a few people who are not tripping seems a wild hole to plug. Besides, if people want to trip, why not give them a strong dose of acid, instead of messing about with drums."

"You can tell he's a barrister," said Seamus amiably.

"I'm all for people having hobbies," said his father. "I just think they should explore them in the comfort of their own homes."

"Sadly, Patrick," said Seamus, "some homes are not that comfortable."

"I know the feeling," said his father. "Which reminds me, do you think we could clear out some of those books, advertisements, brochures, bric-a-brac."

"Surely," said Seamus, "surely."

His father and Seamus got up to leave and Robert realized that he was going to be left alone with Julia.

"I'll help," he said, following them around the terrace. His father led the way into the hall and stopped almost immediately.

"These fluttering leaflets," he said, "advertising other centers, other institutes, healing circles, advanced drumming courses— they're really wasted on us. In fact, this whole notice board," he continued, unhooking it from the wall, "despite its attractive cork surface and its multicolored drawing pins, might as well not be here."

"No problem," said Seamus, embracing the notice board.

Although his father's manner remained supremely controlled, Robert could feel that he was intoxicated with rage and contempt. Seamus clouded over when Robert tried to make out what he was feeling, but eventually he groped his way to the terrible conclusion that Seamus pitied his father. Knowing that he was in charge, Seamus could afford to indulge the fury of a betrayed child. His repulsive pity saved him from feeling the impact of Patrick's fury, but Robert found himself caught between the punching bag and the punch and, feeling frightened and useless, he slipped out of the front door, while his father marched Seamus on to the next offense.

Outside, the shadow of the house was spreading to the flower beds on the edge of the terrace, indicating to some effortless part of his mind that the middle of the afternoon had arrived. The cicadas scratched on. He could see without looking, hear without listening; he was aware that he was not thinking. His attention, which usually bounced from one thing to another, was still. He pushed to test its resistance but he didn't push too hard, knowing that he could probably make himself pinball around again if he tried. His mind was glazed over, like a pond drowsily repeating the pattern of the sky.

The funny thing was that by imagining a pond he had started disturbing the trance it was being compared to. Now he wanted to go to the pond at the top of the steps, a stone semicircle of water at the end of the drive, where the goldfish would be hiding under a shield of reflection. That was right, he didn't want to go around the house with his father and Seamus, he wanted to scatter bread on the water to see if he could make that slippery Catherine wheel of orange fish break the surface. He ran into the kitchen and grabbed a piece of old bread before sprinting up the steps to the pond.

His father had told him that in winter the source gushed out of the pipe and thundered down among the darting fish; it overflowed into the lower ponds and eventually into the stream that ran along the crease of the valley. He wished he could see that one day. By August the pond was only half full. The algae-bearded pipe dripped into greenish water. Wasps and hornets and dragonflies crowded its warm dusty surface, resting on the water-lily pads for a safer drink. The goldfish were invisible unless tempted by food. The best method was to rub two pieces of stale bread together until they disintegrated into fine dry crumbs. Pellets of bread just sank, but the crumbs were held on the surface like dust. The most beautiful fish, the one he really wanted to see, had red and white patches on its skin. The others were all shades of orange, apart from a few small black ones which must either turn orange later on, or die out, because there were no big black ones.

He broke the bread and grated the two halves, watching a rain of light crumbs land on the water and spread out. Nothing happened.

The truth was that he had only seen the swirling frenzy of fish once, and since then either nothing had happened or a solitary fish fed lazily under the wobbling sinking crumbs.

"Fish! Fish! Fish! Come on! Fish! Fish! Fish!"

"Are you calling to your power animal?" said a voice behind him.

He stopped abruptly and swung round. Seamus was standing there, smiling at him benevolently, his tropical shirt blazing in the sun.

"Fish! Fish! Fish!" Seamus called.

"I was just feeding them," mumbled Robert.

"Do you feel you have a special connection with fish?" Seamus asked him, leaning in closer. "That's what a power animal is, you know. It helps you on your journey through life."

"I just like them being fish," said Robert. "They don't have to do anything for me."

"Now fish, for instance, bring us messages from the depths, from under the surface of things." Seamus wriggled his hand through the air. "Ah, it's a magical land here," said Seamus, pushing his elbows back and twisting his neck from side to side with his eyes closed. "My own personal power point, you know, is up there in the little wood, by the bird bath. Do you know the spot? It was your grandmother first pointed it out to me, it was a special place for her, too. The first time I did a journey here, that's where I connected with the non-ordinary reality."

Robert suddenly realized, and as he realized it he also saw its inevitability, that he loathed Seamus.

Seamus cupped his hands around his mouth and howled, "Fish! Fish! Fish!"

Robert wanted to kill him. If he had a car he would run him over. If he had an axe he would cut him down.

He heard the upper door of the house being opened, and then the mosquito door squeaking open as well and out came his mother, holding Thomas in her arms.

"Oh, it's you. Hello, Seamus," said his mother politely. "We were half asleep, and I couldn't work out why a traveling fishmonger was bellowing outside the window."

"We were, you know, invoking the fish," said Seamus.

Robert ran over to his mother. She sat down with him on the low wall around the edge of the pond, away from where Seamus was standing, and tilted Thomas so he could see the water. Robert really hoped the fish didn't come to the surface now, or Seamus would probably think he had made it happen with his special powers. Poor Thomas, he might never see the orange swirl, he might never see the big fish with red and white patches. Seamus was taking away the pond and the wood and the birdbath and the whole landscape from him. In fact, when you thought about it, Thomas had been attacked by his own grandmother from the moment he was born. She wasn't a grand-mother at all; more like a stepmother in a fairy tale, cursing him in his crib. How could she have shown Seamus the birdbath in the wood? He patted Thomas's head protectively. Thomas started to laugh, his surprisingly deep gurgling laugh, and Robert realized that he didn't really know about these things that were driving Robert crazy, and that he needn't know, unless Robert told him.

4

Josh Packer was a boy in Robert's class at school. He had decided (all on his own) that they were best friends. Nobody else could understand why they were inseparable, least of all Robert. If he could have broken away from Josh for long enough he would definitely have made another best friend, but Josh followed Robert around the playground, copied out his spelling tests, and dragged him back to his house for tea. All Josh did outside school was watch television. He had sixty-five channels, whereas Robert only had the free ones. Josh's parents were very rich, so he often had amazing new toys before anyone else had even heard of them. For his last birthday he had been given a real electric jeep, with a DVD player and a miniature television. He drove it around the garden, squashing the flowers and trying to run over Arnie, his dog. Eventually, he crashed into a bush and he and Robert sat in the rain watching the miniature television. When he came around to Robert's flat he said how pathetic the toys were and complained that he was bored. Robert tried to make up games with him but he didn't know how to make things up. He just pretended to be a television character for about three seconds, and then fell over and shouted, "I'm dead."

Jilly, Josh's mother, had telephoned the day before to say that she and Jim had rented a fabulous house in St. Tropez for the whole of August, and why didn't Robert's family come over for a day of fun and games. His parents said it would be good for him to spend a day with someone of his own age. They said it would be an adventure for them as well, because they had only met Josh's parents once at the school sports day. Even then Jim and Jilly were too busy making rival movies of Josh's races to talk much. Jilly showed them how her videocam could make the whole thing go in slow motion, which wasn't really necessary as Josh came in last anyway.

Now that they were actually on their way, Robert's father was ranting at the wheel of the car. He seemed to be much grumpier since Julia had left. He couldn't believe that they were spending a day of their precious holiday in a traffic jam, in a heat wave, crawling into this "world-famous joke of a town."

Robert was sitting next to Thomas, who was in his old car seat facing the wrong way, with only the stained fabric of the back seat to entertain him. Robert made barking noises as he climbed Thomas's leg with a small toy dog. Thomas couldn't have been less interested. Why should he be? thought Robert. He hasn't seen a real dog yet. Mind you, if he was only curious about things he'd seen before, he'd still be trapped in a whirlpool of birth-room lights.

When they finally found the right street, Robert was the one who spotted the tilted script of LES MIMOSAS scrawled across a rustic tile. They thrummed down the ribbed concrete to a parking lot already congested with Jim's private motor show: a black Range Rover, a red Ferrari, and an old cream convertible with cracked leather seats and bulbous chrome fenders. His father found a space for their Peugeot next to a giant cactus, its serrated tongues sticking out in every direction.

"A neo-Roman villa decorated by a disciple of Gauguin's syphilitic twilight," said his father. "What more could one ask?" He slipped into his golden advertising voice, "Situated in St.Tro-pay's most prestigious gated community, only six hours drive from Brigitte Bardot's legendary pet cemetery . . ."

"Sweetheart," interrupted his mother.

There was a tap on the window.

"Jim!" said his father warmly, as he wound down the window.

"We're just off to buy some inflatables for the pool," said Jim, lowering the videocam with which he'd been filming their arrival. "Does Robert want to come along?"

Robert glanced at Josh slumped in the back of the Range Rover. He could tell that he was playing with his Gameboy.

"No, thanks," he said. "I'll help unpack the car."

"You've got him well trained, haven't you?" said Jim. "Jilly's poolside, catching some rays. Just follow the garden path."

They walked through a whitewashed colonnade daubed with Pacific murals, and down a spongy lawn toward the pool, perfectly concealed under a flotilla of inflatable giraffes, fire engines, footballs, racing cars, hamburgers, Mickeys, Minnies, and Goofies, his father lopsided by the baby chair in which Thomas still slept, and his mother like a mule, her sides bulging with bags. Jilly lay stunned on a white and yellow sun bed, flanked by two glistening strangers, all three of them in wigs of Walkman and mobile phone wires. His father's shadow roused Jilly as it fell across her baking face.

"Hi, there!" she said, unhooking her headphones. "I'm sorry, I was in a world of my own."

She got up to greet her guests, but was soon staggering backward, staring at Thomas, a hand sprawled over her heart.

"Oh, my God," she gasped, "your new one is beau-tiful. I'm sorry, Robert," she dug her long shiny nails into his shoulders to help steady him, "I don't want to fan the flames of sibling rivalry, but your little brother is something really special. Aren't you a special one?" she said, swooping down toward Thomas. "He's going to make you dead jealous," she warned his mother, "with all the girls throwing themselves at his feet. Look at those eyelashes! Are you going to have another one? If mine looked like that, I'd have at least six. I sound greedy, don't I? But I can't help it, he's so love-ly. He's made me forget myself, I haven't introduced you to Christine and Roger yet. As if they cared. Look at them, they're in a world of their own. Go on, wake up!" She pretended to kick Roger. "Roger's a business partner of Jim's," she filled them in, "and Christine's from Australia. She's four months pregnant."

She shook Christine awake.

"Oh, hi," said Christine. "Have they arrived?"

Jilly introduced everybody.

"I was just telling them about the pregnancy," she explained to Christine.

"Oh, yeah. Actually, I think we're in major denial about it," said Christine. "I just feel a little heavier, that's all, as if I'd drunk four liters of Evian, or something. I mean, I don't even feel sick in the mornings. The other day Roger said, 'Do you wanna go skiing in January? I've got to be in Switzerland on business any-way,' and I said, 'Sure, why not?' We'd both forgotten that that's the week I'm supposed to be giving birth!"

Jilly hooted with laughter and rolled her eyes skyward.

"I mean, is that absentminded, or what?" said Christine. "Mind you, pregnancy really does your brain in."

"Look at them," said Jilly, pointing to Robert's mother and father, "they're absolutely gobsmacked—they're loving parents."

"So are we," protested Christine, "You know how we are with Megan. Megan's our two-year old," she explained to the guests. "We've left her with Roger's mother. She's just discovered rage— you know the way they discover emotions and then work them for all they're worth, until they get on to the next one."

"How interesting," said Robert's father, "so you don't think emotions have anything to do with how a child is feeling—they're just layers in an archeological dig. When do they discover joy?"

"When you take them to Legoland," said Christine.

Roger woke up groggily, clasping his earpiece.

"Oh, hi. Sorry, I've got a call."

He got up and started to pace the lawn.

"Have you brought your nanny?" asked Jilly.

"We haven't got one," said Robert's mother.

"That's brave," said Jilly. "I don't know what I'd do without Jo. She's only been with us a week and she's already part of the family. You can dump your lot on her, she's marvelous."

"We quite like looking after them ourselves," said his mother.

"Jo!" shouted Jilly. "Jo-o-euh!"

"Tell them it's a mixed leisure portfolio," said Roger. "Don't give them any more details at this stage."

"Jo!" Jilly called again. "Lazy bitch. She spends the whole day gawping at *Hello* magazine and eating Ben and Jerry's ice cream. A bit like her employer, you might say, hem-hem, but it's costing me a fortune, whereas *she's* getting paid."

"I don't care what they told Nigel," said Roger, "it's none of their bloody business. They can keep their noses out of it."

Jim came striding down the lawn, glowing with successful shopping. Tubby Josh followed behind, a tangle of dragging feet. Jim got out a foot pump and unfolded the plastic skin of another inflatable on the flagstones next to the pool.

"What did you get him?" asked Jilly, staring furiously at the house.

"You know he had his heart set on the ice-cream cone," said Jim, pumping up a strawberry cornetto. "And I got him the Lion King."

"And the machine gun," said Josh pedantically.

"Inland Revenue," said Jim to Robert's father, jerking his chin toward Roger, "breathing down his neck. He may want some legal advice over lunch."

"I don't work when I'm on holiday," said his father.

"You don't work much when you're not on holiday," said Robert's mother.

"Oh dear, do I detect marital conflict?" said Jim, filming the strawberry cornetto as it unwrinkled on the ground.

"Jo!" screamed Jilly.

"I'm here," called a big freckly girl in khaki shorts emerging from the house. The words "Up For It" danced on the front of her T-shirt as she bobbed down the lawn.

Thomas woke up screaming. Who could blame him? The last thing he knew he had been in the car with his lovely family, and now he was surrounded by shouting strangers with blacked-out eyes; a nervous herd of monsters jostling brightly in the chlorinated air, another one swelling at his feet. Robert couldn't stand it either.

"Who's a hungry young man?" said Jo, leaning in on Thomas. "Oh, he's beautiful, isn't he?" she said to Robert's mother. "He's an old soul, you can tell."

"Get these two parked in front of a video," said Jilly, "so we can have a bit of peace and quiet. And send Gaston down with a bottle of rosé. You'll love Gaston," she told Robert's mother. "He's a genius. A real old-fashioned French chef. I've put on about three stone since we arrived, and that was only a week ago. Never mind. We've got Heinrich coming to the rescue this afternoon—he's the personal trainer, great big German hunk, gives you a proper old workout. You should join me, help to get your figure back after the pregnancy. Not that you don't look great."

"Is that what you want," his mother asked Robert, "to watch a video?"

"Yeah, sure," he said, desperate to get away.

"It's difficult to see how he could swim," admitted his father, "with all the inflatable food in the pool."

"Come on!" said Jo, sticking a hand out on each side. She seemed to think that Josh and Robert were going to take a hand each and skip up the hill with her.

"Isn't anybody going to hold my hand?" howled Jo, in a fit of mock blubbing.

Josh joined his pudgy palm with hers, but Robert managed to stay free, following at a little distance, fascinated by Jo's pouting khaki bottom.

"We're entering the video cave," said Jo, making spooky noises. "Right! What are you two going to watch? And I don't want any fighting."

"*The Adventures of Sinbad*," shouted Josh.

"Again! Crikey!" said Jo, and Robert couldn't help agreeing with her. He liked to watch a good video five or six times, but when he knew all the dialogue by heart and each shot was like a drawer full of identical socks, he started to feel a twinge of reluctance. Josh was different. He started out with a sort of sullen greed for a new video and only developed real enthusiasm somewhere around the twentieth viewing. Love, an emotion he didn't throw around lightly, was reserved for *The Adventures of Sinbad*, now seen over a hundred times, far too many of them with Robert. Videos were Josh's daydreams, Robert's daydream was solitude. How could he escape from the video cave? When you're a child nobody leaves you alone. If he ran away now, they would send out a search party, round him up, and entertain him to death. Maybe he could just lie there and think while Josh's borrowed imagination flickered on the wall. The whine of the rewind was slowing down and Josh had collapsed back into the dent already made by his breakfast viewing and resumed munching the bright orange cheese puffs scattered on the table next to him. Jo started the tape, switched off the light and left discreetly. Josh was no fast-forward vandal: the warning about video piracy,

the previews of films he had already seen, the plugs for mer-
chandised toys he had already discarded, and the message from
the Video Standards Authority were not allowed to rush past like
so many ugly suburbs before a train breaks out into the bovine
melancholy of true countryside; they were appreciated in their
own right, granted their own dignity, which suited Robert fine,
since the rubbish now pouring from the screen was too familiar
to make any impact on his attention at all.

He closed his eyes and let the poolside inferno dissipate.
After a few hours of other people, he had to get the pileup of
impressions out of him one way or another; by doing impersonations, or working out how things worked, or just trying to
empty his mind. Otherwise the impressions built up to a critical
density and he felt as if he were going to explode.

Sometimes, when he was lying in bed, a single word like
"fear" or "infinity" flicked the roof off the house and sucked
him into the night, past the stars that had been bent into bears
and ploughs, and into a pure darkness where everything was
annihilated except the feeling of annihilation. As the little capsule of his intelligence disintegrated, he went on feeling its burning edges, its fragmenting hull, and when the capsule flew apart
he was the bits flying apart, and when the bits turned into atoms
he was the flying apart itself, growing stronger instead of fading,
like an evil energy defying the running out of everything and
feeding on waste, and soon enough the whole of space was a
waste-fueled rush and there was no place in it for a human mind;
but there he was, still feeling.

He would reel down the corridor to his parents' bedroom,
choking. He would do anything to make it stop, sign any contract, take any vow, but he knew it was useless, he knew that he
had seen something true, that he couldn't change it, only ignore
it for a while, cry in his mother's arms, and let her put the roof
back on and introduce him to some kinder words.

It was not that he was unhappy. It was just that he had seen something and sometimes it was truer than anything else. He first saw it when his grandmother had a stroke. He hadn't wanted to abandon her but she could hardly speak and so he had spent a lot of time imagining what she was feeling. Everybody said you had to be loyal, so he stuck at it. He held her hand for a long time and she gripped his. He didn't like it but he didn't let go. He could tell that she was frightened. Her eyes were dimmed. Part of her was relieved; she had always had trouble communicating, now nobody expected her to make the effort. Part of her was already gone, back to the source, perhaps, or at least far from the material plane about which she had such chronic doubts. What he could get close to was the part of her that was left behind wondering, now that she couldn't help keeping them, if she wanted all those secrets after all. Illness had blown her apart like a dandelion clock. He had wondered if he would end up like that, a few seeds sticking to a broken stem.

"This is my favorite bit," said Josh, lovestruck. Pirates were boarding Sinbad's ship. The ship's parrot flew in the face of the meanest-looking pirate. He staggered around disoriented and was effortlessly tipped overboard by Sinbad's men. Shot of pleased parrot squawking.

"Hmm," said Robert. "Listen, I'll be back in a minute."

Josh paid no attention to his departure. Robert scanned the corridor for Jo, but she was not there. He retraced the route they had come in by, and when he got to the garden door, saw that the grown-ups were no longer around the pool. He slipped outside and hooked around to the back of the house. The tailored lawn petered out to a carpet of pine needles and a couple of big dustbins. He sat down and leaned back against the ridged bark of the pine, unsupervised.

He wondered who was wasting the most time by spending a day with the Packers, not counting the Packers themselves who were always wasting more time than anybody, and usually had a film to prove it. Thomas was only sixty days old, so it was the biggest waste of time for him, because one day was one sixtieth of his life, whereas his father, who was forty-two, was wasting the smallest proportion of his life. Robert tried to work out what proportion of their lives a day was for each of them. The calculations were hard to hold in his mind, so he imagined different sizes of wheels in a clock. Then he wondered how to include the opposite facts: that Thomas had his whole life ahead of him, whereas his parents had quite a lot of theirs behind them, so that one day was less wasteful for Thomas because he had more days left. That created a new set of wheels—red instead of silver—his father's spinning around and Thomas's turning with a stately infrequent click. He still had to include the different qualities of suffering and the different benefits for each of them, but that made his machine fantastically complicated and so, in one salutary sweep, he decided that they were all suffering equally, and that none of them had got anything out of it at all, making the value of the day a nice fat zero. Hugely relieved, he got back to visualizing the rods connecting the two sets of wheels. It all looked quite like the big steam engine in the science museum, except that paper came out at one end with a figure for the units of waste. It turned out, when he read the figures, that he was wasting more time than anyone else. He was horrified by this result, but at the same time quite pleased. Then he heard Jo's dreadful voice calling his name.

For a moment he froze with indecision. The trouble was that hiding only made the search party more frantic and furious. He decided to act casual and amble around the corner just in time to hear Jo bawling his name for the second time.

"Hi," he said.

"Where have you been? I've been looking for you everywhere."

"You can't have been, or you would have found me," he said.

"Don't get smart with me, young man," said Jo. "Have you been fighting with Josh?"

"No," he said. "How could anyone fight with Josh? He's just a blob."

"He's not a blob, he's your best friend," said Jo.

"No he isn't," he said.

"You *have* been fighting," said Jo.

"We haven't," he insisted.

"Well, anyway, you can't just go off like that."

"Why not?"

"Because we all worry about you."

"I worry about my parents when they go away, but that doesn't stop them," he remarked. "Nor should it."

He was definitely winning this argument. In an emergency, his father could send Robert to court on his behalf. He imagined himself in a wig, bringing the jury around to his way of seeing things, but then Jo squatted down in front of him and looked searchingly into his eyes.

"Do your parents go away a lot?" she asked.

"Not really," he said, but before he could tell her that they had never both been out of the house for more than about three hours, he found himself swept into her arms and crushed against the words "Up For It," without fully understanding what they meant. He had to tuck his shirt in again after she had pulled it out of his trousers with her consoling back rub.

"What does 'Up For It' mean?" he asked when he got his breath back.

"Never you mind," she said, round-eyed. "Come on! Lunchtime!"

She marched him into the house. He couldn't exactly refuse to hold her hand now that they were practically lovers.

A man in an apron was standing beside the lunch table.

"Gaston, you're spoiling us rotten," said Jilly reproachfully. "I'm putting on a stone just looking at these tarts. You should have your own television program. Vous sur le television, Gaston, make you beaucoup de monnaie. Fantastique!"

The table was crowded with bottles of pink wine, two of them empty, and a variety of custard tarts; a custard tart with bits of ham in it, a custard tart with bits of onion in it, a custard tart with curled-up tomatoes on it, and a custard tart with curled-up courgettes on it.

Only Thomas was safe, breast-feeding.

"So you've rounded up the stray," said Jilly. She whipped her hand in the air and burst into song, "Round 'em up! Bring 'em in! Raw-w H-ide!"

Robert felt prickles of embarrassment breaking out all over his body. It must be desperate being Jilly.

"He's used to being alone a lot, is he?" said Jo, challenging his mother.

"Yes, when he wants to be," said his mother, not realizing that Jo thought he might as well be living in an orphanage.

"I was just telling your parents they ought to take you to see the real Father Christmas," said Jilly, dishing out the food. "Concorde from Gatwick in the morning, up to Lapland, snow-mobiles waiting, and whoosh, you're in Father Christmas's cave twenty minutes later. He gives the children a present, then back on the Concorde and home in time for dinner. It's in the Arctic Circle, you see, which makes it more real than mucking about in Harrods."

"It sounds very educational," said his father, "but I think the school fees will have to take priority."

"Josh would murder us if we didn't take him," said Jim.

"I'm not surprised," said his father.

Josh made the sound of a massive explosion and punched the air.

"Smashing through the sound barrier," he shouted.

"Which one of these tarts do you fancy?" Jilly asked Robert.

They all looked equally disgusting.

He glanced at his mother with her copper hair spiraling down toward the suckling Thomas, and he could feel the two of them blending together like wet clay.

"I want what Thomas is having," he said. He hadn't meant to say it out loud, it just slipped out.

Jim, Jilly, Roger, Christine, Jo, and Josh brayed like a herd of donkeys. Roger looked even angrier when he was laughing.

"Mine's a breast milk," said Jilly, raising her glass drunkenly.

His parents smiled at him sympathetically.

"I'm afraid you're on solids now, old man," said his father. "I've got used to wishing I was younger, but I didn't expect you to start quite yet. You're still supposed to be wishing you were older."

His mother let him sit on the edge of her chair and kissed him on the forehead.

"It's perfectly normal," Jo reassured his parents, whom she knew had hardly ever seen a child. "They're not usually that direct about it, that's all." She allowed herself a last hiccup of laughter.

Robert tuned out of the babble around him and gazed at his brother. Thomas's mouth was busy and then quiet and then busy, massaging the milk from their mother's breast. Robert wanted to be there, curled up in the hub of his senses, before he knew about things he had never seen—the length of the Nile, the size of the moon, what they wore at the Boston Tea Party—before he was bombarded by adult propaganda, and measured his experience against it. He wanted to be there, too, but he wanted to take his sense of self with him, the sneaky witness of the very thing that had no witnesses. Thomas was not witnessing himself doing things, he was just doing them. It was an impossible task to join him there as Robert was now, like somersaulting and standing still at the same time. He had often brooded on that idea and although he didn't end up thinking he could do it, he felt the impossibility receding as the muscles of his imagination grew more tense, like a diver standing on the very edge of the board before he springs. That was all he could do: drop into the atmosphere around Thomas, letting his desire for observation peel away as he got closer to the ground where Thomas lived, and where he had once lived as well. It was hard to do it now, though, because Jilly was on to him again.

"Why don't you stay here with us, Robert?" she suggested. "Jo could drive you back tomorrow. You'd have more fun playing with Josh than going home and being dead jealous of your baby brother."

He squeezed his mother's leg desperately.

Eventually Gaston returned, distracting Jilly with the dessert, a slimy mound of custard in a puddle of caramel.

"Gaston, you're ruining us," wailed Jilly, slapping his incorrigible, egg-beating wrist.

Robert leaned in close to his mother. "*Please* can we go now,*"* he whispered in her ear.

"Right after lunch," she whispered back.

"Is he pleading with you?" said Jilly, wrinkling her nose.

"As a matter of fact he is," said his mother.

"Go on, let him have a sleepover," insisted Jilly.

"He'll be well looked after," said Jo, as if this was some kind of novelty.

"I'm afraid we can't. We have to go and see his grandmother in her nursing home," said his mother, not mentioning that they were going there in three days time.

"It's funny," said Christine, "Megan doesn't seem to feel any jealousy yet."

"Give her a chance," said his father, "she's only just discovered rage."

"Yeah," laughed Christine. "Maybe it's because I'm not really owning my pregnancy."

"That must help," sighed his father. Robert could tell that his father was now viciously bored. Immediately after lunch, they left the Packers with an urgency rarely seen outside a fire brigade.

"I'm starving," he said, as their car climbed up the driveway. They all burst out laughing.

"I wouldn't dream of criticizing your choice of friend," said his father, "but couldn't we just get the video instead."

"I didn't chose him," Robert protested, "he just . . . stuck to me."

He spotted a restaurant by the roadside where they had a late lunch of extremely excellent pizzas and salad and orange juice. Poor Thomas had to have milk again. That was all he ever got, milk, milk, milk.

"My favorite was the London house speech," said Robert's father. He put on a very silly voice, not particularly like Jilly's but like her attitude. "It looked huge when we bought it, but by the time we put in the guest suite and the exercise room and the sauna and the home office and the cinema, you know, there really wasn't that much room."

"Room for what?" asked his father, amazed. "Room for room. This is the room room, for having room in. Next time we climb onto our coat hangers in London to sleep like a family of bats, let's appreciate that we're not just a few bedrooms away from real civilization, but a room room away."

"I said to Jim," his father continued imitating Jilly, "I hope we can afford this, because I like the lifestyle—the restaurants, the holidays, the shopping—and I'm not going to give them up. Jim assures me that we can afford both."

"And this was the killer," said his father—"He knows that if we can't afford it, *I'll divorce him*." She's un-fucking-believable. She isn't even attractive."

"She is amazing," said his mother. "But I felt in their own quiet way that Christine and Roger had a lot to offer, too. When I said that I used to talk to my children when I was pregnant, she said" (his mother put on a shrill Australian accent), 'Hang on! A baby is after the birth. I'm not going to talk to my pregnancy. Roger would have me committed.'"

Robert imagined his mother talking to him when he had been sealed up in her womb. Of course he wouldn't have known what her blunted syllables were meant to mean, but he was sure he would have felt a current flowing between them, the contraction of a fear, the stretch of an intention. Thomas was still close to those transfusions of feeling; Robert was getting explanations instead. Thomas still knew how to understand the silent language which Robert had almost lost as the wild margins of his mind fell under the sway of the verbal empire. He was standing on a ridge, about to surge downhill, getting faster, getting taller, getting more words, getting bigger and bigger explanations, cheering all the way. Now Thomas had made him glance backward and lower his sword for a moment while he noticed everything that he had lost as well. He had become so caught up in building sentences that he had almost forgotten the barbaric days when thinking was like a splash of color landing on a page. Looking back he could still see it: living in what would now feel like pauses: when you first open the curtains and see the whole landscape covered in snow and you catch your breath and pause before breathing out again. He couldn't get the whole thing back, but maybe he wouldn't rush down the slope quite yet, maybe he would sit down and look at the view.

"Let's get out of this sorry town," said his father, chucking back his small cup of coffee.

"I've just got to change him first," said his mother, gathering up a bulging bag covered in sky-blue rabbits.

Robert looked down at Thomas, slumped in his chair, staring at a picture of a sailing boat, not knowing what a picture was and not knowing what a sailing boat was, and he could feel the drama of being a giant trapped in a small incompetent body.

5

Walking down the long, easily washed corridors of his grandmother's nursing home, the squeak of the nurse's rubber soles
made his family's silence seem more hysterical than it was.
They passed the open door of a common room where a roar-
ing television masked another kind of silence. The crumpled,
paper-white residents sat in rows. What could be making death
take so long? Some looked more frightened than bored, some
more bored than frightened. Robert could still remember from
his first visit the bright geometry decorating the walls. He
remembered imagining the apex of a long yellow triangle stab-
bing him in the chest, and the sharp edge of that red semicircle slicing through his neck.

This year they were taking Thomas to see his grandmother
for the first time. She wouldn't be able to say much, but then neither would Thomas. They might get on really well.

When they went into the room, his grandmother was sitting
in an armchair by the window. Outside, too close to the window,
was the thick trunk of a slightly yellowing poplar tree and
beyond it, the bluish cypress hedge that hid part of the car park.

Noticing the arrival of her family, his grandmother organized her face into a smile, but her eyes remained detached from the process, frozen in bewilderment and pain. As her lips broke open he saw her blackened and broken teeth. They didn't look as if they could manage anything solid. Perhaps that was why her body seemed so much more wasted than when he had last seen her.

They all kissed his grandmother's soft, rather hairy face. Then his mother held Thomas close to his grandmother and said, "This is Thomas."

His grandmother's expression wavered as she tried to negotiate between the strangeness and the intimacy of his presence. Her eyes made Robert feel as if she was scudding through an overcast sky, breaking briefly into clear space and then rushing back through thickening veils into the milky blindness of a cloud. She didn't know Thomas and he didn't know her, but she seemed to have a sense of her connection with him. It kept disappearing, though, and she had to fight to get it back. When she was about to speak, the effort of working out what to say in these particular circumstances wiped her out. She couldn't remember who she was in relation to all the people in the room. Tenacity didn't work anymore; the harder she grasped at an idea, the faster it shot away. Finally, uncertainly, she wrapped her fingers around something, looked up at his father, and said, "Does . . . he . . . like me?"

"Yes," said Robert's mother instantly, as if this was the most natural question in the world.

"Yes," said his grandmother, the pool of despair in her eyes flooding back into the rest of her face. It wasn't what she had meant to ask, but a question which had broken through. She sank back into her chair.

After what he had heard that morning Robert was struck by her question, and by the fact that it seemed to be addressed to his father. On the other hand, he was not surprised that his mother had answered it instead of him.

That morning he had been playing in the kitchen while his mother was upstairs packing a bag for Thomas. He hadn't noticed that the monitor was still on, until he heard Thomas waking up with a few short cries, and his mother going into Thomas's bedroom and talking to him soothingly. Before he could gauge whether she was even sweeter to Thomas when he was not around, his father's voice came blasting over the receiver.

"I can't believe this fucking letter."

"What letter?" asked his mother.

"That scumbag Seamus Dourke is trying to get Eleanor to make the gift of this property absolute during her lifetime. I had arranged for the solicitor to put it on an elastic band of debt. In her will the debt is waived and the house is transferred irrevocably to the charity, but during her lifetime the charity has been lent the value of this property, and if she recalls the debt the place returns to her. She agreed to set things up that way on the grounds that she might get ill and need the money to look after herself, but needless to say, I also hoped she would come to her senses and realize that this joke charity was doing a lot of harm to us and no good to anyone else, except Seamus. Talk about the luck of the Irish. There he was, a National Health nurse changing bedpans in County Meath, until my mother airlifted him from the emerald isle and made him the sole beneficiary of an enormous tax-free income from a new-age hotel masquerading as a charity. It makes me sick, completely sick."

His father was shouting by now.

"Sweetheart, you're ranting," said his mother. "Thomas is getting upset."

"I have to rant," said his father, "I've just seen this letter. She was always a lousy mother, but I thought she might take a holiday toward the end of her life, feel that she'd achieved enough by way of betrayal and neglect, and that it was time to have a break, play with her grandchildren, let us stay in the house, that sort of thing. What really terrifies me is realizing how much I loathe her. When I read this letter, I tried to loosen my shirt so that I could breathe, but then I realized it was already loose enough, I just felt as if a noose was tightening around my neck, a noose of loathing."

"She's a confused old woman," said Robert's mother.

"I know."

"And we're seeing her later today."

"I know," said his father, much more quietly now, almost inaudibly. "What I really loathe is the poison dripping from generation to generation. My mother felt disinherited because of her stepfather getting all her mother's money, and now, after thirty years of consciousness-raising workshops and personal growth programs, she has found Seamus Dourke to stand in for her stepfather. He's really just the incredibly willing instrument of her unconscious. It's the monotony that drives me mad. I'd rather cut my throat than inflict the same thing on my children."

"You won't," his mother answered.

"If you can imagine anything . . ."

Robert had leaned closer to the monitor, trying to make out his father's fading voice, only to hear it growing louder behind him as his parents made their way downstairs.

". . . the result would be my mother," his father was saying.

"King Lear and Mrs. Jellyby," his mother laughed.

"On the heath," said his father, "a quick rut between the feeble tyrant and the fanatical philanthropist."

He had run from the kitchen, not wanting his parents to know that he had heard their conversation on the monitor. He sat on the knowledge all morning, but when his grandmother had stared at his father, as if she was talking about him, and asked, "Does he like me?" Robert couldn't help having the mad idea that she had overheard the same conversation as him.

Although he didn't understand everything his father had said that morning, he understood enough to feel cracks opening in

the ground. And now, in the silence that followed his grandmother's shrewd unintentional question, he could feel her misery, and he could feel his mother's desire for harmony, and he
could feel the strain in his father's self-restraint. He wanted to
do something to make everything all right.

His grandmother was taking about half an hour to ask if
Thomas had been christened yet.

"No," said his mother, "we're not having a formal christen-
ing. The trouble is that we don't really think that children are
steeped in sin, and a lot of the ceremony seems to be based on
the idea that they're fallen and need to be saved."

"Yes," said his grandmother. "No."

Thomas started to shake the tiny silver dumbbell he had
rediscovered in the creases of his chair. It made a strange high
tinkling sound as he waved it jerkily around his head. Soon
enough, he banged it against his forehead. After a delay in which
he seemed to be trying to work out what had happened, he
started to cry.

"He doesn't know whether he hit himself or whether the
dumbbell hit him," said Robert's father.

His mother took sides against the dumbbell and said,
"Naughty dumbbell," kissing Thomas's forehead.

Robert hit himself on the side of the head and fell off his
grandmother's bed theatrically. Thomas wasn't as amused as he
had hoped he would be.

His grandmother held her arms out in pleading sympathy, as
if Thomas was expressing something that she felt as well, but
didn't want to be reminded of. Robert's mother lifted Thomas
gently into his grandmother's lap. Seduced by the novelty of his
position, Thomas stopped crying and looked searchingly at his
grandmother. She seemed to be calmed by his presence. He sat
on her lap, giving her what she needed, and they sank together
into speechless solidarity. The rest of the family fell silent as
well, not wanting to show up the nonspeakers. Robert felt his

father hovering over his grandmother, resisting saying what was on his mind. In the end it was his grandmother who spoke, not quite fluently but much better than before, as if her speech, abandoning the hopelessly blocked highway of longing, had stolen out under cover of darkness and silence.

"I want you to know," she said, "that I'm very . . . unhappy . . . at not being able to communicate."

His mother reached out and touched her knee.

"It must be horrible for you," said his father.

"Yes," said his grandmother, staring at the faraway floor.

Robert didn't know what to do. His father hated his own mother. He couldn't join him and he couldn't condemn him. His grandmother had done her family some wrong, but she was suffering horribly. Robert could only fall back on how things were before they had been darkened by his father's disappointment. Those cloudless days when he was just meant to love his grandmother; he was not sure they had ever existed, but he was sure they didn't exist now. It was still too unfair to gang up against his frightened grandmother, even if she was leaving the house to Seamus.

He hopped down from the bed and sat on the arm of his grandmother's chair, taking her hand in his, like he used to when she first fell ill. That way she could tell him things without having to speak, her thoughts flooding into him in pictures.

The bridges were burned and broken and everything his grandmother wanted to say got banked up on one side of a ravine, never taking form, never moving on. She felt a perpetual pressure, a scratching behind her eyeballs, like a dog pleading to be let in, a fullness that could only escape in tears and sighs and jagged gestures.

Under the bruise of feeling there was a brutal instinct to stay alive, like a run-over snake thrashing on a hot road, or blind roots pumping sap into a bleeding stump.

Why was she being tortured? They had sown her into a sack and thrown her into the bottom of a boat, chains wrapped around her feet. She must have done something very bad to be teased by the oarsmen as they rowed her out into the bay. Something very bad, which she couldn't remember.

He tried to break off. It was too much. He didn't let go of her hand, he just tried to close down, but it was impossible to break the connection completely.

He noticed that his grandmother was crying. She gave his hand a squeeze.

"I am . . . no." She couldn't say it. A carefully threaded thought unstrung itself and scattered across the floor. She couldn't get it back. Something opaque clung to her all the time. Her head had been sealed in a dirty plastic bag; she wanted to tear it off but her hands were tied.

"I . . . am," she tried again. "Brave. Yes."

The evening light was on the other side of the building and the room was growing dimmer. They were all lost for words, except for Thomas who had none to lose. He leaned against his grandmother's arms, looking at her with his cool objective gaze. His example balanced the atmosphere. They sat in the fading light of the almost peaceful room, feeling sympathetic and a little bored. Robert's grandmother sank into a quieter anguish, like someone deep in the broken springs of a chair, watching a dust storm coat the world in a blunt gray film.

After knocking on the door and not waiting for a reply, a nurse squeaked in with a trolley of food and slid a clattering tray onto the mobile table next to the bed. Robert's mother lifted Thomas back into her arms, while his father wheeled the table into position and removed the tin hood from the main dish. The sweaty gray fish and leaky ratatouille might have made a greedy man pause, but for his grandmother, who would rather have starved to death anyway, all food was equally unwelcome, and so she gave Robert's hand a last squeeze and broke the circuit which had introduced so many violent pictures into his imagination, and picked up her fork with the strange flat obedience of despair. She maneuvered a flake of fish onto her fork and began to lift it toward her mouth. Then she stopped and lowered the fork again, staring at his father.

"I can't . . . find my mouth," she said with emergency precision.

His father looked frustrated, as if his mother had found a trick to stop him from being angry with her, but Robert's mother immediately picked up the fork and smiled and said, "Can I help you, Eleanor?" in the most natural way.

His grandmother's shoulders crumpled a little farther at the thought that it had come to that. She nodded and his mother started to feed her, still holding Thomas on her other arm. His father, temporarily frozen, came to his senses and took Thomas from Robert's mother.

After a few more mouthfuls his grandmother shook her head and said, "No" and leaned back in her chair exhausted. In the silence that followed, his father handed Thomas back to his mother and sat down next to his grandmother.

"I hesitate to mention this," said his father, pulling a letter out of his pocket.

"I think you should keep on hesitating," said his mother quickly.

"I can't," he said to her, "hesitate any longer." He turned back to Robert's grandmother. "Brown and Stone have written to me saying that you intend to make an outright gift of Saint Nazaire to the Foundation. I just want to say that I think that leaves you very exposed. You can barely afford to stay here and if you needed any more medical care, you would go broke very quickly."

Robert hadn't thought his grandmother could look any more unhappy, but somehow her features managed to yield a fresh impression of horror.

"I . . . really . . . I . . . really . . . no."

She covered her face with her hands and screamed.

"I really do object . . ." she wailed.

His mother put her arm around his grandmother without glancing at his father. His father put the letter back in his pocket and looked at his shoes with perfect contempt.

"It's all right," said his mother. "Patrick just wants to help you, he's worried that you may give too much away too soon, but nobody's questioning that you can do what you like with the Foundation. The lawyers only told him because you've asked him to help you in the past."

"I . . . need . . . to rest now," said his grandmother.

"We'll leave then," said his mother.

"Yes."

"I'm sorry I've upset you," sighed his father. "I just don't see what the hurry is: Saint Nazaire is going to the Foundation in your will anyway."

"I think we should drop this subject," said his mother.

"Fine," he agreed.

Robert's grandmother allowed herself to be kissed by each of them in turn. Robert was the last to say goodbye to her.

"Don't . . . leave me," she said.

"Now?" he asked, confused.

"No . . . don't . . . no." She gave up.

"I won't," he said.

Any discussion of their visit to the nursing home seemed too hazardous, and they started the drive home in silence. Soon enough, though, his father's determination to talk took over. He tried to keep things general, he tried to keep away from the subject of his mother.

"Hospitals are very shocking places," he said, "full of poor deluded fools who aren't looking for groundless celebrity or obscene quantities of money, but think the point of life is to help other people. Where do they get these ideas from? We must send them on an empowerment weekend workshop with the Packers."

Robert's mother smiled.

"I'm sure Seamus could organize it, give it a shamanic angle," said his father, dragged irresistibly out of his orbit. "Mind you, although hospitals may be awash with cheerful saints, I would rather shoot myself in the head than experience the erosion of self we witnessed this afternoon."

"I thought Eleanor did very well," said his mother. "I was very moved when she said that she was brave."

"What can drive a man mad is being forced to have the emotion which he is forbidden to have at the same time," said his father. "My mother's treachery forced me to be angry, but then her illness forced me to feel pity instead. Now her recklessness makes me angry again but her bravery is supposed to smother my anger with admiration. Well, I'm a simple sort of a fellow, and the fact is that I remain *fucking angry*," he shouted, banging the steering wheel.

"Who is King Lear?" asked Robert from the backseat.

"Did you overhear our conversation this morning?" asked his mother.

"Yes."

"Eavesdropping," said his father.

"No, I wasn't," he objected. "You left the monitor on."

"Oh, yes," said his mother, "so I did. Anyway, it hardly matters now, does it, darling?" she asked his father sweetly. "Since you're screaming that you're 'fucking angry' at the top of your voice."

"King Lear," said his father, "is a petulant tyrant in Shakespeare who gives everything away and is then surprised when Goneril and Regan—or Seamus Dourke, as I prefer to think of them—refuse him the care he requires and boot him out."

"And who's Mrs. Jellybean?"

"Jellyby. She's a compulsive do-gooder who writes indignant letters about orphans in Africa, while her own children fall into the fireplace at the other end of the drawing room."

"And what's a rut?"

"Well, the idea is that if you combined these two characters you would get someone like Eleanor."

"Oh," said Robert, "it's quite complicated."

"Yes," said his father. "The thing is that Eleanor is trying to buy herself a front row seat in heaven by giving all her money to 'charity' but, as you can see, she has in fact bought herself a ticket to hell."

"I don't think it's that clever to turn Robert against his grandmother," said his mother.

"I don't think it was that clever of her to make it inevitable."

"You're the one who feels betrayed—she's your mother."

"She's lied to all of us," his father insisted. "At every stage she told me that such and such a thing was destined for Robert, but one by one these little concessions to family feeling were ripped from their pedestals and sucked into the black hole of the Foundation."

Robert's mother let some time pass in silence and then said, "Well, at least we didn't have *my* mother to stay this year."

"Yes, you're right," said his father, "we must cultivate gratitude."

The atmosphere settled down a little after this moment of harmony. They climbed the lane toward the house. The sunset was simple that evening, without clouds to make mountains and chambers and staircases, just a clear pink light around the hilltops, and an edge of moon hanging in the darkening sky. As they rumbled down the rough drive, Robert felt a sense of home which he knew he must learn to set aside. Why was his grandmother causing so much trouble? The scramble for a front-row seat in heaven seemed unbearably expensive. He looked at Thomas in his baby chair and wondered if he was closer to "the source" than the rest of them, and whether it was a good thing if he was. His grandmother's impatience to be reabsorbed into a luminous anonymity suddenly filled him with the opposite impatience: to live as distinctively as he could before time nailed him to a hospital bed and cut out his tongue.

AUGUST 2001

6

By day, when Patrick heard the echoing bark of the unhappy dog on the other side of the valley, he imagined his neighbor's shaggy Alsatian running back and forth along the split-cane fence of the yard in which he was trapped, but now, in the middle of the night, he thought instead of all the space into which the rings of yelping, howling sound were expanding and dissipating. The crowded house compressed his loneliness. There was no one he could go to, except possibly, or rather impossibly (or, perhaps, possibly), Julia, back again after a year.

As usual, he was too tired to read and too restless to sleep. The tower of books on his bedside table seemed to provide for every mood, except the mood of agitated despair he was invariably in. *The Elegant Universe* made him nervous. He didn't want to read about the curvature of space, when he was already watching the ceiling shift and warp under his exhausted gaze. He didn't want to think about the neutrinos streaming through his flesh— it seemed vulnerable enough already. He had started but finally had to abandon Rousseau's *Confessions*. He had all the persecution mania he could handle without importing anymore. A novel pretending to be the diary of one of Captain Cook's officers on his first voyage to Hawaii was too well researched to bear any resemblance to life. Weighed down by the tiny variation of emblems on the Victualing Board's biscuits, Patrick had started to feel thoroughly depressed, but when a second narrative, written by a descendent of the first narrator, living in twenty-first century Plymouth and taking a holiday in Honolulu, had set up a ludic counterpoint with the first narrative, he thought he was going to go mad. Two works of history, one a history of salt and the other a history of the entire world since 1500 B.C., competed for a place at the bottom of the pile.

As usual, Mary had gone to sleep with Thomas, leaving Patrick split between admiration and abandonment. Mary was such a devoted mother because she knew what it felt like not to have one. Patrick also knew what it felt like, and as a former beneficiary of Mary's maternal overdrive, he sometimes had to remind himself that he wasn't an infant anymore, to argue that there were real children in the house, not yet horror trained; he sometimes had to give himself a good talking to. Nevertheless, he waited in vain for the maturing effects of parenthood. Being surrounded by children only brought him closer to his own childishness. He felt like a man who dreaded leaving harbor, knowing that under the deck of his impressive yacht there is only a dirty little twin-stroke engine: fearing and wanting, fearing and wanting.

Kettle, Mary's mother, had arrived that afternoon and, as usual, immediately found a source of friction with her daughter.

"How was your flight?" asked Mary politely.

"Ghastly," said Kettle. "There was an awful woman next to me on the plane who was terribly proud of her breasts, and kept sticking them in her child's face."

"It's called breast-feeding, Mummy," said Mary.

"Thank you, darling," said Kettle. "I know it's all the rage now, but when I was having children the talk was of getting one's figure back. A clever woman was the one who went to a party looking as if she'd never been pregnant, not the one with her breasts hanging out, at least not for breast-feeding."

As usual, the bottle of Tamazepan squatted on his bedside table. He definitely had a Tamazepan problem, namely, that it wasn't strong enough. The side effects, the memory loss, the dehydration, the hangover, the menace of nightmarish withdrawals, all that worked beautifully. It was just the sleep that was missing. He went on swallowing the pills in order not to confront the withdrawal. He remembered, in the distant past, a leaflet saying not to take Tamazepan for more than thirty consecutive days. He had been taking it every night for three years in larger and larger doses. He would be "perfectly happy," as people said when they meant the opposite, to suffer horribly, but he never seemed to find the time. Either it was one of the children's birthdays, or he was appearing in court, already hungover, or some other enormous duty required the absence of hallucination and high anxiety. Tomorrow, for instance, his mother was coming to lunch. Both mothers at once: not an occasion for bringing on any additional psychosis.

And yet he still cherished the days when additional psychosis had been his favorite pastime. His second year at Oxford was spent watching the flowers pulse and spin. It was during that summer of alarming experiments that he had met Julia. She was the younger sister of a dull man on the same staircase in Trinity. Patrick, already in the early stages of a mushroom trip, had been hurriedly refusing his invitation to tea, when he saw through the half-open door a neck-twistingly pretty girl hugging her knees in the window seat. He veered toward a "quick cup of tea" and spent the next two hours staring idiotically at the unfairly lovely Julia, with her rose-pink cheeks and dark blue eyes. She wore a raspberry T-shirt which showed her nipples, and faded blue jeans frayed open a few inches under the back pocket and above her right knee. He swore to himself that when she was old enough he would seduce her, but she preempted his timid resolution by seducing him the same evening. They had made time-lapse, slow-motion, and technically illegal (she was only sixteen the following week) love. They had fallen upward, disappeared down rabbit holes, watched clocks go anticlockwise, and run away from policemen who weren't chasing them. When they went to Greece he helped to stash the acid in his favorite hiding place: between her legs. He thought that things would cascade from one adventure to another, but now the stammering ecstasy of their love-making seemed like a miracle of freedom belonging to a lost world. Nothing had ever been as spontaneously intimate again, especially not, he kept reminding himself, conversation with the harder, drier Julia who was staying with him now. And yet, there she was, just down the corridor, bruised but still pretty. Should he go? Should he risk it? Should they mount a joint retrospective? Would the intensity come back once their bodies intertwined? The idea was insane. He would have to walk past Robert, the insomniac observation freak, past the ferocious Kettle, past Mary who hovered like a dragonfly over the surface of sleep, in case she missed the slightest inflection of her baby's distress, and then into Julia's room (the corner of her door scraped the floor), which had probably already been invaded by her daughter Lucy anyway. He was paralyzed, as usual, by equal and opposite forces.

Everything was as usual. That was depression: being stuck, clinging to an out-of-date version of oneself. During the day, when he played with the children, he was very close to being what he appeared to be, a father playing with his children, but at night he was either aching with nostalgia or writhing with self-rejection. His youth had sprinted away in its Airmax Nike trainers (only Kettle's youth still wore winged sandals), leaving a swirl of dust and a collection of fake antiques. He tried to remind himself what his youth had really been like, but all he could remember was the abundance of sex and the sense of potential greatness, replaced, as his view closed in on the present, by the disappearance of sex and the sense of wasted potential. Fearing and wanting, fearing and wanting. Perhaps he should take another twenty milligrams of Tamazepan. Forty milligrams, as long as he drank a lot of red wine for dinner, sometimes purchased a couple of hours of sleep; not the gorgeous oblivion which he craved, but a sweaty, turbulent sleep laced with nightmares. Sleep, in fact, was the last thing he wanted if it was going to usher in those dreams: strapped to a chair in the corner of the room watching his children being tortured while he screamed curses at the torturer, or begged him to stop. There was also a diet version, the Nightmare Lite, in which he threw himself in front of his sons just in time to have his body shredded by gunfire, or dismembered by ravenous traffic. When he wasn't woken by these shocking images, he dozed off dreamlessly, only to wake a few minutes later, gasping for air. The price he paid for the sedation he needed to drop off was that his breathing seized up, until an emergency unit in his back brain sent a screaming ambulance to his frontal lobes and jolted him back into consciousness.

His dreams, dreadful enough in their own right, were almost always accompanied by a defensive analytic sequel. Oliver, his psychoanalyst friend, had said this was called "lucid dreaming," in which the dreamer acknowledged that he was dreaming. What was he protecting his children from? His own sense of being tortured, of course. The in-dream dream seminars always reached such reasonable conclusions.

He was obsessed, it was true, with stopping the flow of poison from one generation to the next, but he already felt that he had failed. Determined not to inflict the causes of his suffering on his children, he couldn't protect them from the consequences. Patrick had buried his own father twenty years ago and hardly ever thought about him. At the peak of his kindness David had been rude, cold, sarcastic, easily bored; compulsively raising the hurdle at the last moment to make sure that Patrick cracked his shins. It would have been too flagrant for Patrick to become a disastrous father, or to get a divorce, or to disinherit his children; instead they had to live with the furious, sleepless consequence of those things. He knew that Robert had inherited his midnight angst and refused to believe that there was a midnight angst gene which furnished the explanation. He remembered talking endlessly about his insomnia at a time when Robert had wanted to copy everything about him. He also saw, with a mixture of guilt and satisfaction and guilt about the satisfaction, the gradual shift in Robert from empathy and loyalty toward hatred and contempt for Eleanor and her philanthropic cruelty.

One great relief was that they wouldn't be seeing the Packers this year. Josh had been taken out of school for three weeks and lost the habit of pretending that he and Robert were best friends. During that period of heady freedom, Patrick and Robert had run into Jilly in Holland Park and found out that she was getting a divorce from Jim.

"The glitter's off the diamond," she admitted. "But at least I get to keep the diamond," she added with a triumphant little hoot. "It's awful about Roger being sent to prison. Hadn't you heard? It's an open prison, one of the posh ones. Still, it isn't great, is it? They got him for fraud and tax evasion. Basically, for doing what everyone else does, but not getting away with it. Christine's in bits, with the two kids and everything. She can't even afford a nanny. I said to her, "Get a divorce, it really bucks you up." Mind you, I forgot she wouldn't be getting a huge settlement. I don't know how much it *does* buck you up without a fortune thrown in. I sound awful, don't I? But you've got to be realistic. The doctor's put me on these pills, I can't stop talking. You'd better just walk away, or I'll have you pinned down here all day listening to me wittering on. It's funny, though, thinking of us last year, all sitting around the pool in St. Trop, having the time of our lives, and now everyone going their separate ways.

Still, we've got the children, haven't we? That's the main thing. Don't forget that Josh is still your best friend," she shouted at Robert as they left.

Thomas had started speaking over the last year. His first word was "light," followed soon afterward by "no." All those atmospheres evaporated and got so convincingly replaced, it was hard to remember the beginning, when he was speaking not so much to tell a story as to see what it was like to come out of silence into words. Amazement was gradually replaced by desire. He was no longer amazed by seeing, for instance, but by seeing what he wanted. He spotted a broom hundreds of yards down the street, before the rest of them could even see the sweeper's fluorescent jacket. Hoovers hid behind doors in vain; desire had given him X-ray vision. Nobody could wear a belt for long if he was in the room, it was commandeered for an obscure game in which Thomas, looking solemn, waved the buckle around, humming like a machine. If they ever made it out of London, his parents sniffed the flowers and admired the view, Robert looked for good climbing trees, and Thomas, who wasn't yet far enough from nature to have turned it into a cult, hurtled across the lawn toward the limp coils of a hose lying almost invisibly in the uncut grass.

At his first birthday party last week, Thomas had been attacked for the first time by a boy called Eliot. A commotion suddenly drew Patrick's attention to the other side of the drawing room. Thomas, who was walking along unsteadily with his wooden rabbit on a string, had just been pushed over by a bruiser from his playgroup, and had the string wrenched from his hand. He let out a cry of indignation and then burst into tears. The thug wandered off triumphantly with the undulating rabbit clattering behind him on uneven wheels.

Mary swooped down and lifted Thomas off the ground. Robert went over to check that he was all right, on the way to recapture the rabbit.

Thomas sat on Mary's lap and soon stopped crying. He looked thoughtful, as if he was trying to introduce the novelty of being attacked into his frame of reference. Then he wriggled off Mary's knee and back down to the ground.

"Who was that dreadful child?" said Patrick. "I don't think I've ever seen such a sinister face. He looks like Chairman Mao on steroids."

Before Mary could answer, the bruiser's mother came over.

"I'm sorry about that," she said. "Eliot is so competitive, just like his dad. I hate to repress all that drive and energy."

"You're relying on the penal system for that," said Patrick.

"He should try knocking me over," said Robert, practicing his martial arts moves.

"Let's not go global with this rabbit thing," said Patrick.

"Eliot," said the bruiser's mother, in a special false voice, "give Thomas his rabbit back."

"No," growled Eliot.

"Oh, dear," said his mother, delighted by his tenacity.

Thomas had transferred his focus to the fire tongs which he was dragging noisily out of their bucket. Eliot, convinced that he must have stolen the wrong thing, abandoned the rabbit and headed for the tongs. Mary picked up the string of the rabbit and handed it to Thomas, leaving Eliot revolving next to the bucket, unable to decide what he should be fighting for. Thomas offered the rabbit string to Eliot who refused it and waddled over to his mother with a cry of pain.

"Don't you want the tongs?" she asked coaxingly.

Patrick hoped he would handle things more wisely with Thomas than he had with Robert, not infuse him with his own anxieties and preoccupations. The hurdles were always raised at the last moment. He was so tired now. The hurdles always raised . . . of course . . . he would think that . . . he was chasing his tail now . . . the dog was barking on the other side of the valley . . . the inner and outer worlds plowing into each other . . . he was almost falling asleep . . . perchance to dream . . . fuck that. He sat up and finished the thought. Yes, even the most enlightened care carried a shadow. Even Johnny (but then, he was a child psychologist) reproached himself for making his children feel that he really understood them, that he knew what they were feeling before they knew themselves, that he could read their unconscious impulses. They lived in the panoptic prison of his sympathy and expertise. He had stolen their inner lives. Perhaps the kindest thing Patrick could do was to break up his family, to offer his children a crude and solid catastrophe. All children had to break free in the end. Why not give them a hard wall to kick against, a high board to jump from. Christ, he really must get some rest.

After midnight, the wonderful Dr. Zemblarov was never far from his thoughts. A Bulgarian who practiced in the local village, he spoke in extremely rapid, heavily accented English. "In our culture, we have only this," he would say, signing an elaborate prescription, "*la pharmacologie*. If we lived in the *Pacifique*, maybe we could dance, but for us there is only the chemical manipulation. When I go back to Bulgaria, for example, I take *de l'amphetamine*. I drive, I drive, I drive, I see my family, I drive, I drive, I drive, and I come back to Lacoste." The last time Patrick had hesitantly asked for more Tamazepan, Dr. Zemblarov reproached him for being so shy. "*Mais il faut toujours demander.* I take it myself when I travel. *L'administration* want to limit us to thirty days, so I will put 'one in the evening and one at night,' which naturally is not true, but it will avoid you to come here so often. I will also give you Stillnox, which is from another family—the hypnotics! We also have the barbiturate family," he added with an appreciative smile, his pen hovering over the page.

No wonder Patrick was always tired, and could only offer short bursts of childcare. Today, Thomas had been in pain. Some more teeth were bullying their way through his sore gums, his cheeks were red and swollen and he was rushing about looking for distractions. In the evening, Patrick had finally contributed a quick tour of the house. Their first stop was the socket in the wall under the mirror. Thomas looked at it longingly and then anticipated his father by saying, "No, no, no, no, no." He shook his head earnestly, piling up as many "no's" as he could between him and the socket, but desire soon washed away the little dam of his conscience, and he lunged toward the socket, improvising a plug with his small wet fingers. Patrick swept him off his feet and hauled him farther down the corridor. Thomas shouted in protest, planting a couple of sharp kicks in his father's testicles.

"Let's go and see the ladder," gasped Patrick, feeling it would be unfair to offer him anything much less dangerous than electrocution. Thomas recognized the word and calmed down, knowing that the frail, paint-splattered aluminum ladder in the boiler room had its own potential for injury and death. Patrick held him lightly by the waist while he monkeyed up the steps, almost pulling the ladder back on them. As he was lowered to the ground, Thomas burst into a drunken run, reeling his way toward the boiler. Patrick caught him and prevented him from crashing into the water tank. He was completely exhausted by now. He'd had enough. It wasn't as if he hadn't contributed to the baby care. Now he needed a holiday. He staggered back into the drawing room, carrying his wriggling son.

"How are you?" asked Mary.

"Done in," said Patrick.

"I'm not surprised, you've had him for a minute and a half."

Thomas hurtled toward his mother, buckling at the last minute. Mary caught him before his head hit the floor and put him back on his feet.

"I don't know how you cope without a nanny," said Julia.

"I don't know how I would cope with one. I've always wanted to look after the children myself."

"Motherhood takes some people that way," said Julia. "I must say, it didn't in my case, but then I was so *young* when I had Lucy."

To show that she too went mad in the sun-drenched south, Kettle had come down to dinner wearing a turquoise silk jacket and a pair of lemon-yellow linen trousers. The rest of the household, still wearing their sweat-stained shirts and Khaki trousers, left her just where she wanted to be, the lonely martyr to her own high standards.

Thomas slapped his hands over his face as she came in.

"Oh, it's too sweet," said Kettle. "What's he doing?"

"Hiding," said Mary.

Thomas whipped his hands away and stared at the others with his mouth wide open. Patrick reeled back, thunderstruck by his reappearance. It was Thomas's new game. It seemed to Patrick the oldest game in the world.

"It's so relaxing having him hide where we can all see him," said Patrick. "I dread the moment when he feels he has to leave the room."

"He thinks we can't see him because he can't see us," said Mary.

"I must say, I do sympathize," said Kettle. "I rather wish people saw things exactly as I do."

"But you know that they don't," said Mary.

"Not always, darling," said Kettle.

"I'm not sure that it's a story of the self-centered child and the well-adjusted adult," Patrick had made the mistake of theorizing. "Thomas knows that we don't see things as he does, otherwise he wouldn't be laughing. The joke is the shift in perspective. He expects us to flow into his point of view when he covers his face, and back into our own when he whips his hands away. We're the ones who are stuck."

"Honestly, Patrick, you always make everything so intellectual," Kettle complained. "He's just a little boy playing a game.

Apropos of hiding," she said, in the manner of someone taking the wheel from a drunken driver, "I remember going to Venice with Daddy before we were married. We were trying to be discreet because one was expected to make an effort in those days. Well, of course the first thing that happened was that we ran into Cynthia and Ludo at the airport. We decided to behave rather like Thomas and pretend that if we didn't look at them they couldn't see us."

"Was it a success?" asked Patrick.

"Not at all. They shouted our names across the airport at the top of their voices. I would have thought it was perfectly obvious that we didn't want to be spotted, but tact was never Ludo's forte. Anyway, we made all the right noises."

"But Thomas does want to be spotted, that's his big moment," said Mary.

"I'm not saying it's exactly the same situation," said Kettle, with a little splutter of irritation.

"What are the 'right noises'?" Robert had asked Patrick on the way into dinner.

"Anything that comes out of Kettle," he replied, half hoping she would hear.

It didn't help that Julia was so unfriendly to Mary, not that it would have helped if she had been friendly. His loyalty to Mary was not in question (or was it?); what was in question was whether he could last without sex for one more second. Unlike the riotous appetites of adolescence, his present cravings had a tragic tinge, they were cravings for the appetites, metacravings, wanting to want. The question now was whether he would be able to sustain an erection, rather than whether he could ever get rid of the damn thing. At the same time the cravings had to cultivate simplicity, they had to collapse into an object of desire, in order to hide their tragic nature. They were not cravings for things which he could get, but for capacities which he would never have back. What would he do if he did get Julia?

Apologize for being exhausted, of course. Apologize for being tied up. He was having (get it off your chest, dear, it'll do you good) a midlife crisis, and yet he wasn't, because a midlife crisis was a cliché, a verbal Tamazepan made to put an experience to sleep, and the experience he was having was still wide awake—at three-thirty in the fucking morning.

He didn't accept any of it, the reduced horizons, the fading faculties. He refused to buy the pebble spectacles which his Magoo-Standard eyesight pleaded for. He loathed the fungus which seemed to have invaded his bloodstream, blurring everything. The impression of sharpness which he still sometimes gave was a simulation. His speech was like a jigsaw puzzle he had done a hundred times, he was just remembering what he had done before. He didn't make fresh connections anymore. All that was over.

From down the corridor, he heard Thomas starting to cry. The sound sandpapered his nerves. He wanted to console Thomas. He wanted to be consoled by Julia. He wanted Mary to be consoled by consoling Thomas. He wanted everyone to be all right. He couldn't bear it any longer. He threw the bedclothes aside and paced the room.

Thomas soon settled down, but his cries had set off a reaction which Patrick could no longer control. He was going to go to Julia's room. He was going to turn the narrow allotment of his life into a field of blazing poppies. He opened the door slowly, lifting it on its hinges so that it didn't whine. He pulled it closed again with the handle held down so that it didn't click. He released the tongue slowly into the groove. The corridor was glowing with child-friendly light. It was as bright as a prison yard. He walked down it, heel-to-toe, all the way to the end, to Lucy's partially open door. He wanted to check first that she was still in her room. Yes. Fine. He doubled back to Julia's door. His heart was thumping. He felt terrifyingly alive. He leaned close to the door and listened.

What was he going to do next? What would Julia do if he went into her room? Call the police? Pull him into bed whispering, "What took you so long?" Perhaps it was a little tactless to wake her at four in the morning. Maybe he should make an appointment for the following evening. His feet were getting cold, standing on the hexagonal tiles.

"Daddy."

He turned around and saw Robert, pale and frowning in the doorway of his bedroom.

"Hi," whispered Patrick.

"What are you doing?"

"Good question," said Patrick. "Well, I heard Thomas crying . . ." that much was true. "And I wondered if he was all right."

"But why are you standing outside Julia's room?"

"I didn't want to disturb Thomas if he had gone back to sleep," Patrick explained. Robert was too intelligent for this rubbish, but perhaps he was a shade too young to be told the truth. In a couple of years Patrick could offer him a cigar and say, "I'm having this rather awkward *mezzo del camin* thing, and I need a quick affair to buck me up." Robert would slap him on the back and say, "I completely understand, old man. Good luck and happy hunting." In the meantime, he was six years old and the truth had to be hidden from him.

As if to save Patrick from his predicament, Thomas let out another wail of pain.

"I think I'd better go in," said Patrick. "Poor Mummy has been up all night."

He smiled stoically at Robert. "You'd better get some sleep," he said, kissing him on the forehead.

Robert turned back into his room, unconvinced.

The safety plug in Thomas's cluttered room cast a faint orange glow across the floor. Patrick picked his way toward the bed into which Mary carried Thomas every night out of his hated crib, and lowered himself onto the mattress, pushing half a dozen soft toys onto the floor. Thomas writhed and twisted, trying to find a comfortable position. Patrick lay on his side, teetering on the edge of the bed. He certainly wasn't going to get any sleep in this precarious sardine tin, but if he could just let his mind glide along, he might get some rest; if he could go omnogogic, gaining the looseness of dreams without their tyranny, that would be something. He was just going to forget about the Julia incident. What Julia incident?

Perhaps Thomas wouldn't be a wreck when he grew up. What more could one ask?

He was beginning to glide along in half thoughts . . . quarter thoughts, counting down . . . down.

Patrick felt a violent kick land on his face. The warm metallic rush of blood flooded his nose and the roof of his mouth.

"Jesus," he said, "I think I've got a nose bleed."

"Poor you," mumbled Mary.

"I'd better go back to my room," he whispered, rolling backward onto the floor. He replaced Thomas's velveteen bodyguards and clambered to his feet. His knees hurt. He probably had arthritis. He might as well move into his mother's nursing home. Wouldn't that be cozy?

He slouched back down the corridor, pressing his nostril with the knuckle of his index finger. There were spots of blood on his pajamas: so much for the field of poppies. It was five in the morning now, too late for one half of life and too early for the other. No prospect of sleep. He might as well go downstairs, drink a gallon of healthy, organic coffee and pay some bills.

7

Kettle, wearing dark glasses and an enormous straw hat, was already sitting at the stone table. Using her expired boarding pass as a bookmark, she closed her copy of James Pope-Hennesy's biography of Queen Mary and put it down next to her plate.

"It's like a dream," said Patrick, easing his mother's wheelchair into position, "having you both here at the same time."

"Like . . . a . . . dream," said Eleanor, generalizing.

"How are you, my dear?" asked Kettle, bristling with indifference.

"Very . . ."

The effort that Eleanor put into producing, after some time, a high-pitched "well" gave an impression of something quite different, as if she had seen herself heading toward "mad" or "miserable" and just managed to swerve at the last moment. Her radiant smile uncovered the dental bomb site Patrick had so often begged her to repair. It was no use: she was not about to waste money on herself while she could still draw a charitable breath. The tiny amount of spare income she had left was being saved up for Seamus's sensory-privation tanks. In the meantime, she was well on her way to depriving herself of the sensation of eating. Her tongue curled and twisted among shattered crags, searching forlornly for a whole tooth. There were several no-go areas too sensitive for food to enter.

"I'm going to help with the lunch," said regretful, duty-bound Patrick, bolting across the lawn like a swimmer hurrying to the surface after too long a dive.

He knew that it was not really his mother he needed to escape but the poisonous combination of boredom and rage he felt whenever he thought about her. That, however, was a long-term project. "It may take more than one lifetime," he warned himself in a voice of simpering tenderness. Just looking at the next few minutes, he needed to put as many literal-minded yards between himself and his mother as he could manage. That morning, in the nursing home, he had found her sitting by the door with her bag on her knees, looking as if she had been ready for hours. She handed him a faint pencil-written note. It said that she wanted to transfer Saint Nazaire to the Foundation straight away and not, as things stood, after her death. He had managed to postpone things last year, but could he manage it again? The note said she "needed closure" and wanted his help and his "blessing." Seamus's rhetoric had left its fingerprints all over the prose. No doubt he had a closure ritual lined up, a Native American trance dance, which would close its own closure with a macrocosmic and microcosmic, a father sky and mother earth, a symbolic and actual, an immediate and eternal booting out of Patrick and his family from Saint Nazaire. At the center of a dogfight of contradictory emotions, Patrick could sometimes glimpse his longing to get rid of the fucking place. At some point he was going to have to drop the whole thing, he was going to have to come back to Saint Nazaire for a healing drum weekend, to ask Seamus to help him let go of his childhood home, to put the "trans" into what seemed so terribly personal.

As he crossed from the terrace into the olive grove, Patrick imagined himself extolling to a group of neo-shamen and neo-shawomen the appropriateness, the challenge, and "I never would have believed this possible, but I have to use the word 'beauty,' of coming back to this property in order to achieve closure in the letting go process (sighs of appreciation). There was a time when I resented and, yes, I must admit, hated Seamus and the Foundation and my own mother, but my loathing has been miraculously transformed into gratitude, and I can honestly say (little catch in his throat) that Seamus has been not only a wonderful teacher and drum guide, but also my truest friend (the pitter-patter of applause and rattles)."

Patrick ditched his little fantasy with a sarcastic yelp and sat down on the ground with his back to the house, leaning against the knotted gray trunk of an old bifurcating olive tree that he had used all his life to hide and to think. He had to keep reminding himself that Seamus was not a straightforward crook who had cheated a little old lady out of her money. Eleanor and Seamus had corrupted each other with the extravagance of their good intentions. Seamus might have continued to do some good, changing bedpans in Navan—the only town in Ireland to be spelled the same way backward—and Eleanor could have lived on Ryvita and given her income to the blind, or to medical research, or to the victims of torture, but instead they had joined forces to produce a monument of pretension and betrayal. Together they were going to save the world. Together they were going to heighten consciousness by dumbing down an already dangerously dumb constituency. Whatever good there was in Seamus was being destroyed by Eleanor's pathological generosity, and whatever good had been in Eleanor was being destroyed by Seamus's inane vision.

What had turned Eleanor into such a goody-goody? Patrick felt that Eleanor's loathing for her own mother was at the root of her overambitious altruism. Eleanor had told him the story of being taken by her mother to her first big party. It took place in Rome just after the Second World War. Eleanor was a fifteen-year-old girl back for the holidays from her boarding school in Switzerland. Her mother, a rich American and a dedicated snob, had divorced Eleanor's dissolute, charming, and untitled father and married a dwarfish and ill-tempered French duke, Jean de Valencay, obsessed with questions of rank and genealogy. On the tattered stage of a near-communist Republic, and entirely subsidized by his wife's recent industrial wealth, he was all the keener to insist on the antiquity of his bloodline. On the night of the party, Eleanor sat in her mother's immense Hispano-Suiza, parked next to a bombed-out building, around the corner from the glowing windows of Princess Colonna's house. Her stepfather had been taken ill but, languishing in an ornate Renaissance bed, which had been in his family since his wife bought it for him the month before, he made his wife swear that she wouldn't enter the princess's house until after the Duchessa di Dino, over whom she had precedence. Precedence, it turned out, meant that her mother had to arrive late. They waited in the car. In the front, next to the driver, was a footman, periodically sent around to check if the inferior duchessa had arrived. Eleanor was a shy and idealistic girl, happier talking to the cook than to the guests who were being cooked for, but she was still quite impatient and curious about the party.

"Can't we just go? We're not even Italian."

"Jean would kill me," said her mother.

"He can't afford to," said Eleanor.

Her mother froze with fury. Eleanor regretted what she had just said, but also felt a twinge of adolescent pride at giving precedence to honesty over tact. She looked out of the glass cage of her mother's car and saw a tramp stumbling toward them in torn brown clothes. As he grew closer, she saw the skeletal sharpness of his face, the outsized hunger in his eyes. He shuffled up to the car and tapped on the window, pointing pleadingly to his mouth, raising his hands in prayer, pointing again to his mouth.

Eleanor looked over at her mother. She was staring straight ahead, waiting for an apology.

"We've got to give him some money," said Eleanor. "He's starving."

"So am I," said her mother without turning her head. "If this Italian woman doesn't show up soon, I'm going to go crazy."

She tapped the glass separating her from the front seat and waved impatiently at the footman.

When they eventually got inside the house, Eleanor spent the party in her first flush of philanthropic fever. Her rejection of her mother's values fused with her idealism to produce an intoxicating vision of herself as a barefoot saint: she was going to dedicate her life to helping others, as long as they weren't related to her. A few years later, her mother speeded Eleanor along the path of self-denial by allowing herself to be bullied, as she lay dying of cancer, into leaving almost all of her vast fortune outright to Eleanor's stepfather. He had protested that the original will, in which he only had the use of her fortune during his lifetime, was an insult to his honor since it implied that he might cheat his stepdaughters by disinheriting them. He, in turn, broke the promise he had made to his dying wife and left the loot to his nephew. Eleanor was by then too implicated in her spiritual quest to admit how bewildered she was about the loss of all that money. The resentment was being passed on to Patrick, carefully preserved like one of the antiques which Jean loved to collect at his wife's expense. Her mother had liked dukes whereas Eleanor liked would-be witch doctors, but regardless of the social decline the essential formula remained the same: rip off the children for the sake of some cherished self-image, the *grande dame,* or the holy fool. Eleanor had pushed on to the next generation the parts of her experience she wanted to get rid of: divorce, betrayal, mother-hatred, disinheritance; and clung to an idea of herself as part of the world's salvation, the Aquarian Age, the return to primitive Christianity, the revival of shamanism—the terms shifted over the years, but Eleanor's role remained the same: heroic, optimistic, visionary, proud of its humility. The result of her psychological apartheid was to keep both the rejected and aspirant parts of herself frozen. On the night of that Roman party, she had borrowed some money from a family friend and dashed outside to find the starving tramp whose life she was going to save. A few corners later, she found that the streets had not recovered as quickly from six years of war as the merrymakers she had left behind. She couldn't help feeling conspicuous among the rats and the rubble, dressed in her sky-blue ball gown with a large banknote gripped in her eager fist. Shadows shifted in a doorway, and a splash of fear sent her shivering back to her mother's car.

Sixty years later, Eleanor still hadn't worked out a realistic way to act on her desire to be good. She still missed the feast without relieving the famine. When things went wrong, and they always did, the bad experiences were not allowed to inform the passionate teenager; they were exiled to the bad experience dump. A secret half of Eleanor grew more bitter and suspicious, so that the visible half could remain credulous and eager. Before Seamus there had been a long procession of allies. Eleanor handed her life over to them with complete trust and then, within a few hours of their last moment of perfection, they were suddenly rejected, and never mentioned again. What exactly they had done to deserve exile was never mentioned either. Illness was producing a terrifying confluence of the two selves, which Eleanor had gone to such trouble to keep apart. Patrick was curious to know whether the cycle of trust and rejection would remain intact. After all, if Seamus crossed over into the shadows,

Eleanor might want to dismantle the Foundation as vehemently as she had wanted to set it up. Maybe he could delay things for another year. There he was, still hoping to hang on to the place.

Patrick could still remember wandering around the rooms and gardens of his grandmother's half dozen exemplary houses. He had watched a world-class fortune collapse into the moderate wealth that his mother and his aunt Nancy enjoyed from a relatively minor inheritance they received before their mother caved in to the lies and bullying of her second husband. Eleanor and Nancy looked rich to some people, living at good addresses, one in London and one in New York, each with a place in the country, and neither of them needing to work, or indeed shop, wash, garden, or cook for themselves, but in the history of their own family they were surviving on loose change. Nancy, who still lived in New York, combed the catalogs of the world's auction houses for images of the objects she should have owned. On the last occasion Patrick visited her on Sixty-ninth Street, she had scarcely offered him a cup of tea before getting out a sleek black catalog from Christie's, Geneva. It had just arrived and inside was a photograph of two lead *jardinières*, decorated with gold bees almost audibly buzzing among blossoming silver branches. They had been made for Napoleon.

"We didn't even used to comment on them," said Nancy bitterly. "Do you know what I'm saying? There were so many beautiful things. They used to just sit on the terrace in the rain. A million and a half dollars, that's what the little nephew got for Mummy's garden tubs. I mean, wouldn't you like to have some of these things to give to your children?" she asked, carrying over a new set of photograph albums and catalogs, to syncopate the sale price with the sentimental significance of what had been lost.

She went on decanting the poison of her resentment into him for the next two hours.

"It was thirty years ago," he would point out from time to time.

"But the little nephew sells something of Mummy's every week," she growled in defense of her obsession.

The continuing drama of deception and self-deception made Patrick violently depressed. He was only really happy when Thomas first greeted him with a burst of uncomplicated love, throwing open his arms in welcome. Earlier that morning, he had carried Thomas around the terrace, looking for geckos behind the shutters. Thomas grabbed every shutter as they passed, until Patrick unhooked it and creaked it open. Sometimes a gecko shot up the wall toward the shelter of a shutter on the upper floor. Thomas pointed, his mouth rounded with surprise. The gecko was the trigger to the real event, the moment of shared excitement. Patrick tilted his head until his eyes were level with Thomas's, naming the things they came across. "Valerian . . . Japonica . . . Fig tree," said Patrick. Thomas stayed silent until he suddenly said, "Rake!" Patrick tried to imagine the world from Thomas's point of view, but it was a hopeless task. Most of the time, he couldn't even imagine the world from his own point of view. He relied on nightfall to give him a crash course in the real despair that underlay the stale, remote, patchily pleasurable days. Thomas was his antidepressant, but the effect soon wore off as Patrick's lower back started to ache and he caved in to his terror of early death, of dying before the children were old enough to earn a living, or old enough to handle the bereavement. He had no reason to believe that he would die prematurely; it was just the most flagrant and uncontrollable way of letting his children down. Thomas had become the great symbol of hope, leaving none for anyone else.

Thank goodness Johnny was coming later in the month. Patrick felt sure that he was missing something which Johnny could illuminate for him. It was easy to see what was sick but it was so difficult to know what it meant to be well.

"Patrick!"

They were after him. He could hear Julia calling his name. Perhaps she could come and join him behind the olive tree, give him a very quick blow job, so that he felt a little lighter and calmer during lunch. What a great idea. Standing outside her door last night. The tangle of shame and frustration. He clambered to his feet. Knees going. Old age and death. Cancer. Out of his private space into the confusion of other people, or out of the confusion of his private space into the effortless authority of his engagement with others. He never knew which way it would go.

"Julia. Hi, I'm over here."

"I've been sent to find you," said Julia, walking carefully over the rougher ground of the olive grove. "Are you hiding?"

"Not from you," said Patrick. "Come and sit here for a few seconds."

Julia sat down next to him, their backs against the forking trunk.

"This is cozy," she said.

"I've been hiding here since I was a child. I'm surprised there isn't a dent in the ground," said Patrick. He paused and weighed up the risks of telling her.

"I stood outside your door last night at four in the morning."

"Why didn't you come in?" said Julia.

"Would you have been pleased to see me?"

"Of course," she said, leaning over and kissing him briefly on the lips.

Patrick felt a surge of excitement. He could imagine pretending to be young, rolling around among the sharp stones and the fallen twigs, laughing manfully as mosquitoes fed on his naked flesh.

"What stopped you?" asked Julia.

"Robert. He found me hesitating in the corridor."

"You'd better not hesitate next time."

"Is there going to be a next time?"

"Why not? You're bored and lonely; I'm bored and lonely."

"God," said Patrick. "If we got together, there would be a terrifying amount of boredom and loneliness in the room."

"Or maybe they have opposite electrical charges and they'd cancel each other out."

"Are you positively or negatively bored?"

"Positively," said Julia. "And I'm absolutely and positively lonely."

"You may have a point then," smiled Patrick. "There's something very negative about *my* boredom. We're going to have to conduct an experiment under strictly controlled conditions to see whether we achieve a perfect elimination of boredom or an overload of loneliness."

"I really should drag you back to lunch now," said Julia, "or everyone will think we're having an affair."

They kissed. Tongues. He'd forgotten about tongues. He felt like a teenager hiding behind a tree, experimenting with real kissing. It was bewildering to feel alive, almost painful. He felt his pent-up longing for closeness streaming through his hand as he placed it carefully on her belly.

"Don't get me going now," she said, "it's not fair."

They climbed groaning to their feet.

"Seamus had just arrived when I came to get you," said Julia, brushing the dust off her skirt. "He was explaining to Kettle what went on during the rest of the year."

"What did Kettle make of that?"

"I think she's decided to find Seamus charming so as to annoy you and Mary."

"Of course she has. It's only because you've got me all flustered that I hadn't worked that out already."

They made their way toward the stone table, trying not to smile too much or to look too solemn. Patrick felt himself sliding back under the microscope of his family's attention. Mary smiled at him. Thomas threw out his arms in welcome. Robert gazed at him with his intimidating, knowledgeable eyes. He picked up Thomas and smiled at Mary, thinking, "A man may smile and smile and be a villain." Then he sat down next to Robert, feeling as he did when he defended an obviously guilty client in front of a famously difficult judge. Robert noticed everything. Patrick admired his intelligence, but far from short-circuiting his depression as Thomas did, Robert made him more aware of the subtle tenacity of the destructive influence that parents had on their children—that he had on his children. Even if he was an affectionate father, even if he wasn't making the gross mistakes his parents had made, the vigilance he invested in the task created another level of tension, a tension which Robert had picked up. With Thomas he would be different—freer, easier, if one could be free and easy while feeling unfree and uneasy. It was all so hopeless. He really must get a decent night's sleep. He poured himself a glass of red wine.

"It's good to see you, Patrick," said Seamus, rubbing him on the back.

Patrick felt like punching him.

"Seamus has been telling me all about his workshops," said Kettle. "I must say they sound absolutely fascinating."

"Why don't you sign up for one?" said Patrick. "It's the only way you'll see the place in the cherry season."

"Ah, the cherries," said Seamus. "Now, they're something really special. We always have a ritual around the cherries—you know, the fruits of life."

"It sounds very profound," said Patrick. "Do the cherries taste any better than they would if you experienced them as the fruits of a cherry tree?"

"The cherries . . ." said Eleanor. "Yes . . . no . . ." She rubbed out the thought hastily with both hands.

"She loves the cherries. They're grand, aren't they?" said Seamus, clasping Eleanor's hand in his reassuring grip. "I always take her a bowl in the nursing home, freshly picked, you know."

"A handsome rent," said Patrick, draining his glass of wine.

"No," said Eleanor, panic-stricken, "no rent."

Patrick realized he was upsetting his mother. He couldn't even go on being sarcastic. Every avenue was blocked. He poured himself another glass of wine. One day he was going to have to drop the whole thing, but just for now he was going to go on fighting; he couldn't stop himself. Fight with what, though? If only he hadn't gone to such trouble to make his mother's folly legally viable. She had handed him, without any sense of irony, the task of disinheriting himself, and he had carried it out carefully. He had sometimes thought of putting a hidden flaw in the foundations. He had sat in the multijurisdictional meetings with *notaires* and solicitors, discussing ways of circumventing the forced inheritance of the Napoleonic code, the best way to form a charitable foundation, the tax consequences and the accountancy procedures, and he had never done anything except refine the plan to make it stronger and more efficient. The only way out was that elastic band of debt which Eleanor was now proposing to snip. He had really put it in for her protection. He had tried to set aside the hope that she would take advantage of it, but now that he was about to lose that hope, he realized that he had been cultivating it secretly, using it to keep him at a small but fatal distance from the truth. Saint Nazaire would soon be gone forever and there was nothing he could do about it. His mother was an unmaternal idiot and his wife had left him for Thomas. He still had one reliable friend, he sobbed silently, splashing more red wine into his glass. He was definitely going to get drunk and insult Seamus, or maybe he wasn't. In the end, it was even harder to behave badly than to behave well. That was the trouble with not being a psychopath. Every avenue was blocked.

A scene was unfolding around him, no doubt, but his attention was so submerged that he could hardly make out what was
going on. If he clawed his way up the slippery well shaft, what
would he find anyway, except Kettle extolling Queen Mary's
child-rearing methods, or Seamus radiating Celtic charisma?
Patrick looked over the valley, a gauntlet of memory and associ-
ation. In the middle of the view was the Mauduits's ugly farm-
house, its two big acacia trees still growing in the front yard.
When he was a child he had often played with the oafish Marcel
Mauduit. They used to fashion spears out of the pale-green
bamboos that flanked the stream at the bottom of the valley.
They flung them at little birds, which managed to leave several
minutes before the bamboo clattered onto the abandoned
branch. When Patrick was six years old Marcel invited him to
watch his father beheading a chicken. There was nothing more
curious and amusing than watching a chicken run around in silly
circles looking for its head, Marcel explained. You really had to
see it for yourself. The boys waited in the shade of the acacia
trees. An old hatchet was stuck at a handy angle among the criss-
cross cuts on the surface of a brownish plane tree stump. Marcel
danced around like an Indian with a tomahawk, pretending to
decapitate his enemies. In the distance, Patrick could hear the
panic in the chicken coop. By the time Marcel's father arrived,
gripping a hen by the neck, her wings beating uselessly against
his vast belly, Patrick was beginning to side with her. He wanted
this one to get away. He could see that she knew what was going
on. She was held down sideways, her neck stuck over the edge of
the stump. Monsieur Mauduit brought the hatchet down so that
her head flopped neatly at his feet. Then he put the rest of her
quickly on the ground and with an encouraging pat, set her off
on a frantic dash for freedom, while Marcel jeered and laughed
and pointed. Elsewhere, the hen's eyes stared at the sky and
Patrick stared at her eyes.

With his fourth glass of wine, Patrick found his imagination tilting toward Victorian melodrama. Dark scenes formed of their own accord, but he did nothing to stop them. He saw the bloated figure of a drowned Seamus floating in the Thames. His mother's wheelchair seemed to have lost control and was bouncing down the coastal path toward a Dorset cliff. Patrick noted the magnificent National Trust backdrop as she pitched forward over the edge. One day he really must drop the whole thing, get real, get contemporary, accept the facts, but just for the moment he would go on imagining himself putting the last touches to a forged will, while Julia, seated on the edge of his desk, bemused him with the complexity of her undergarments. Just for now, he would have another little splash of wine.

Thomas leaned forward in Mary's lap, and with her usual perfect intuition, she immediately handed him a biscuit. He sank back on her chest convinced, as he was hundreds of times a day, that he would never need something without being given it. Patrick scanned himself for jealousy, but it wasn't there. There was plenty of dark emotion but no rivalry with his infant son. The trick was to keep up a high level of loathing for his own mother, leaving no room to feel jealous of Thomas getting the solid foundations his father so obviously lacked. Thomas leaned forward a second time and, with an inquiring murmur, held out his biscuit to Julia, offering her a bite. Julia looked at the wet and blunted biscuit, made a face and said, "Yuck. No thank you very much."

Patrick suddenly realized that he couldn't make love to someone who missed the point of Thomas's generosity so completely. Or could he? Despite his revulsion, he felt his lust running on, not unlike a beheaded chicken. He had now achieved the pseudo-detachment of drunkenness, the little hillock before the swamps of self-pity and memory loss. He saw that he really must get well, he couldn't go on this way. One day he was going to drop the whole thing, but he couldn't do that until he was ready, and he couldn't control when he would be ready. He could, however, get ready to be ready. He sank back in his chair and agreed at least to that: his business for the rest of the month was to get ready to be ready to be well.

8

"How are you?" asked Johnny, lighting a cheap cigar.

The flaring match brought a patch of color into the black-and-white landscape cast by the moonlight. The two men had come outside after dinner to talk and smoke. Patrick looked at the gray grass and then up at a sky bleached of stars by the violence of the moon. He didn't know where to begin. The previous evening he had somehow managed to transcend the "Yuck" incident, stealing into Julia's bed after midnight and staying there until five in the morning. He had slept with Julia in a speculative haze, which his impulsiveness and greed failed to abolish. Too busy asking himself what adultery felt like, he had almost forgotten to notice what Julia felt like. He wondered what it meant to be back inside a woman who, apart from the relatively faint reality of her limbs and skin, was above all a site of nostalgia. What it certainly did not mean was Time Regained. Being a pig in the trough of a disreputable emotion turned out to fall short of the spontaneous timelessness of involuntary memory and associative thinking. Where were the uneven cobblestones and silver spoons and silver doorbells of his own life? If he stumbled across them, would floating bridges spring into being, with their own strange sovereignty, belonging to neither the original nor the repeated, the past nor the fugitive present, but to some kind of enriched present capable of englobing the linearity of time? He had no reason to think so. He felt deprived not only of the ordinary magic of intensified imagination, but of the even more ordinary magic of immersion in his own physical sensations. He wasn't going to scold himself for a lack of particularity in experiencing his sexual pleasure. All sex was prostitution for both participants, not always in the commercial sense, but in the deeper etymological sense that they stood in for something else. The fact that this was sometimes done so effectively that there were weeks or months in which the object of desire and the person one happened to be in bed with seemed identical, could not prevent the underlying model of desire from beginning to drift away, sooner or later, from its illusory home. The strangeness of Julia's case was that she stood in for herself, as she had been twenty years ago, a pre-drift lover.

"Sometimes a cigar is just a cigar," said Johnny, realizing that Patrick didn't want to answer his question.

"When's that?" said Patrick.

"Before you light it—after that, it's a symptom of unreconstructed orality."

"I wouldn't be having this cigar unless I'd given up smoking," said Patrick. "I want to make that absolutely clear."

"I completely understand," said Johnny.

"One of the burdens of being a psychologist," said Patrick, "is that if you ask someone how they are, they tell you. Instead of saying that I feel fine, I have to give you the real answer: *not* fine."

"Not fine?"

"Bad, chaotic, terrified. My emotional life seems to cascade into wordlessness in every direction, not only because Thomas hasn't taken up words yet and Eleanor has already been abandoned by them, but also, internally, I feel the feebleness of everything I can control surrounded by the immensity of everything I can't control. It's very primitive and very strong. There's no wood left for the fire that keeps the wild animals at bay, that sort of thing. But also something even more confusing—the wild animals are a part of me that's winning. I can't stop them from destroying me without destroying them, but I can't destroy them without destroying myself. Even that makes it sound too organized. It's really more like a cartoon of cats fighting: a spinning blackness with exclamation Patrick's flying off it."

"You sound as if you have a good grasp of what's going on," said Johnny.

"That should be a strength, but since I'm trying to communicate how little grasp I have of what's going on, it's a hindrance."

"It's not a hindrance to your telling me about the chaos. It's only a hindrance if you're trying to manifest it."

"Perhaps I do want to manifest it, so that it takes some concrete form, instead of it being this enormous state of mind."

"I'm sure it does take some concrete form."

"Hmm . . ."

Patrick scanned the concrete forms, the insomnia, the heavy drinking, the bouts of overeating, the constant longing for solitude, which, if achieved, made him desperate for company, not to mention (or should he mention it? He felt the heavy gravitational field of confession surrounding Johnny) last night's adulterous incident. He could remember only a few hours ago concluding that it had been a mistake, and beginning to imagine the mature discussion he was going to have with Julia. Now that the tide of alcohol was rising again, he was becoming more and more convinced that he had simply gone to bed with the wrong attitude. He must do better. He would do better.

"I must do better," said Patrick.

"Do what better?"

"Oh, everything," said Patrick vaguely.

He certainly wasn't going to tell Johnny, and then have his inflamed appetites placed in some pathological context, or worse, in a therapeutic program. On the other hand, what was the point of his friendship with Johnny if it wasn't truthful? They had been friends for thirty years. Johnny's parents had known his parents. They knew each other's lives in depth. If Patrick had been wondering whether to commit suicide, he would have asked Johnny's opinion. Maybe he could shift the conversation away from his own mental health and onto one of their favorite topics: the way that time was grinding down their generation. Their shorthand for this process was "the retreat from Moscow," thanks to the vivid picture they both had of the straggling survivors of Napoleon's army limping, bloodstained and bootless, through a landscape of frozen horses and dying men. Out of professional curiosity, Johnny had recently attended a reunion dinner of their year at school. He reported back to Patrick. The captain of the First Eleven was now a crack-head. The most brilliant student of their year was buried in the middle ranks of the civil service. Gareth Williams couldn't come because he was in a mental hospital. Their most "successful" contemporary was the head of a merchant bank who, according to Johnny, "failed to register on the authenticity graph." That was the graph that Johnny cared about, the one that would determine whether, in his own eyes, he ended up in a roadside ditch or not.

"I'm sorry to hear that you've been feeling bad," said Johnny, before Patrick could get him onto the safe ground of collective disappointment, sellout, and loss.

"I slept with Julia last night," said Patrick.

"Did that make you feel better?"

"It made me wonder if I was feeling better. It was perhaps just a little bit too cerebral."

"That's what you 'must do better.'"

"Exactly. I didn't know whether to tell you. I thought I might have to stop if we worked out exactly what was going on."

"You've worked it out already."

"Up to a point. I know that Thomas is making me revisit my own infancy in a way that Robert never did. Maybe it's the prominence of that old prop, a mother who needs mothering, which has lent so much authenticity to this revival. In any case, a deep sense of ancestral gloom stalks the night, and I would rather spend it with Julia who, instead of the primal chaos I feel on my own, offers the relatively innocuous death of youth."

"It all sounds very allegorical—Primal Chaos and the Death of Youth. Sometimes a woman is just a woman."

"Before you light her up?"

"No, no, that's a cigar," said Johnny.

"Honestly, there are no easy answers. Just when you think you've worked something out . . ."

Patrick could hear the whining of a mosquito in his right ear. He turned his head and blew smoke in its direction. The sound stopped.

"Obviously, I would love to have real, embodied, fully present experiences—especially of sex—" Patrick went on, "but, as you've pointed out, I'm taking refuge in an allegorical realm where everything seems to represent a well-known syndrome or conflict. I remember complaining to my doctor about the side effects of the Ribavirin he prescribed for me. "Oh, yes, that's known," he said with a kind of tremendous, uninfectious calm. Mind you, when I told him about a side effect that wasn't known, he dismissed it by saying, 'I've never heard of that before.' I think I'm trying to be like him, to immunize myself against experience by concentrating on phenomena. I keep thinking, 'That's known,' when in fact I feel the opposite, that it's alien and menacing and out of control."

Patrick felt a sharp sting. "Fucking mosquitoes," he said, slapping the back of his neck rather too hard. "I'm being eaten alive."

"I've never heard of that before," said Johnny skeptically.

"Oh, it's *known*," Patrick assured him. "It's quite standard among the highlanders of Papua, New Guinea. The only question is whether they make you eat yourself alive."

Johnny let this prospect drown in silence.

"Listen," said Patrick, leaning forward, and speaking more rapidly than before, "I'm not in any serious doubt that everything I'm going through at the moment corresponds with the texture of my infancy in some way. I'm sure that my midnight angst resembles some free fall I felt in my crib when, for my own good, and so as to save me from becoming a manipulative little monster, my parents did exactly what suited them and ignored me. As you know, my mother only paves the road to hell with the best intentions, so we can assume that my father was the advocate of the character-building advantages of a will-breaking upbringing. But how can I really know and what good would it do me to find out?"

"Well, for a start, you're not using your powers of persuasion to keep Mary away from Thomas. Without any sense of connection with your own infancy, you almost certainly would be. It's true that the hardest maps to draw up are the very early ones, the first two years. We can only work with inferences. If, for example, someone had an acute intolerance of being kept waiting, felt a perpetual hunger, which eating turned into a bloated despair, and was kept awake by hypervigilance . . ."

"Stop! Stop!" sobbed Patrick. "It's all true."

"That would imply a certain quality of early care," Johnny went on, "different from the kind of omnipotent fantasy world that Eleanor wants to perpetuate with her 'non-ordinary reality' and her 'power animals.' We are always 'the veils that veil us from ourselves,' but looking into infancy, with no memories and no established sense of self, it's *all veils*. If the privation is bad enough, there's nobody there to have the insights. It's a question of reinforcing the best false self you can lay your hands on—the authenticity project is not an option. But that's not your case. I think you can afford to lose control, to go into the free fall. If the past was going to destroy you it already would have."

"Not necessarily. It might have been waiting for just the right moment. The past has all the time in the world. It's only the future which is running out."

He emptied the wine bottle into his glass.

"And the wine," he added.

"So," said Johnny, "you're going to try to 'do better' tonight?"

"Yes. My conscience isn't rebelling in quite the way I expected. I'm not trying to punish Mary by going to bed with Julia—I'm just looking for a little tenderness. I think Mary would almost be relieved if she knew. It's a burden to someone like her not being able to give me what I need."

"You're really doing her a favor," said Johnny.

"Yes," said Patrick, "I don't like to boast about it, but I'm helping her out. She won't need to feel guilty about abandoning me."

"If only more people had your sense of generosity," said Johnny.

"I think quite a lot of people do," said Patrick. "Anyway, these philanthropic impulses run in my family."

"All I feel like saying," said Johnny, "is that there's no point to your free fall unless it produces some insight. This is the time for Thomas to develop secure attachment. If you can make it through to his third birthday without destroying your marriage or making Mary feel depressed, that would be a great achievement. I think Robert is already well grounded. Anyway, he has that amazing talent for mimicry, which he uses to play with whatever weighs on his mind."

Before Patrick had time to respond, he heard the screen door swing open and snap back again on its magnetic strip. Both men fell silent and waited to see who was coming out of the house.

"Julia," said Patrick, as she came into view, swishing across the gray grass, "come and join us."

"We've all been wondering what you're up to," said Julia. "Are you baying at the moon, or working out the meaning of life?"

"Neither," said Patrick, "there's too much baying in this valley already, and we worked out the meaning of life years ago. 'Walk tall and spit on the graves of your enemies.' Wasn't that it?"

"No, no," said Johnny. "It was 'love thy neighbor as thyself.'"

"Oh, well, given how much I love myself, it amounts to pretty much the same thing."

"Oh, darling," said Julia, resting her hands on Patrick's shoulders, "are you your own worst enemy?"

"I certainly hope so," said Patrick. "I dread to think what would happen if somebody else turned out to be better at it than me."

Johnny ground his crackling, splitting cigar into the ashtray.

"I might head for bed," he said, "while you decide who's grave to spit on."

"Eenee, meenee, minee, mo," said Patrick.

"Do you know, Lucy's generation doesn't say, 'Catch a nigger by the toe' anymore; they say, 'Catch a tiger by the toe.' Isn't it sweet?"

"Have they rewritten 'Rock a Bye Baby' as well? Or is the cradle still allowed to fall?" asked Patrick. "God," he added, looking at Johnny, "it must be difficult for you hearing a person's unconscious breaking through every sentence."

"I try not to hear it," said Johnny, "when I'm on holiday."

"But you don't succeed."

"I don't succeed," smiled Johnny.

"Has everyone gone to bed?" asked Patrick.

"Everyone except Kettle," Julia replied. "She wanted to have a little heart to heart; I think she's in love with Seamus. She's been to tea in his cottage for the last two afternoons."

"She *what?*" said Patrick.

"She's stopped talking about Queen Mary's widowhood and started talking about 'opening up to one's full potential.'"

"That bastard. He's going to try to get Mary disinherited as well," said Patrick. "I'm going to have to kill him."

"Wouldn't it be more efficient to kill Kettle before she changes her will?" asked Julia.

"Good thinking," said Patrick. "My judgment was clouded by emotion."

"What is this?" said Johnny. "An evening with the Macbeths? What about just letting her open to her full potential?"

"Jesus," said Patrick, "who have you been reading recently? I thought you were a realist, not a human potential moron who claims to see El Dorados of creativity in every flower arrangement. Even in the hands of a psychotherapeutic genius, Kettle's peak would be joining a Tango class in Cheltenham, but with Seamus her 'full potential' is to be fully ripped off."

"The potential, which Kettle hasn't realized—and she's not alone," said Johnny, "has nothing to do with hobbies, or even achievements, it's to do with being able to enjoy anything at all."

"Oh, that potential," said Patrick. "You're right, of course, we all need to work on that."

Julia grazed his thigh discreetly with her fingernails. Patrick felt a half erection creep its way into the most inconvenient possible position among the folds of his underwear. Not particularly wanting to struggle with his trousers in front of Johnny, he waited confidently for the problem to disappear. He didn't have to wait long.

Johnny got to his feet and said good night to Patrick and Julia.

"Sleep well," he added, starting out toward the house.

"One may be too busy opening up to one's full potential," said Patrick in a racy version of his Kettle voice.

As soon as they heard Johnny entering the house, Julia climbed astride Patrick's lap, facing him with her hands dangling lightly over his shoulders.

"Does he know?" she asked.

"Yes."

"Is that a good idea?"

"He won't tell anyone."

"Maybe, but now it's too late for us not to tell anyone. I can't believe we're already into who knows what, that's all. We've only just been to bed together and it's already a problem of knowledge."

"It's always a problem of knowledge."

"Why?"

"Because there was this garden, right? And this apple tree . . ."

"Oh, honestly, that has nothing to do with it. That's a different kind of knowledge."

"They came together. In the absence of God, we have the omniscience of gossip to keep us preoccupied with who knows what."

"I'm not in fact preoccupied with who knows what, I'm preoccupied with how we feel for each other. I think you want it to be about knowledge because you're more at home in your head than in your heart. Anyhow, you didn't have to tell Johnny."

"Whatever," said Patrick, suddenly drained of all desire to prove a point or win an argument. "I often think there should be a superhero called Whateverman. Not an action hero like Superman or Spiderman, but an inaction hero, a hero of resignation."

"Is there a comma between 'Whatever' and 'Man'?

"Only when he can be bothered to speak, which, believe me, isn't often. When someone screams, 'There's a meteor headed straight for us! It's the end of all life on Earth!' he says, 'Whatever, man' with a comma in between. But when he is invoked, during an episode of ethnic cleansing, or paranoid schizophrenia, as in, 'this is a job for Whateverman,' it's all in one word."

"Does he have a cloak?"

"God, no. He wears the same old jeans and T-shirt year in year out."

"And this fantasy is all in the service of not admitting that you were wrong to tell Johnny."

"It was wrong if it upset you," said Patrick. "But when my oldest friend asked me what was going on, it would have been glib to leave out the most important fact."

"Poor darling, you're just too—"

"Authentic," Patrick interrupted. "That's always been my trouble."

"Why don't you bring some of that authenticity upstairs?" asked Julia, leaning forward and giving Patrick a long slow kiss.

He was grateful that she made it impossible for him to answer her question. He wouldn't have known what to say. Was she mocking his shallow disembodied presence the night before? Or hadn't she noticed? The problem of other minds. Christ, he was at it again. They were kissing. Get into it. Picture of himself getting into it. No, not the picture, the thing in itself. Whatever that was. Who was to say that authenticity lay in being oblivious to the reflective aspect of the mind? He was speculative. Why suppress that in favor of what was, in the end, just a picture of authenticity, a cliché of into-it-ness?

Julia broke off the kiss.

"Where have you gone?" she asked.

"I was lost in my head," he admitted. "I think I was thrown by your request for me to bring my authenticity upstairs—there's just so much of it, I'm not sure I can manage."

"I'll help," said Julia.

They untangled themselves and walked back into the house, holding hands, like a couple of moonstruck teenagers.

When they reached the landing and were about to slip into Julia's bedroom, they heard stifled giggling from Lucy's bedroom, followed by a crescendo of hushing. Transformed from furtive lovers into concerned parents, they walked down the corridor with a new authority. Julia tapped gently on the door and immediately pushed it open. The room was dark, but light from the corridor fell across a crowded bed. All of Lucy's indispensable soft toys, her white rabbit and her blue-eyed dog and, incredibly, the chipmunk she had chewed religiously since her third birthday, were scattered in various buckled postures across the bedspread, and replaced, inside the bed, by a live boy.

"Darling?" said Julia.

The children made no sound.

"It's no use pretending to be asleep. We heard you down the corridor."

"Well," said Lucy, sitting up suddenly, "we're not doing anything wrong."

"We didn't say you were," said Julia.

"This is the most outrageous subplot," said Patrick. "Still, I don't see why they shouldn't sleep together if they want to."

"What's a subplot?" asked Robert.

"Another part of the main story," said Patrick, "reflecting it in some more or less flagrant way."

"Why are *we* a subplot?" asked Robert.

"You're not," said Patrick. "You're a plot in your own right."

"We've just got so much to talk about," said Lucy, "we just couldn't wait until tomorrow."

"Is that why you two are still up?" asked Robert. "Because you've got so much to talk about. Is that why you said we were a subplot?"

"Listen, forget I ever said it," said Patrick. "We're all each other's subplots," he added, trying to confuse Robert as much as possible.

"Like the moon going around the Earth," said Robert.

"Exactly. Everyone thinks they're on the Earth, even when they're on somebody else's moon."

"But the Earth goes around the sun," said Robert. "Who's on the sun?"

"The sun is uninhabitable," said Patrick, relieved that they had traveled so far from the original motive of his comment. "Its only plot is to keep us going around and round."

Robert looked troubled and was about to ask another question when Julia interrupted him.

"Can we return to our own planet for a second?" she asked. "I suppose I don't mind you sharing a bed, but remember we're going to Aqualand tomorrow, so you must go straight to sleep."

"What else would we do?" said Lucy, starting to giggle. "Smudging?"

She and Robert made sounds of extravagant revulsion and collapsed in a heap of limbs and laughter.

9

Patrick ordered another double espresso and watched the waitress weave her way back to the bar, only momentarily transfixed by a vision of her sprawled across one of the tables, gripping its sides while he fucked her from behind. He was too loyal to linger over the waitress when he was already involved in a fantasy about the girl in the black bikini on the other side of the cafe, her eyes closed and her legs slightly parted, absorbing the beams of the morning sun, still as a lizard. He might never recover from the look of intense seriousness with which she had examined her bikini line. An ordinary woman would have reserved that expression for a bathroom mirror, but she was a paragon of self-absorption, running her finger along the inside edge of her bikini, lifting it and realigning it still closer to the center, so that it interfered as little as possible with the total nudity which was her real object. The mass of holiday makers on the Promenade Rose, shuffling forward to claim their coffin-sized plot of beach, might as well not have existed; she was too fascinated by the state of her tan, her wax job, her waist line, too in love with herself to notice them. He was in love with her, too. He was going to die if he didn't have her. If he was going to be lost, and it looked as if he was, he wanted to be lost inside her, to drown in the little pool of her self love—if there was room.

Oh, no, not that. Please. A piece of animated sports equipment had just walked up to her table, put his pack of red Marlboros and his mobile phone next to her mobile phone and her pack of Marlboro Lights, kissed her on the lips and sat down, if that was the right term for the muscle-bound bouncing with which he eventually settled into the chair next to hers. Heartbreak. Disgust. Fury. Patrick skimmed over the ground of his immediate emotions and then forced himself upward into the melancholy sky of resignation. Of course she was spoken for a million times over. In the end it was a good thing. There could be no real dialogue between those who still thought that time was on their side, and those who realized that they were dangling from its jaws, like Saturn's children, already half-devoured. Devoured. He could feel it: the dull efficiency of a praying mantis tearing arcs of flesh from the still living aphid it has clamped between its forelegs; the circular hobbling of a wildebeest, reluctant to lie down with the lion who hangs confidently from his neck. The fall, the dust, the last twitch.

Yes, in the end it was a good thing that Bikini Girl was spoken for. He lacked the pedagogic patience and the particular kind of vanity which would have enabled him to opt for the cheap solution of being a youth vampire. It was Julia who had got him used to sex during her fortnight's stay, and it was among the time refugees of her blighted generation that he must look for lovers. With the possible exception, of course, of the waitress who was now weaving her way back toward him. There was something about the shopworn sincerity of her smile which suited his mood. Or was it the stubborn pout of the labial mould formed by her jeans? Should he get a shot of brandy to tip into his espresso? It was only ten-thirty in the morning, but there were already several misty-cold glasses of beer blazing among the round tables. He only had two days of holiday left. They might as well be debauched. He ordered the brandy. At least that way she would be back soon. That's how he liked to think of her, weaving back and forth on his behalf, tirelessly attending to his clumsy search for relief.

He turned toward the sea, but the harsh glitter of the water blinded him and, while he shielded his eyes from the sun, he found himself imagining all the people on that body-packed curve of blond sand, shining with protective lotions, playing with bats and balls, lolling in the placid bay, reading on their towels and mattresses, all being blasted by a fierce wind and blown into a fine veil of sparkling sand, and the collective murmur, pierced by louder shouts and sharper cries, falling silent.

He must rush down that beach to shelter Mary and the children from ruin, give them a few more seconds of life with the decomposing shield of his own body. He struggled so hard to get away from his roles as a father and a husband, only to miss them the moment he succeeded. There was no better antidote to his enormous sense of futility than the enormous sense of purpose which his children brought to the most obviously futile tasks, such as pouring buckets of seawater into holes in the sand. Before he managed to break away from his family, he liked to imagine that once he was alone he would become an open field of attention, or a solitary observer training his binoculars on some rare species of insight usually obscured by the mass of obligations that swayed before him like a swarm of twittering starlings. In reality solitude generated its own roles, not based on duty but on hunger. He became a café voyeur, drunk with desire, or a calculating machine compulsively assessing the inadequacy of his income.

Was there any activity which didn't freeze into a role? Could he listen without being a listener, think without being a thinker? No doubt there was a flowing world of present participles, of listening and thinking, rushing along beside him, but it was part of the grim allegorical tinge of his mentality that he sat with his back to this glittering torrent, staring at a world of stone. Even his affair with Julia seemed to have *The Sorrows of Adultery* carved on its plinth. Instead of thrilling him with his own audacity, it reminded him of how little he had left. After they had started sleeping together, his days were spent sprawled on a poolside lounger, feeling that he might as well have been splayed in a roadside ditch, discouraging the excitement of some hungry rats rather than turning down the demands of his adorable children. His guilt-fueled bouts of charm toward Mary were as flagrant as his row-picking arguments. The margin of freedom he had gained with Julia was soon filled with the concrete of another role. She was his mistress, he was her married man. She would struggle to get him away, he would struggle to keep her in the mistress slot without tearing his family apart. They were already in a perfectly structured situation, with ultimately opposed interests. Its currency was deception: of Mary, of each other, and of themselves. It was only in the immediate greed of a bed that they could find any common ground. He was amazed by the amount of defeat and inconvenience that already surrounded his affair with Julia. The only sane action would be to end it straight away, to define it as a summer fling and not try to elaborate it into a love affair. The terrible thing was that he had already lost control of the situation. He only felt well when he was in bed with her, when he was inside her, when he was coming inside her. Kneeling on the floor, that had been good, when she had sat in the armchair with her knees up and her legs spread. And the night of the thunderstorm, the air awash with free ions, when she stood in the window, gasping at the lightning and he stood behind her and . . . and here came his brandy, thank God.

He smiled at the waitress. What was the French for, "How about it, darling?" Something, something, something, *chérie.* He'd better stick to the French for "same again"—stay on safe ground. Yes, he was lost because he liked everything about Julia:

the smell of tobacco on her breath, the taste of her menstrual blood. He couldn't rely on revulsion of any sort to set him free. She was kind, she was careful, she was accommodating. He was going to have to rely on the machine of their situation to grind them down, as he knew it would.

"*Encore la même chose*," he called to the waitress, swirling his finger over his empty glass while she unloaded her tray at a nearby table. She nodded. She was the waitress, and he was the waiter waiting for the waitress. Everyone had their role.

He could feel the *fin de saison*, the lassitude of the beaches and restaurants, the sense that it was time to get back to school and to work, back to the big cities; and among the residents, relief at the subsiding numbers, the fading heat. All his guests had left Saint Nazaire. Kettle had left in triumph, knowing she would be the first to return. She had signed up for Seamus's Basic Shaman workshop and then, in a kind of shopper's euphoria, decided to stay on for the Chi Gong course given by a ponytailed martial artist whose photograph she pored over whenever there was someone to watch her. Seamus had given her a book called *The Power of Now*, which she kept facedown beside her deck chair, not as reading material, obviously, but as a badge of allegiance to the power that now ran Saint Nazaire. She had taken him up for the simple reason that it was the most annoying thing she could think of doing. It occupied the time when she was not criticizing Mary for the way she brought up the children. Mary had learned to walk away, to make herself unavailable for half days at a time. Kettle had never known what to do with those fallow periods until she decided to become a fan of Seamus's Transpersonal Foundation. *The Power of Now* only disappeared when Anne Whitling, an old friend of Kettle's, wearing her own vast straw hat with an Isadora Duncan length scarf trailing dangerously behind it, talked her way down the coast from one of the fashionable Caps. Her profound inability to listen to anyone else was unhappily married to a hysterical concern about what other people thought of her. When Thomas started babbling excitedly to Mary about the hose that was coiled next to the pool house, Anne said, "What's he saying? What's he saying? If he's saying my nose is too big, I'm going to commit." This charming abbreviation, which Patrick had never heard before, made him imagine bloodstained articles about men's fear of commitment. Should he commit to his marriage? Or commit to Julia? Or just commit?

How could he go on feeling so awful? And how could he stop? Stealing a picture from his senile mother was one obvious way to cheer himself up. The last two valuable paintings she owned were a pair of Boudins, making up complementary views of the beach at Deauville, and worth approximately two hundred thousand pounds. He had to rap himself over the knuckles for assuming that he would inherit the Boudins in "the normal course of events." Only three days ago, just after waving an exhilarating farewell to Kettle, he had received another of Eleanor's faint, painstaking, pencil-written notes, saying that she wanted the Boudins sold and the money used to build Seamus's sensory-privation annex. Things just weren't moving along fast enough for the Kubla Khan of the mindless realms.

He could imagine himself in some distant past thinking he ought to "keep the Boudins in the family," feeling sentimental about those banked-up clouds, the atmosphere of a lost yet vividly present world, the cultural threads radiating from those Normandy beaches. Now they might as well have been two cash dispensers in the wall of his mother's nursing home. If he was going to have to walk away from Saint Nazaire, it would put a spring in his step to know that the sale of the Boudins and the sale of the London flat and a preparedness to move to Queen's Park, would allow him to save Thomas from the converted cupboard in which he now slept and offer him an ordinary-sized children's bedroom in a terraced house on a main road, no more than a two-hour traffic jam from his brother's school. Anyway, the last thing he needed was a view of a beach at the other end of France when he could so easily admire the carcinogenic inferno of Les Lecques through the amber lens of his second cognac. "The sea meets the sky here as well, thank you very much, Monsieur Boudin," he muttered to himself, already a little light-headed.

Did Seamus know about the note? Had he written it himself? Whereas Patrick was simply going to ignore Eleanor's request to make the gift of Saint Nazaire absolute in her own lifetime, he was going to make a more drastic refusal in the case of the Boudins: steal them. Unless Seamus had written evidence that Eleanor wanted to give the paintings to the Foundation, any contest would come down to his word against Seamus's. Luckily, Eleanor's post-stroke signature looked like an incompetent forgery. Patrick felt confident that he could run legal circles around the visionary Irishman, even if he was unable to win a popularity contest against him when it was judged by his own mother. It was really, he assured himself, as he briskly ordered a *"dernier cognac,"* like a man with better things to do than get blind drunk before lunch, really just a question of how to unhook these two oily ATMs from the wall.

The light on the Promenade Rose rained down on him like a shower of hot needles. Even behind his dark glasses his eyeballs ached. He was really quite . . . the coffee and the brandy . . . a little jet engine whistle. "Walkin' on the beaches / Lookin' at the peaches / Na, na-na, na-na-na-na-na." Where was that from? Press Retrieve. Nothing happens as usual. Gerald Manley Hopkins? He cackled wildly.

He must have a cigar. Must have, must have, must have, on a must have basis. When was a cigar just a cigar? Before you must have it.

With any luck, he should arrive back at the Tahiti Beach (Irish accent) just in toyem for a syphilised battle of whine. "God bless Seamus," he added piously, making a puking sound at the foot of a squat bronze lamppost. Puns: the symptom of a schizoid personality.

Here was the Tabac. The red cylinder. Whoops. *"Pardon, Madame."* What was it with these big, tanned, wrinkly French women with chunky gold jewelry, orange hair and caramel-colored poodles? They were *everywhere.* Unlock the glass cabinet. *"Celui-la,"* pointing to a Hoyo de Monterey. The little guillotine. Snip. Do you have something more serious at the back of the shop? *Un vrai guillotine. Non, non, Madame, pas pour les cigars, pour les clients!* Snap.

More hot needles. Hurry to the next patch of pine shade. Maybe he should have one more teeny weeny brandy before going back to his family. Mary and the boys, he loved them so much, it made him want to cry.

He stopped at Le Dauphin. Coffee, cognac, cigar. Just as well to get these chores out of the way, then he'd be free to enjoy the rest of the day. He lit his cigar and as the thick smoke trickled back out of his mouth, he felt he was being shown a pattern, like a rug unrolling in a rug shop. He had taken Mary, a good woman, and made her into an instrument of torture, a weird echo of Eleanor forty years ago: never available, always exhausted by her dedication to an altruistic project which didn't include him. He had achieved this by the ironic device of rejecting the sort of woman who would have made a bad mother, like Eleanor, and choosing one who was such a good mother that she was incapable of letting one drop of her love escape from her children. He could see that his obsession with not having enough money was only the material form of his emotional privation. He had known these facts for years, but just at that moment he felt that his grasp of them was especially subtle and clear and that his understanding gave him complete mastery of the situation. A second mouthful of heavy blue Cuban smoke drifted into the air. He was entranced by the sense of his own detachment, as if he had been set free by an instinctual expertise, like a sea bird who breaks into flight just before a wave crashes onto the rock where it was perched.

The feeling passed. With only orange juice for breakfast, the six espressos and four glasses of brandy were having a bar brawl in his stomach. What was he doing? He had given up smoking. He flung the cigar toward the gutter. Whoops. *"Pardon, Madame."* My God, it was the same woman, or almost the same woman. He might have set fire to her poodle. The newspaper headlines didn't bear thinking about . . . *Anglais intoxiqué . . . incendie de caniche . . .* He must call Julia. He could live without her as long as he knew that she couldn't live without him. That was the deal the furiously weak made between their permanent disappointment and their temporary consolations. He looked at it with some disgust but knew that he would sign the contract anyway. He must make sure she was waiting for him, missing him, longing for him, and expecting him in her flat on Monday night.

The nearest phone booth, a doorless and piss-scented waste-paper basket, was smoldering in full sunlight on the next corner. The blue plastic burned his hand as he dialed the number.

"I can't come to the phone at the moment, but please leave a message . . ."

"Hello? Hello? It's Patrick. Are you hiding behind your machine? . . . Okay, I'll call you tomorrow. I love you." He'd almost forgotten to say that.

So, she wasn't in. Unless she was in bed with another man, sniggering at his tentative phone message. If he had one thing to say to the world, it was this: never, never have a child without first getting a reliable mistress. And don't be deceived by the false horizons—"when the breast-feeding is over; when he spends the whole night in his own bed; when he goes to university." Like a team of runaway horses, the empty promises hauled a man over shattered stone and giant cactuses, while he prayed for the tangled reins to snap. It was all over, there was no comfort in marriage, just duty and obligation. He sank down on the nearest bench, needing to pause before he saw his family again. The cerulean huts and parasols of the Tahiti Beach were already in view, tunneling deep into his memory. He had been Thomas's age when he first went there and Robert's when his memories became most intense: those pedalo rides, which he expected to grind up on African beaches; jumping up and down on the sand castles carefully assembled for him by foreign au pairs; being allowed to order his own drinks and ice creams as his chin cleared the wooden counter for the first time. As a teenager, he had taken books to the beach. They helped to hide his bulging trunks while he stared from behind his wraparound shades at the first blush of topless sunbathing to pass over the pale sands of Les Lecques. Since then the Tahiti had grown thinner and thinner, until the whole beach was nearly abolished by the sea. In his twenties, he had watched the municipality rebuild it with thousands of tons of imported pebbles. Every Easter sand was dredged from the bay and spread over the artificial beach by teams of bulldozers, and every winter storms clawed it back into the bay.

He leaned forward and rested his chin on his hands. The initial impact of the coffee and brandy was dying out, leaving him only with a doomed nervous energy, like a flung stone bouncing over the water a few times before sinking beneath its surface. He looked wearily at the simulacrum of the original beach, if "original" was the word for the beach he had known when he was the same age as his children were now. He let this pitifully local definition melt away, and tumbled back through geological time to the perfect boredom of the first beach, with its empty rock pools and its simple molecules not knowing what to do with themselves for billions of years on end. Can anyone think of anything to do other than jostle around? Rows of blank faces, like asking a group of old friends to suggest a new restaurant on a Sunday night. Seen from this primal shore, the emergence of

human life looked like Géricault's *Raft of the Medusa*, greenish
ghosts drowning in a frigid ocean of time.

He really needed another drink to recover from the chaos of
his imagination. And some food. And some sex. He needed to
get grounded, as Seamus would say. He needed to rejoin his own
species, the rows and rows of belching animals on the beach with
only a razor blade or a wax job between them and a great thick
pelt; paying with agonizing back pains for their pretentious
upright posture, but secretly longing to hobble along with their
knuckles dragging in the sand, squealing and grunting, fighting
and fucking. Yes, he needed to get real. Only consideration for
the white-haired old lady with swollen ankles farther down the
bench prevented him from raining punches on his clenched pec-
torals and letting out a territorial bellow. Consideration and, of
course, his growing sense of liverish gloom and midday hangover.

He hauled himself up and scraped his way along the last few
hundred yards to the Tahiti. Swaying toward him over the
smooth pink concrete, an almost naked girl with overpoweringly
perfect breasts and a diamond nestling in her navel, locked her
eyes onto his and smiled, raising both her arms, ostensibly to
wrap her long blonde hair into a loose coil above her head, but
really to simulate the way her limbs would be arranged if she
were lying on a bed with her arms thrown back. Oh, God, why
was life so badly organized? Why couldn't he just hoist her onto
a hot car hood and tear off that turquoise excuse for a bikini
bottom? She wanted it, he wanted it. Well, anyway, he wanted it.
She probably wanted exactly what she had, the power to disturb
every heterosexual man—and let's not forget our lesbian col-
leagues, he added with mayoral unction—who she scythed
through as she strolled back and forth between her depressing
boyfriend and her nippy little car. She walked by, he staggered
on. She might as well have chopped off his genitals and chucked
them in the sand. He could feel the blood running down his legs,

hear the dogs squabbling over the unexpected meat. He wanted to sit down again, to lie down, to bury himself deep underground. He was finished as a man. He envied the male spider who was eaten straight after fertilizing the female, rather than consumed bit by bit like his human counterpart.

He paused at the head of the broad white ladder that led down to the Tahiti Beach. He could see Robert running back and forth with a bucket, trying to fill a leaking moat. Thomas was lying in his mother's arms, sucking his thumb, holding his raggie and watching Robert with his strange objective gaze. They were happy because they had the undivided attention of their mother, and he was unhappy because he had her undivided inattention. That, at least, was the local reason, but hardly the original beach of his unhappiness. Never mind the original beach. He had to step down onto this one and be a father.

"Hello, darling," said Mary, with that permanently exhausted smile in which her eyes didn't participate. They inhabited a harder world in which she was trying to survive the ceaseless demands of her sons, and the destructive effect on a solitary nature of spending years without a moment of solitude.

"Hi," said Patrick. "Shall we have lunch?"

"I think Thomas is about to fall asleep."

"Right," said Patrick, sinking down onto his lounger. There was always a good reason to frustrate his desires.

"Look," said Robert, showing Patrick a swelling on his eyelid, "I got a mosquito bite."

"Don't be too hard on mosquitoes," sighed Patrick, "only the pregnant females whine, whereas women never stop whining, even after they've had several children."

Why had he said that? He seemed to be full of zoological misogyny today. If anyone was whining it was him. It certainly wasn't true of Mary. He was the one who suffered from a seething distrust of women. His sons had no reason to share it.

He must try to pull himself together. The least he could do was to contain his depression.

"I'm sorry," he said, "I don't know why I said that. I'm feeling awfully tired."

He smiled apologetically all around.

"It looks as if you need some help with that moat," he suggested to Robert, picking up a second bucket.

They walked back and forth, pouring seawater into the sand until Thomas fell asleep in his mother's arms.

AUGUST 2002

10

From the blue paddling pool where he had been playing contentedly a moment before, Thomas suddenly dashed across the sand, glancing over his shoulder to see if his mother was following him. Mary pushed her chair back and bolted after him. He was so fast now, faster every day. He was already on the top step and only had to cross the Promenade Rose to reach the traffic. She leaped up three steps at a time and just caught him as he reached the corner of the parked car that hid him from the drivers cruising along the seaside road. He kicked and wriggled as she lifted him in the air.

"Never do that," she said, almost in tears. "Never do that. It's *so* dangerous."

Thomas gurgled with laughter and excitement. He had discovered this new game yesterday when they arrived back at the Tahiti Beach. Last year he used to double back if he got more than three yards away from her.

As Mary carried him from the road to the parasol he shifted into another mode, sucking his thumb, and patting her face affectionately with his palm.

"Are you all right, Mama?"

"I'm upset that you ran into the road."

"I'm going to do something so dangerous," said Thomas proudly. "Yes, I am."

Mary couldn't help smiling. Thomas was so charming.

How could she say she was sad when she was happy the next minute? How could she say she was happy when a minute later she wanted to scream? She had no time to draw up a family tree of every emotion that rushed through her. She had spent too long in a state of shattering empathy, tuned in to her children's vagrant moods. She sometimes felt she was about to forget her own existence completely. She had to cry to reclaim herself. People who didn't understand thought that her tears were the product of a long suppressed and mundane catastrophe, her terminal exhaustion, her huge overdraft or her unfaithful husband, but they were in fact a crash course in the necessary egotism of someone who needed to get a self back in order to sacrifice it again. She had always been like that. Even as a child she only had to see a bird land on a branch in order for its wild heartbeat to replace her own. She sometimes wondered if her selflessness was a distinction or a pathology. She had no final answer to that either. Patrick was the one who worked in a world where judgments and opinions had to be given with an air of authority.

She sat Thomas down in the stacked plastic chairs of his place at the table.

"No, Mama, I don't want to sit in the double chairs," said Thomas, climbing down and smiling mischievously as he set off toward the steps again. Mary recaptured him immediately and lifted him back into the chairs.

"No, Mama, don't pick me up, it's really unbearable."

"Where do you pick up these phrases?" Mary laughed.

Michelle, the owner, came over with their grilled dorade and looked at Thomas reproachfully.

"*C'est dangereux ça,*" she scolded him.

Yesterday Michelle had said she would have spanked her children for running toward the road like that. Mary was always getting useless advice. She couldn't spank Thomas under any circumstances. Apart from the nausea she felt at the idea, she thought that punishment was the perfect way of masking the lesson it was supposed to enforce; all the child remembered was the violence, replacing the parent's justified distress with his own.

Kettle was a supreme source of useless advice, fed by the deep wells of her own uselessness as a mother. She had always tried to smother Mary's independent identity. It was not that she had treated Mary as a doll—she was too busy being one herself to do that—but as a kind of venture capital fund: someone who was initially worthless, but who might one day pay off, if she married a big house or a big name. She had made it clear that marrying a barrister who was about to lose a medium-sized house abroad fell short of the bonanza she had in mind. Kettle's disappointment in the adult Mary was only the sequel to the disappointment she felt at her birth. Mary was not a boy. Girls who weren't boys were such a letdown. Kettle pretended that Mary's father was desperate for a boy, whereas the desperation had really belonged to her own father, a soldier who preferred trench warfare to female company and only agreed to the minimum necessary contact with the weaker sex in the hope of producing a male heir. Three daughters later he retired to his study.

Mary's father, on the contrary, had been delighted with her just as she was. His shyness intermeshed with hers in a way that set them both free. Mary, who hardly spoke for the first twenty years of her life, loved him for never making her feel that her silence was a failure. He understood that it came from a kind of over-intensity, a superabundance of impressions. The gap between her emotional life and social convention was too wide for her to cross. He had been the same way when he was young, but gradually learned to present something that was not quite himself to the world. Mary's violent authenticity brought him back to his own core.

Mary remembered him vividly but her memories were embalmed by his early death. She was fourteen when he died of cancer. She was "protected" from his illness by an ineffectual secrecy, which made the situation more worrying than it was anyway. The secrecy had been Kettle's contribution, her substitute for sympathy. After Henry died, Kettle told Mary to "be brave." Being brave meant not asking for sympathy now either. There would have been no point in asking for it, even if the opportunity had not been blocked. Their experiences were essentially so different. Mary was utterly lost in loss, lost in imagining her father's suffering, lost in the madness of knowing that only he could have understood her feelings about his death. At the same time, confusingly, so much of their relationship had been spent in silent communion that there seemed to be no reason for it to stop. Kettle only appeared to be sharing the same bereavement. She was in fact suffering from the latest installment of her inevitable disappointment. It was so unfair. She was too young to be a widow, and too old to start again on acceptable terms. It was in the wake of her father's death that Mary had got the full measure of her mother's emotional sterility and learned to despise her. The crust of pity that she had formed since then had grown thinner when she had children of her own. It was now in constant danger of being torn apart by fresh eruptions of fury.

Kettle's most recent contribution had been to apologize for not getting Thomas a present for his second birthday. She had searched "high and low" (translation: rung Harrods) "for some of those marvelous reins you used to have as a child." After Harrods let her down, she was too tired to look for anything else. "They're bound to come back into fashion," she said, as if she might give Thomas a pair when he was twenty or thirty, or whenever the world came to its senses and started stocking child reins again.

"I suppose Granny's a great disappointment to you, not getting you any reins," she said to Thomas.

"No, I don't want any reins," said Thomas, who had taken to ritually contradicting the latest statement he heard. Kettle, not knowing this, was astonished.

"Nanny used to swear by them," she resumed.

"And I used to swear at them," said Mary.

"You didn't as a matter of fact," said Kettle. "Unlike Thomas, you weren't encouraged to swear like a drunken sailor."

It was true that the last time they had visited Kettle in London, Thomas had said, "Oh, no! Bloody fucking hell, my washing machine is on again," and then pretended to turn it off by pressing the disconnected bell next to Kettle's fireplace.

He had heard Patrick say, "bloody fucking hell" that morning, after reading a letter from Sotheby's. The Boudins, it turned out, were fakes.

"What a waste of moral effort," said Patrick.

"It wasn't a waste. You didn't know they were fakes before you decided not to steal them."

"I know, that's just it: it would have been such an easy decision if I had known. "Steal from my own mother? Never!" I could have thundered right at the beginning, instead of spending a year wondering whether to be some kind of intergenerational Robin Hood, correcting an imbalance with my virtuous crime. My mother managed to make me hate myself for being honorable," said Patrick, clasping his head between his hands. "How conflicted was that? And how unnecessary."

"What's Dada talking about?" asked Thomas.

"I'm talking about your fucking grandmother's fake paintings."

"No, she's not my fucking grandmother," said Thomas, shaking his head solemnly.

"Seamus is not the first person to have bamboozled her into parting with the little money that *my* fucking grandmother left her. Some art dealer in Paris pulled off that facile trick thirty years ago."

"No, she's not your fucking grandmother," said Thomas, "she's my fucking grandmother."

Property was another thing Thomas had taken up recently. For a long time he had no sense of owning things, now everything belonged to him.

She was alone with Thomas for the first week of August. Patrick was detained in London by a difficult case, which she suspected should be called *Julia vs. Mary*, but was pretending to be called something else. How could she say she was jealous of Julia when the next moment she was not? Sometimes, in fact, she was grateful to her. She didn't want Patrick to be taken away, nor did she think he would be. Mary was both naturally jealous and naturally permissive, and the only way these two sides of her could collaborate was by cultivating the permissiveness. That way Patrick never really wanted to leave her, and so her jealousy was satisfied as well. The flow chart looked simple enough, except for two immediate complications. First, there were the times when she was overwhelmed with nostalgia for the erotic life they had shared before she became a mother. Her passion had peaked, naturally, when it was organizing its own extinction, during the time when she was trying to get pregnant. Secondly, she was angered when she felt that Patrick was deliberately worsening their relations in order to invigorate his adultery. There it was: he needed sex, she couldn't provide it, he was going to look elsewhere. Infidelity was a technicality, but disloyalty introduced a fundamental doubt, a terminal atmosphere.

It was the first time Robert had been away from home for more than a night. He was devastatingly relaxed on his first evening at his friend Jeremy's when they spoke on the telephone. Of course she was pleased, of course it was a sign of his confidence in his parents' love that he felt the love was there even when they were not. Still, it was strange to be without him. She could remember him at Thomas's age, when he still ran away in order to be chased and still hid in order to be found. Even then he had been more introspective than Thomas, more burdened. He had been, on the one hand, the inhabitant of a pristine paradise that Thomas would never know, and on the other hand, a prototype. Thomas had benefited from learned mistakes and the more precise hopes that followed them.

"I've had enough now," said Thomas, starting to climb down from his chairs.

Mary waved at Michelle but she was serving another customer. She held back a plate of chips for this moment. If Thomas saw them earlier he ate no fish, if he saw them now he stayed for a second five-minute sitting. Mary couldn't catch Michelle's attention and Thomas continued his descent.

"Do you want some chips, darling?"

"No, Mama, I don't. Yes, I do want some chips," Thomas corrected himself.

He slipped and bumped his chin against the tabletop.

"Mama take you," he said, spreading his arms out.

She lifted him up and sat him on her lap, rocking him gently. Whenever he was hurt he reverted to calling himself "you," although he had discovered the proper use of the first-person singular six months ago. Until then, he had referred to himself as "you" on the perfectly logical grounds that everyone else did. He also referred to others as "I," on the perfectly logical grounds that that was how they referred to themselves. Then one week "you want it" turned into "I want it." Everything he did at the moment—the fascination with danger, the assertion of ownership, the ritual contradiction, the desire to do things for himself—was about this explosive transition from being "you" to being "I," from seeing himself through his parents' eyes to looking through his own. Just for now, though, he was having a grammatical regression, he wanted to be "you" again, his mother's creature.

"It's so difficult because your will is what gets you through life," Sally had said last night. "Why would you want to break your child's will? That's what our mothers wanted to do. That's what it meant to be 'good'—being broken."

Sally, Mary's American friend, was her greatest ally; also a mother showered in useless advice, also determined to give her children uncompromised support, to roll the boulder of her own upbringing out of the way so that they could run free. This task was surrounded by hostile commentary: stop being a door-mat; don't be a slave to your children; get your figure back; keep your husband happy; get back "out there"; go to a party, spending your whole time with your children drives you literally mad; increase your self-esteem by handing your children over to some-one else and writing an article saying that women should not feel guilty about handing their children over to someone else; don't spoil your children by giving them what they want; let the little tyrants cry themselves to sleep, when they realize that crying is useless they'll stop; anyway, children love boundaries. Below this layer came the confusing rumors: never use acetaminophen, always use acetaminophen, acetaminophen stops homeopathy from working, homeopathy doesn't work, homeopathy works for some things but not for others; an amber necklace stops their teeth hurting; that rash could be an allergy to cow's milk, it could be an allergy to wheat, it could be an allergy to the air quality, London has become five times more polluted in the last ten years; nobody really knows, it'll probably just go away. Then there were the invidious comparisons and the plain lies: my daughter sleeps all through the night; she hasn't needed nappies since she was three weeks old; his mother breast-fed him till he was five; we're so lucky, they've both got guaranteed places at the Acorn; her best friend at school is Cilla Black's granddaughter.

When all these distractions could be ignored, Mary tried to hack through the dead wood of her own conditioning, through the overcompensation, through the exhaustion and the irritation and the terror, through the tension between dependency and independence, which was alive in her as well as her children, which she had to recognize but could give no time to, and get back, perhaps, to the root of an instinct for love, and try to stay there and to act from there.

She felt that Sally was roped to the same cliff face as her, and that they could rely on each other. Sally had sent through a fax last night but Mary hadn't had time to read it yet. She had torn it from the fax machine and squeezed it into her rucksack. Perhaps when Thomas had a sleep—when he had a sleep, that moment into which the rest of life was supposed to be artfully crammed. By the time it came around, she was usually too desperate for sleep herself to break away from his rhythm and do anything different.

The chips had already lost their power to hold Thomas and he was climbing back down the chairs. Mary took his hand and let him lead her back to the steps he had dashed up earlier. They wandered down the Promenade Rose together hand in hand.

"It's lovely and smooth on my feet," said Thomas. "Oh," he suddenly stopped in front of a row of wilted cactuses, "what's that called?"

"It's some kind of cactus, darling. I don't know the specific name."

"But I want to know the specific name," said Thomas.

"We'll have to look it up in my book when we get home."

"Yes, Mama, we'll . . . Oh! What's that boy doing?"

"He's got a water pistol."

"For watering the flowers."

"Well, yes, that would be a good use for it."

"It's for watering the flowers," he informed her.

He loosened his hand and walked ahead of her. Although they were constantly together, she often didn't get to look at him for hours on end. He was either too close for her to see the whole of him, or she was focused on the dangerous elements in the situation and had no time to appreciate the rest. Now she could see him whole, without anxiety, looking adorable with his hooped blue T-shirt and khaki trousers and his determined walk. His face was astonishingly beautiful. She sometimes worried about the kind of attention it would attract, and the kind of impact he would get used to having. She could remember when he had first opened his eyes in the hospital. They were blazing with an inexplicably strong sense of intention; a drive to make sense of the world, in order to house another kind of knowledge which he already had. Robert had arrived with a completely different atmosphere, a sense of emotional intensity, of trouble that needed working out.

"Oh," said Thomas, pointing, "What's that funny man doing?"

"He's putting on his mask and snorkel."

"It's my mask and snorkel."

"Well, it's very nice of you to let him use it."

"I let him use it," said Thomas. "He can use it, Mama."

"Thank you, darling."

He marched on. He was being munificent now, but in about ten minutes his energy would collapse and everything would start to go wrong.

"Shall we go back to the beach and have a little rest?"

"I don't want a little rest. I want to go to the playground. I love the playground so much," he said, breaking into a run.

The playground was uninhabitable at this time of day, its dangerous climbing frame led to a metal slide hot enough to fry an egg on. Next to it, a plastic pony squeaked unbearably on a coiled spring. When they arrived at the wooden gate, Mary reached out and swung it open for Thomas.

"No, Mama, I do it," he said with a sudden wail of misery.

"Okay, okay," said Mary.

"No, I do it," said Thomas, pulling open with some difficulty the gate, made heavier by a metal plaque displaying eight playground rules, four times as many rules as rides. They made the transition to a pink rubber surface masquerading as tarmac. Thomas climbed the curved bars up to the platform above the slide, and then dashed over to the other opening, opposite a fireman's pole, which he couldn't possibly get down on his own. Mary hurried around the climbing frame to meet him. Would he really jump? Was he really going to misjudge his capacities to that extent? Was she pumping fear into a situation where only play was needed? Was it an instinct to anticipate disaster, or was every other mother in the world more relaxed than her? Was it worth pretending to be relaxed, or was pretense always a bad thing? Once Mary was standing beside the pole, Thomas moved back to the slide and quickly pulled himself down. He tipped over at the end of his run and banged his head on the edge. The shock fused with his exhaustion to produce a long moment of silence; his face flushed and he let out a long scream, his pink tongue quivering in his mouth, and his eyes thickly glazed with tears. Mary felt, as usual, that a javelin had been flung into her chest. She picked him up in her arms and held him close, reassuring them both.

"Raggie with a label," he sobbed. She handed him a Harrington square with the label still on it. A raggie without a label was not just unconsoling but doubly upsetting because of its tantalizing resemblance to the ones which still had labels.

She walked back swiftly to the beach, carrying him in her arms. He shuddered and grew quiet, clasping Raggie and sucking his thumb with the same hand. The adventure was over, the exploration had gone to its limit and ended the only way it could, involuntarily. She lay him down on a mattress under a parasol and curled up next to him, closing her eyes and lying completely still. She heard him suck his thumb more intensely as he settled, and then she could tell from the change in his breathing that he had fallen asleep. She opened her eyes.

Now she had an hour, perhaps two, in which to answer letters, pay her taxes, keep in touch with her friends, revive her intellect, take some exercise, read a good book, think of a brilliant money-making scheme, take up yoga, see an osteopath, go to the dentist, and get some sleep. Sleep, remember sleep? The word had once referred to great haunches of unconsciousness, six, eight, nine-hour slabs; now she fought for twenty-minute scraps of disturbing rest, rest which reminded her that she was fundamentally done in. Last night she was kept awake by an overwhelming terror that some harm would come to Thomas if she fell asleep. She was rigid with resistance all night, like a sentry who knows that death is the penalty for nodding off on his watch. Now she really had to get some muddling, hangover-like afternoon sleep, soaked in unpleasant dreams, but first she was going to read Sally's fax, as a sign of her independence, which she often felt was even less well established than Thomas's, since she couldn't test its limits as wildly as he could. It was a practical fax, as Sally had warned her, with the dates and times of her arrival at Saint Nazaire, but then at the end Sally added, "I came across this quotation yesterday, from Alexander Herzen. 'We think the purpose of a child is to grow up because it does grow up. But its purpose is to play, to enjoy itself, to be a child. If we merely look to the end of the process, the purpose of life is death.'"

Yes, that was what she had wanted to say to Patrick when they had been alone with Robert. Patrick had been so concerned with shaping Robert's mind, with giving him a transfusion of skepticism, that he had sometimes forgotten to let him play, enjoy himself and be a child. He let Thomas follow his own course, partly because he was preoccupied with his own psychological survival, but also because Thomas's desire for knowledge outstripped any parental ambition. With him, she thought, as she closed her eyes after a last glance at Thomas's sleeping face, it was so clear that playing and enjoying himself were identical with learning to master the world around him.

11

"Where has my willie gone?" said Thomas, lying on his blue towel after his bath.

"It's disappeared," said Mary.

"Oh! There it is, Mama," he said, uncrossing his legs.

"That's a relief," said Mary.

"It certainly is a relief," said Thomas.

After playing in his bath he was reluctant to get back into the padded cell of a nappy. Pajamas, the dreadful sign that he was expected to go to sleep, sometimes had to wait until he was asleep to be put on. Any sense that Mary was in a hurry made him take twice as long to go to bed.

"Oh, no! My willie's disappeared again," said Thomas. "I really am upset about it."

"Are you, darling?" said Mary, noticing him experiment with the phrase she had used yesterday when he threw a glass on the kitchen floor.

"Yes, Mama, it's driving me crazy."

"Where can it have gone?" asked Mary.

"I don't believe it," he said, pausing for her to appreciate the gravity of the loss. "Oh, there it is!" He gave a perfect imitation of the reassured cheerfulness with which she rediscovered a milk bottle or a lost shoe.

He started to jump up and down and then dropped onto the bed, rolling among the pillows.

"Be careful," said Mary, watching him bounce too near the metal guards that surrounded the edge of the bed.

It was hard to stay ready for a sudden catch, to keep scanning for sharp corners and hard edges, to let him go to the limit of his adventure. She really wanted to lie down now, but the last thing she should do was to show any sign of exasperation or impatience.

"I am an acrobat at the circus," said Thomas, trying to do a forward roll but keeling over. "Mama say, 'Be careful little monkey.'"

"Be careful little monkey." Mary repeated her line obediently. She must get him a director's chair and a megaphone. He was always being told what to do; now it was his turn.

She felt drained by the long day, most of all by visiting Eleanor in her nursing home. Mary had tried to mask her sense of shock when she arrived with Thomas in Eleanor's room. All of Eleanor's upper teeth were missing from one side of her mouth and only three dangled like black stalactites from the other. Her hair, which she used to have washed every other day, was reduced to a greasy chaos stuck to her now visibly bumpy skull. As Mary leaned over to kiss Eleanor, she was assailed by a stench that made her want to reach for the portable changing mat she carried in her rucksack. She must restrain her maternal drive, especially in the presence of a proven champion of maternal self-restraint.

Eleanor's decay was underlined by her loss of equality with Thomas. Last year, neither of them could talk properly or walk steadily; Eleanor had lost enough teeth to leave her with roughly the same number as Thomas had gained; her new need for incontinence pads matched his established need for nappies. This year, everything had changed. Thomas wouldn't need nappies for much longer, Eleanor needed more than she was currently using; only his back molars still had to work their way through, her back molars would soon be the only teeth she had left; he was getting so fast that his mother could hardly keep up, Eleanor could hardly keep herself up in her chair and would soon be bedridden. Mary paused on top of the icy slopes of potential conversation. The already strained assumption that they shared an enthusiasm for Thomas's progress now looked like a covert insult. It was no use reminding her of Robert either, her former ally, now the disciple of his father's hostility.

"Oh, no!" said Thomas to Eleanor, "Alabala stole my halumbalum."

Thomas, who was so often stuck with adults in a traffic jam of incomprehensible syllables, sometimes answered back with a little private language of his own. Mary was used to this sweet revenge and also intrigued by the emergence of Alabala, a recent creation who seemed to be falling into the classic role of doing naughty things to and for Thomas, and was accompanied by his conscience, a character called Felan. She looked up at Eleanor with a smile. It was not returned. Eleanor stared at Thomas with horror and suspicion. What she saw was not the ingenuity of a child but the harbinger of her worst fear: that soon, on top of being unable to make herself understood, she would not be able to understand anybody else. Mary moved in quickly.

"He doesn't only talk nonsense," she said. "One of his favorite phrases at the moment—I think you'll detect Patrick's influence—" she tried another complicit smile, "is 'absolutely unbearable.'"

Eleanor's body lurched forward a couple of inches. She gripped the wooden arms of her chair and looked at Mary with furious concentration.

"Absolute-ly un-bearable," she spat out, and then fell back, adding a high, faint, "Yes."

Eleanor turned again toward Thomas, but this time she looked at him with a kind of greed. A moment ago, he seemed to be announcing the storm of gibberish that would soon enshroud her, but now he had given her a phrase which she understood perfectly, a phrase she couldn't have managed on her own, describing exactly how she felt.

Something similar happened when Mary read out a list of audiobooks that Eleanor might want sent from England. Eleanor's method for choosing the books bore no obvious relation to their authors or categories. Mary droned through the titles of works by Jane Austen and Proust, Jeffrey Archer and Jilly Cooper, without any signs of interest from Eleanor. Then she read out the title, *Ordeal of Innocence*, and Eleanor started nodding her head and flapping her hands acquisitively, as if she were splashing water onto her chest. *Harvest of Dust* elicited the same surges of excitement. Stimulated by these unexpected communications, Eleanor remembered the note she had written earlier, and handed it to Mary with her shaking, liver-spotted hand.

Mary made out the faint words, in pencil-written block capitals, WHY SEAMUS DOES NOT COME?

Mary suspected the reason, but could hardly believe it. She hadn't expected Seamus to be so flagrant. His opportunism always seemed to be blended with the genuine delusion that he was a good man, or at least a strong desire to be mistaken for one. And yet here he was, only a fortnight after the final transfer of Saint Nazaire to the Foundation, dropping his benefactor like a sack on a skip.

She remembered what Patrick had said when he finally used the power of attorney his mother had given him to sign over the house: "These people who want to crawl unburdened to their graves, just don't make it. There is no second childhood, no license for irresponsibility." He then got blind drunk.

Mary looked at Eleanor's face. It was impacted with misery. Her eyes were veiled like the eyes of a recently dead fish, but in her case the dullness seemed to stem from the effort of staying disconnected from reality. Mary could see now that her missing teeth were really a suicidal gesture, with the violent passivity of a hunger strike. They could so easily have been replaced, it must have taken great stubbornness to stay in the vortex of self-neglect, week after week, as they fell out, one by one, ignoring the medical profession, the antidepressants, the nursing home, and the remains of her own will to live.

Mary felt pierced by a sense of tragedy. Here was a woman who had abandoned her family for a vision and for a man, and now the man and the vision had abandoned her. She could remember Eleanor telling her, when she could still speak adequately, that she and Seamus had known each other in "previous lifetimes." One of these previous lifetimes had taken place on something called a "skelig," some kind of Irish seaside mound, which Seamus had taken Eleanor to see early in his financial courtship, on that unforgettable, blustery day when he took her hand and said, "Ireland needs you." Once Eleanor realized, in a "past life recall," that she had lived as Seamus's wife on the very skelig they visited, during the Dark Ages, when Ireland was a beacon of Christianity in that muddle of pillage and migration, her immediate family, with whom she had a relatively shallow past, began to slip from view. And once Seamus visited Saint Nazaire, he realized that France needed him even more than Ireland needed Eleanor. The house had been a convent in the seventeenth century, and a second "past life recall" established that Eleanor was (it seemed obvious once you were told) the Mother Superior. The noun, Mary remembered thinking, had stayed stuck in front of the adjective ever since. Seamus, amazingly, was the abbot of a local monastery at exactly the same time. And so they had been thrown together again, this time in a "spiritual friendship," which had been misinterpreted and caused a great scandal in the area.

When Eleanor told her all this, in an oppressive parody of girls' talk, Mary decided not to argue. Eleanor believed more or less anything, as long as it was untrue. It was part of her charitable nature to rush belief to the unbelievable, like emergency aid. She clearly needed to inhabit these historical novels to make up for the disappointment of a passion which was not being acted out in the bedroom (it had evolved too much for that) but was having a thrilling enough time at the Land Registry. It had all seemed so ridiculous to Mary at the time, now she wished she could stick back the peeling wallpaper of Eleanor's credulity. Under the dreadful sincerity of the original confession was that need to be needed, which Mary recognized so well.

"I'll ask him," she said, covering Eleanor's hand gently with her own. Although she hadn't seen him yet, she knew that Seamus was in his cottage. "Perhaps he's been ill, or in Ireland."

"Ireland," Eleanor whispered.

When they were walking back to the car, Thomas stopped and shook his head. "Oh, dear," he said, "Eleanor is not very well."

Mary loved his straightforward sympathy for suffering. He hadn't yet learned to pretend that it wasn't going on, or to blame the person who was having it. He fell asleep in the car and she decided she might as well go straight to Seamus's cottage.

"Well now that's a terrible thing," said Seamus, "I thought with the family being here and everything, that Eleanor wouldn't want to see me so much. And, to be honest with you, Mary, the Pegasus Press have been breathing down my neck. They want to put my book in their spring catalog. I've got so many ideas, it's just getting them down. Do you think *Drumbeat of My Heart* or *Heartbeat of My Drum* is better?"

"I don't know," said Mary. "It depends which one you mean, I suppose."

"That's good advice," said Seamus. "'Talking of drums, we're very pleased with your mother's progress. She's taken to the soul retrieval work like a duck to water. I just got an e-mail from her saying she wants to come to the autumn intensive."

"Amazing," said Mary. She was nervous that the monitor wouldn't work. The green light seemed to be winking in the usual way, but she had never used it in the car before.

"Soul retrieval is something I think Eleanor could benefit from immensely. I'm just thinking aloud now," said Seamus, swiveling excitedly in his chair and blocking Mary's view of a leathery old Inuit woman, with a pipe dangling from her mouth, that radiated from his computer screen. "If your mother were to lead a ceremony with Eleanor at the center of the circle, that could be hugely powerful with all the, you know, connections." He spread the fingers of both his hands and intermeshed them tenderly.

Poor Seamus, thought Mary, he wasn't really a bad man, he was just a complete idiot. She sometimes became a little competitive with Patrick about who had the most annoying mother. Kettle gave nothing away, Eleanor gave everything away; the results were indistinguishable for the family, except that Mary had "expectations," made fantastically remote by the robustness of her meticulously selfish mother, who thought of nothing but her own comfort, rushed to the doctor every time she sneezed, and "treated" herself to a holiday once a month to get over the disappointment of the last one. Patrick's disinheritance had nudged him ahead in the bad mother stakes, but perhaps Seamus was planning to eliminate that advantage by taking Kettle's money as well. Was he, after all, really a bad man doing a brilliant impersonation of an idiot? It was hard to tell. The connections between stupidity and malice were so tangled and so dense.

"I'm seeing more and more connections," said Seamus, twisting his fingers around each other. "To be honest with you, Mary, I don't think I'll write another book. It can do your head in."

"I bet," said Mary. "I couldn't even begin to write a book."

"Oh, I've done the beginning," said Seamus. "In fact, I've done several beginnings. Perhaps it's all beginnings, do you know what I mean?"

"With each new heartbeat," said Mary. "Or drumbeat."

"That's right, that's right," said Seamus.

Thomas's waking cry burst through the monitor. Mary was relieved to know that she was in range.

"Oh, dear, I'm going to have to leave."

"I'll definitely try to see Eleanor in the next few days," said Seamus, accompanying her to the door of his cottage. "I really appreciate what you said about the heartbeat and being in the moment—it's given me a lot of ideas."

He opened the door, setting off a tinkling of chimes. Mary looked up and saw three Chinese pictographs clustered around a dangling brass rod.

"Happiness, Peace, and Prosperity," said Seamus. "They're inseparable."

"I'm sorry to hear that," said Mary. "I was rather hoping to get the first two on their own."

"Ah, but what is prosperity?" said Seamus, walking with her toward the car. "Ultimately, it's having something to eat when you're hungry. That's the prosperity that was denied to Ireland, for instance, during the 1840s, and that's still denied to millions of people around the world."

"Gosh," said Mary. "There's not a lot I can do about the Irish in the 1840s. But I could give Thomas his 'ultimate prosperity'—or can I go on calling it 'lunch'?"

Seamus threw back his head and let out a guffaw of wholesome laughter.

"I think that would be simpler," he said, giving Mary's back an unwelcome rub.

She opened the door and took Thomas out of his car seat.

"How is the little man?" asked Seamus.

"He's very well," said Mary. "He has a lovely time here."

"Well, I'm sure that's down to your excellent mothering," said Seamus, his hand by now burning a hole in the back of her T-shirt. "But I'd also say that with the soul work, it's very important to create a safe environment. That's what we do here. Now, maybe Thomas is picking that up, you know, at some level."

"I expect he is," said Mary, reluctant to deny Thomas a compliment, even when it was really intended by Seamus for himself. "He's very good at picking things up."

She managed to stand out of Seamus's range, holding Thomas in her arms.

"Ah," said Seamus, framing the two of them with a large parenthetical gesture, 'the mother and child archetype. It makes me think of my own mother. She had the eight of us to look after. At the time I think I was preoccupied with little ways of getting more than my fair share of the attention." He chuckled indulgently at the memory of this younger, less enlightened self. "That was definitely a big dynamic in my family; but looking back from where I'm standing now, what amazes me is how she went on giving and giving. And you know, Mary, I've come to the conclusion that she was tapping into a universal source, into that archetypal mother and child energy. Do you know what I mean? I want to put something about that in my book. It all ties in with the shamanic work—at some level. It's just getting it down. I'd welcome any thoughts about that: moments when you've felt supported by something beyond the level of, you know, personal sacrifice."

"Let me think about it," said Mary, suddenly realizing where Seamus had learned his little ways of getting mothers to hand over their resources to him. "In the meantime, I really must make Thomas some lunch."

"Of course, of course," said Seamus. "Well, it's been grand talking to you, Mary. I really feel that we've connected."

"I feel I've learned a lot as well," said Mary.

She now knew, for instance, that his feeble promise to "try to visit Eleanor in the next few days" meant that he would not visit her today, or tomorrow, or the next day. Why would he waste his "little ways" on a woman who only had a couple of fake Boudins to her name?

She carried Thomas into the kitchen and put him down on the counter. He took his thumb out of his mouth and looked at her with a subtle expression which hovered between seriousness and laughter.

"Seamus is a very funny man, Mama," he said.

Mary burst out laughing.

"He certainly is," she said, kissing him on the forehead.

"He certainly is a very funny man!" said Thomas, catching her laughter. He scrunched up his eyes in order to laugh more seriously.

No wonder she was tired after seeing Eleanor and Seamus on the same day, no wonder it was difficult to extort any more vigilance from her aching body and her blanched mind. Something had happened today, she hadn't quite got the measure of it, but it was one of those sudden dam bursts, which were the only way she ever ended a long period of conflict. She had no time to work it out while Thomas was still bouncing naked in the middle of the bed.

"That was a very big jump," said Thomas climbing to his feet again. "You certainly are impressed, Mama."

"Yes, darling. What would you like to read tonight?"

Thomas stopped in order to concentrate on a difficult task.

"Let's talk reasonably about lollipops," he said, retrieving a phrase from an old book of Patrick's which had got stuck down in Saint Nazaire.

"*Dr. Upping and Dr. Downing?*"

"No, Mama, I don't want to read that."

Mary took *Babar and Professor Grifaton* from the shelf and climbed over the guard onto the bed. They had a ritual of reviewing the day, and Mary threw out the usual question, "What did we do today?" Thomas stopped bouncing as she had hoped.

Thomas lowered his voice and shook his head solemnly.

"Peter Rabbit has been eating my grapes," he said.

"No!" said Mary, shocked.

"Mr. McGregor will be very angry with Seamus."

"Why Seamus? I thought it was Peter Rabbit who took the grapes."

"No, Mama, it was Seamus."

Whatever it was that Thomas was "picking up," it wasn't the sense of a "safe environment" that Seamus had boasted about creating for "the soul work." It was the atmosphere of theft. If Seamus was prepared to treat Eleanor with so little ceremony, when she had set off the prosperity chime in his life with such a resounding tinkle, why would he bother to honor her promises to his defeated rivals? His imagination was teeming with competing siblings, and he had adopted Patrick and Mary for the purposes of triumphing over them in an archaic contest for which neither of them had received his commando training. What was the point of an old woman who couldn't even buy him a sensory-privation tank? And what was the point of her descendants cluttering up his Foundation during August?

12

"But I don't understand," said Robert, watching Mary pack. "Why do we have to leave?"

"You know why," said Mary.

He sat on the edge of the bed, his shoulders rounded and his hands wedged under his thighs. If there had been time, she would have sat beside him and hugged him and let him cry again, but she had to get on with the packing while Thomas was sleeping.

Mary hadn't slept for the last two days, equally tormented by the atmosphere of loss and the longing to leave. Houses, paintings, trees, Eleanor's teeth, Mark's childhood, and her children's holidays: to her tired mind they all seemed to be piled up like the wreckage from a flood. She had spent the last seven years watching Patrick's childhood like a rope inching through his clenched hands. Now she wanted to get the hell out. It was already too late to stop Robert from identifying with Patrick's sense of injustice, but she could still save Thomas from getting tangled in the drama of disinheritance. The family was being split in half and it could only come back together if they left.

Patrick had gone to say goodbye to Eleanor. He had promised not to make any irrevocably bitter speeches in case he never saw her again. If he had enough warning of her death, he would doubtless fly down to hold her hand, but it was unrealistic to think that the rest of them would be checking into the Grand Hotel des Bains to mount a deathbed vigil in the nursing home. Mary had to admit that she looked forward to Eleanor dropping out of their lives altogether.

"Would we get the house if we killed Seamus?" asked Robert.

"No," said Mary. "It would go to the next director of the Foundation."

"That's so unfair," said Robert. "Unless I became the director. Yes! I'm a genius!"

"Except that you would have to direct the Foundation."

"Oh, yeah, that's true," said Robert. "Well, maybe Seamus will repent." He adopted a thick Irish accent, "I can only apologize, Mary. I don't know what came over me, trying to steal the house from you and the little ones, but I've come to moi senses now and I want you to know that, even if you can find it in your heart to forgive me for the agony I've caused you, I shall never be able to forgive myself." He broke down sobbing.

She knew his fake sobbing was close to being real. For the first time since Thomas was born she felt that Robert was the one who needed her most. His great strength was that he was even more interested in playing with what was going on than he was in wasting his time trying to control it—although he did quite a lot of that as well. His playfulness had collapsed for a few days and been replaced entirely by wishing and longing and regretting. Now she saw it coming back. She could never quite get used to the way he pieced together impersonations out of the things he overheard. Seamus had become his latest obsession, and no wonder. She was too exhausted to do anything but give him a laborious smile and fold the swimming trunks she had unpacked for him less than a week before. Everything had happened so fast. On the day he arrived with Robert, Patrick had found a note asking if Kevin and Anette could have "some space" in the house. Seamus had dropped in the next morning at breakfast to get his answer.

"I hope I'm not interrupting," he called out.

"Not at all," said Patrick. "It's good of you to come so quickly. Would you like some coffee?"

"I won't, thank you, Patrick. I've really been abusing the caffeine lately in an attempt to get myself going with the writing, you know."

"Well, I hope you don't mind if I go ahead and abuse some caffeine without you."

"Be my guest," said Seamus.

"Is that what I am?" asked Patrick, like a greyhound out of the slips. "Or are you in fact my guest during this one month of the year? That's the crux of the matter. You know that the terms of my mother's gift included letting us have the house for August, and we're not going to put up with having your friends billeted on us."

"Well, now, 'terms' is a very legalistic way of putting it," said Seamus. "There's nothing in writing about the Foundation providing you with a free holiday. I have a genuine sympathy for the trouble you've had in accepting your mother's wishes. That's why I've been prepared to put up with a lot of negativity from your side."

"We're not discussing the trouble I've had with my mother's wishes, but the trouble you're having with them. Let's not stray from the subject."

"They're inseparable."

"Everything looks inseparable to a moron."

"There's no need to get personal. They're inseparable because they both depend on knowing what Eleanor wanted."

"It's obvious what she wanted. What isn't clear is whether you can accept the part that doesn't suit you."

"Well, I have a more global vision than that, Patrick. I see the problem in holistic terms. I think we all need to find a solution together, you and your family, and Kevin and Anette, and me. Perhaps we could do a ritual expressing what we bring to this community and what we expect to take from it."

"Oh, no, not another ritual. What is it with you people and rituals? What's wrong with having a conversation? When I spent my teenage years in what has become your cottage, there were two bedrooms. Why don't you put your friends up in your own spare room?"

"That's now my study and office space."

"God forbid they should invade your private space."

Thomas wriggled down from Mary's arms and started to explore. His desire to move made her even more aware of how paralyzed the rest of them had become. She took no pleasure in seeing Patrick frozen in a kind of autumnal adolescence: dogmatic and sarcastic, resentful of his mother's actions, still secretly thinking of Seamus's cottage as the teenage den in which he spent half a dozen summers of semi-independence. Only Thomas, because he hadn't been given any coordinates on this particular grid, could slip to the floor and let his mind flow wherever it wanted. Seeing him get away gave Mary a certain remoteness from the scene being played out by Patrick and Seamus, even though she could feel a sullen violence taking over from Seamus's usual inane affability.

"Did you know," said Patrick, addressing Seamus again, "that among the caribou herdsmen of Lapland, the top shaman gets to drink the urine of the reindeer that has eaten the magic mushrooms, and his assistant drinks the urine of the top shaman, and so on, all the way down to the lowest of the low who scramble in the snow, pleading for a splash of twelfth-generation caribou piss?"

"I didn't know that," said Seamus flatly.

"I thought it was your special field," said Patrick, surprised. "Anyhow, the irony is that the *premier cru*, the first hit, is much the most toxic. Poor old top shaman is reeling and sweating, trying to get all the poison out, whereas a few damaged livers later, the urine is harmless without having lost its hallucinogenic power. Such is the human attachment to status, that people will sacrifice their peace of mind and their precious time in order to pickax their way toward what turns out to be a thoroughly poisonous experience."

"That's all very interesting," said Seamus, "but I don't see what it has to do with our immediate problem."

"Only this: that out of what I admit is pride, I am not prepared to be at the bottom of the pissing hierarchy in this 'community.'"

"If you don't want to be part of this community, you don't have to stay," said Seamus quietly.

There was a pause.

"Good," said Patrick. "Now, at least we know what you really want."

"Why don't *you* go away," shouted Robert. "Just leave us alone. This is my grandmother's house, and we have more right to be here than you do."

"Let's calm down," said Mary, resting a hand on Robert's shoulder. "We aren't going to leave in the middle of the children's holidays, whether we come here next year or not. We could compromise over your friends, perhaps. If you sacrifice your office for a week, we could put them up for the last week of our stay. That seems fair enough."

Seamus faltered between the momentum of his anger and his desire to look reasonable.

"I'll have to get back to you on that," he said. "To be honest with you, I'm going to have to process some of the negative feelings I'm having at the moment, before I can come to a decision."

"You process away," said Patrick, getting up to bring the conversation to an end. "Be my guest. Do a ritual."

He moved around the table, and spread his arms as if to herd Seamus out of the house, but then he came to a halt.

"By the way," he said, leaning close, "Mary tells me that you've dropped Eleanor now that she's given you the house. Is that true? After all she's done for you, you might pop in on her."

"I don't need any lectures from you on the importance of my friendship with Eleanor," said Seamus.

"Listen, I know she's not great company," said Patrick, "but that's just part of the treasure trove of things you have in common."

"I've had just about enough of your hostile attitude," said Seamus, his face flushing crimson. "I've tried to be patient—"

"Patient?" Patrick interrupted. "You've tried to billet your sidekicks on us and you've tossed Eleanor on the scrap heap because there's nothing more you can screw out of her. Anyone who thinks that 'patient' is the word to describe that sort of thing, should be doing English as a foreign language rather than signing a book contract."

"I don't have to stand for these insults," said Seamus. "Eleanor and I created this Foundation, and I know that she wouldn't want anything to undermine its success. What's so tragic, in my opinion, is that you don't see how central the Foundation is to your mother's life's purpose, and you don't realize what an extraordinary woman she is."

"You're so wrong," said Patrick. "I couldn't wish for a more extraordinary mother."

"It's fairly obvious where all this is heading," said Mary. "Let's take some time to cool off. I don't see any point in more acrimony."

"But darling," said Patrick, "acrimony is all we've got left."

It was certainly all he had left. She knew that it would fall on her to rescue a holiday from the wreckage left by Patrick's disdain. The expectation that she would be tirelessly resourceful and at the same time completely sympathetic to Patrick, was not one she could either put up with or disappoint.

As she hoisted Thomas into her arms, she felt again the extent to which motherhood had destroyed her solitude. Mary had lived alone through most of her twenties and stubbornly kept her own flat until she was pregnant with Robert. She had such a strong need to distance herself from the flood of others. Now she was very rarely alone, and if she was, her thoughts were commandeered by her family obligations. Neglected meanings piled up like unopened letters. She knew they contained ever more threatening reminders that her life was unexamined.

Solitude was something she had to share with Thomas for the moment. She remembered a phrase Johnny once quoted about the infant being "alone in the presence of its mother." That had stayed with her, and sitting with Thomas after the row between Patrick and Seamus, while he played with his favorite hose, holding it sideways and watching the silvery arc of water splash to the ground, Mary could feel the pressure to encourage him to be useful, to water the plants and to keep the mud from splattering his trousers, but she didn't give in to it, seeing a kind of freedom in the uselessness of his play. He had no outcome in mind, no project or profit, he just liked watching the water flow.

It would have made perfect sense for her to make room for nostalgia now that the departure she had longed for seemed inevitable, but she found herself looking at the garden and the view and the cloudless sky with a cold eye. It was time to go.

Back in the house, she went to her own room for a moment's rest, and found Patrick already sprawled on the bed with a glass of red wine beside him.

"You weren't very friendly this morning," he said.

"What do you mean?" said Mary. "I wasn't unfriendly. You were wrapped up in arguing with Seamus."

"Well, the Thermopylae buzz is wearing off," said Patrick.

She sat down on the edge of the bed and stroked his hand absently.

"Do you remember, back in the old days, when we used to go to bed together in the afternoon?" asked Patrick.

"Thomas has only just gone to sleep."

"You know that's not the real reason. We're not grinding our teeth with frustration, promising we'll jump into bed the moment we get the chance: it isn't even a possibility." Patrick closed his eyes. "I feel as if we're shooting down a gleaming white tunnel . . ." he said.

"That was yesterday, on the way from the airport," said Mary.

"A bone with the marrow sucked out," Patrick persevered. "Nothing is ever the same again, however often you repeat that magical phrase to the waitress in the cocktail bar."

"Never, in my case," said Mary.

"Congratulations," said Patrick, falling abruptly silent, his eyes still closed.

Was she being unsympathetic? Should she be giving him a charity blow job? She felt that these pleas for attention were timed to be impossible, so as to keep him self-righteously unfaithful. Patrick would have been horrified if she had started to make love to him. Or would he? How could she find out while she was incapable of taking any sexual initiative? The whole thing had died for her, and she couldn't blame his affair for the collapse. It had happened the moment Thomas was born. She couldn't help marveling at the strength of the severance. It had the authority of an instinct, redirecting her resources from the spent, enfeebled, damaged Patrick to the thrilling potential of her new child. The same thing had happened with Robert, but only for a few months. This time her erotic life was subsumed in intimacy with Thomas. Her relationship with Patrick was dead, not without guilt and duty turning up at the funeral. She sank down on the bed next to him, stared at the ceiling for a few seconds of empty intensity and then closed her eyes as well. They lay on the bed together, floating in shallow sleep.

"Oh, God," said Mary to Robert, getting up from the floor where she had been kneeling next to the open suitcase, "I still haven't canceled Granny and Sally."

"I must say it's frightfully disappointing," said Robert in his Kettle voice.

"Let's see if you're right," said Mary, sitting down next to him to dial her mother's number.

"Well, I must say it *is* disappointing," said Kettle, making Mary cover the mouthpiece while she tried to suppress her laughter. "Perfect," she whispered to Robert. He raised his arms in triumph.

"Why don't you come anyway?" said Mary to her mother. "Seamus seems to enjoy your company even more than we do. Which is saying a lot," she added after too long a pause.

Sally said she would come to see them all in London instead, and then took the view that it was "great news."

"To an outsider that place looks like a beautiful bell jar with the air being sucked out. You have to get out before you blow up."

"She's happy for us," said Mary.

"Well, gee," said Robert, "I hope she loses her house so we can be happy for her."

When Patrick returned, he put a piece of paper on top of the suitcase Mary was struggling to close and sank down onto the chair by the door. She picked the paper up and saw that it was one of Eleanor's faint pencil-written notes.

MY WORK HERE IS OVER. I WANT TO COME HOME. PLEASE FIND A NURSING HOME IN KEN-SINGTON?

She gave the note to Robert.

"It's difficult to know which sentence gave me most pleasure," said Patrick. "Eleanor's tiny store of unshamanic capital will be dismembered in rather less than a year if she moves to Kensington. After that, if she has the bad taste to stay alive, guess who will be expected to keep her vegetating in the Royal Borough?"

"I like the question mark," said Mary.

"Eleanor's real genius is for putting our emotional and moral impulses into total conflict. Again and again she makes me hate myself for doing the right thing, she makes virtue into its own punishment."

"I suppose we have to protect her from the horror of knowing that Seamus was really only interested in her money."

"Why?" said Robert. "It serves her right."

"Listen," said Patrick, "what I saw today was someone who is terrified. Terrified of dying alone. Terrified that her family will abandon her, as Seamus has done. Terrified that she's fucked up, that she's been sleepwalking through a replica of her mother's behavior. Terrified by the impotence of her convictions in the face of real suffering, terrified of everything. If we agree to her request, she can switch from philanthropy to family. Essentially, neither of them works anymore, but the switch might give her a little relief before she settles back into hell."

Nobody spoke.

"Let's hope that it's purgatory rather than hell," said Mary.

"I'm not very up on these things," said Patrick, "but if purgatory is a place where suffering refines you rather than degrades you, I see no sign of it."

"Well, maybe it can be purgatory for us at least."

"I don't understand," said Robert. "Is Granny going to come and live with us?"

"Not in the flat," said Mary. "In a nursing home."

"And we're going to have to pay?"

"Not yet," she replied.

"But that way Seamus wins completely," said Robert. "He gets the house and we get the cripple."

"She's not a cripple," said Mary, "she's an invalid."

"Oh, sorry," said Robert, "that makes all the difference. Lucky us." Robert put on his compere voice, "Today's lucky winners, the Melrose family from London, will be taking home our fabulous first prize. This amazing *invalid* can't speak, can't walk, *and* she can't control her bowels." Robert made the sound of delirious applause, and then changed to a solemn but consoling tone. "Bad luck, Seamus," he said, putting his arm around an imaginary contestant, "you played well, but in the end, they beat you in the slow death round. You won't be going home empty-handed, though, because we're giving you this private hamlet in the South of France, with thirty acres of gorgeous woodland, a giant swimming pool, and several garden areas for the kiddies to play in . . ."

"That was amazing," said Mary. "Where did that pop up from?"

"I don't think Seamus knows yet," said Patrick. "She made me read a postcard saying that he was going to come and see her after the family had left. So he still hasn't seen her yet."

"And did she look as if that might change her mind?"

"No," said Patrick. "She smiled when she gave me the note."

"The mechanical smile, or the radiant one?"

"Radiant," said Patrick.

"It's worse than we thought," said Mary. "She's not just running away from the truth about Seamus's motives, she's making another sacrifice. The only thing she had left to give him was her absence. It's unconditional love, the thing people usually keep for their children, if they can do it at all. In this case the children are the sacrifice."

"There's an awful Christian stench to it as well," said Patrick. "Being useful and affirming her worthlessness at the same time—all in the service of wounded pride. If she stays here she has to pay attention to Seamus's betrayal, but this way we're the ones who are betrayed. I can't get over her stubbornness. There's nothing like doing God's will to make people pig-headed."

"She can't speak or move," said Mary, "but look at the power she has."

"Yeah," said Patrick. "All this chattering that takes place in between is nothing compared to the crying and groaning that takes place at either end of life. It drives me crazy: we're controlled by one wordless tyrant after another."

"But where are we going for our holidays next year?" asked Robert.

"We can go anywhere," said Patrick. "We're no longer prisoners of this Provencal perfection. We're jumping out of the postcard, we're hitting the road." He sat down next to Robert on the bed. "Bogota! Blackpool! Rwanda! Let your imagination roam. Picture the fugitive Alaskan summer breaking out among the potholes of the tundra. Tierra del Fuego is nice at this time of year. No competition for the beaches there, except from those hilarious, blubbery sea lions. We've had enough of the predictable pleasures of the Mediterranean, with its pedalos and its *pizzas au feu de bois.* The world is our oyster."

"I hate oysters," said Robert.

"Yeah, I slipped up there," said Patrick.

"Well, where do you want to go?" asked Mary. "You can choose anywhere you like."

"America," said Robert. "I want to go to America."

"Why not?" said Patrick. "That's where Europeans traditionally go when they've been evicted."

"We're not being evicted," said Mary, "we're finally getting free."

AUGUST 2003

13

Would America be just like he'd imagined it? Along with the rest of the world, Robert had lived under a rain of American images most of his life. Perhaps the place had already been imagined for him and he wouldn't be able to see anything at all.

The first impression that came his way, while the plane was still on the ground at Heathrow, was a sense of hysterical softness. The flow of passengers up the aisle was blocked by a red-haired woman sagging at the knees under her own weight.

"I cannot go there. I cannot get in there," she panted. "Linda wants me to sit by the window, but I cannot fit in there."

"Get in there, Linda," said the enormous father of the family.

"Dad!" said Linda, whose size spoke for itself.

That certainly seemed typical of something he had seen before in London's tourist spots: a special kind of tender American obesity; not the hard won fat of a gourmet, or the juggernaut body of a truck driver, but the apprehensive fat of people who had decided to become their own air-bag systems in a dangerous world. What if their bus was hijacked by a psychopath who hadn't brought any peanuts? Better have some now. If there was going to be a terrorist incident, why go hungry on top of everything else?

Eventually, the Airbags dented themselves into their seats. Robert had never seen such vague faces, mere sketches on the immensity of their bodies. Even the father's relatively protuberant features looked like the remnants of a melted candle. As she squeezed into her aisle seat, Mrs. Airbag turned to the long queue of obstructed passengers, a brown smudge of tiredness radiating from her faded hazel eyes.

"Thank you for your patience," she groaned.

"It's sweet of her to thank us for something we haven't given her," said Robert's father. "Perhaps I should thank her for her agility."

Robert's mother gave him a warning look. It turned out they were in the row behind the Airbags.

"You're going to have to put the arm rests down for liftoff," Linda's father warned her.

"Mom and me are sharing these seats," giggled Linda. "Our tushes are expanding!"

Robert peeped through the gap in the seats. He didn't see how they were going to get the armrests down.

After meeting the Airbags, Robert's sense of softness spread everywhere. Even the hardness of some of the faces he saw on that warm and waxy arrival afternoon, in the flag-strewn mineral crevasses of Midtown Manhattan, looked to him like the embittered softness of betrayed children who had been told to expect everything. For those who were prepared to be consoled there was always something to eat; a pretzel stall, an ice-cream cart, a food-delivery service, a bowl of nuts on the counter, a snack machine down the corridor. He felt the pressure to drift into the mentality of grazing cattle, not just ordinary cattle but industrialized cattle, neither made to wait nor allowed to.

In the Oak Bar, Robert saw a row of men as pale and spongy as mushrooms, all standing on the broad stalks of their khaki trousers in front of the cigar cabinet. They seemed to be playing at being men. They sniggered and whispered, like schoolboys who were expecting to be caught out, to be made to remove the cushions they had stuffed under their pastel button-down shirts, and unpeel the plastic caps which made them look as if they were already bald. Watching them made Robert feel so grownup. He saw the old lady on the next table drape her powdered lips over the edge of her cocktail glass and suck the pink liquid expertly into her mouth. She looked like a camel trying to hide its braces. In the convex reflection of the black ceramic bowl in the window, he saw people come and go, yellow cabs surge and slip, the spinning wheels of the park carriages approaching until they grew as small as the wheels of a wristwatch, and disappeared.

The park was bright and warm, crowded with sleeveless dresses and jackets hooked over shoulders. Robert felt the heightened alertness of arrival being eroded by exhaustion, and the novelty of New York overlaid by the sense that he had seen this new place a thousand times before. Whereas the London parks he knew seemed to insist on nature, Central Park insisted on recreation. Every inch was organized for pleasure. Cinder paths looped among the little hills and plains, past a zoo and a skating rink, quiet zones, sports fields, and a plethora of playgrounds. Headphoned roller bladers pursued a private music. Teenagers scaled small mounds of bronze gray rocks. A flute player's serpentine music echoed damply under the arch of a bridge. As it faded behind them, it was replaced by the shrill mechanical tooting of a carousel.

"Look, Mama, a carousel!" said Thomas. "I want to go on it. I can't resist doing that actually."

"Okay," said Robert's father with a tantrum-avoiding sigh.

Robert was delegated to take Thomas for a ride, sitting on the same horse as him and fastening a leather belt around his waist.

"Is this a real horse?" said Thomas.

"Yes," said Robert. "It's a huge wild American horse."

"You be Alabala and say it's a wild American horse," said Thomas.

Robert obeyed his brother.

"No, Alabala!" said Thomas sharply, waving his index finger. "It's a carousel horse."

"Whoops, sorry," said Robert as the carousel set in motion.

Soon it was going fast, almost too fast. Nothing about the carousel in Lacoste had prepared him for these rearing, snorting horses, their nostrils painted red and their thick necks twisted out ambitiously toward the park. He was on a different continent now. The frighteningly loud music seemed to have driven all the clowns on the central barrel mad, and he could see that instead of being disguised by a painted sky studded with lights, heavily greased rods were revolving overhead. Along with the violence of the ride, this exposed machinery struck him as typically American. He didn't really know why. Perhaps everything in America would show this genius for being instantly typical. Just as his body was being tricked by a second afternoon, every surprise was haunted by this sense of being exemplary.

Soon after they left the carousel, they came across a vibrant middle-aged woman bent over her lap dog.

"Do you want a cappuccino?" she asked, as if it must be a tremendous temptation. "Are you ready for a cappuccino? Come on! Come on!" She clapped her hands together ecstatically.

But the dog strained backward on his leash, as if to say, "I'm a Dandy Dinmont, I don't drink cappuccino."

"I think that's a clear 'no,'" said Robert's father.

"Shh . . ." said Robert.

"I mean," said Thomas, removing his thumb from his mouth as he reclined in his stroller, "I think that's a clear no." He chuckled. "I mean, it's incredible. The little doggie doesn't want a cappuccino!" He put his thumb back in his mouth and played with the smooth label of his raggie.

After another five minutes his parents were ready to head back to the hotel, but Robert caught a glimpse of some water and ran forward a little farther.

"Look," he said, "a lake."

The landscaping created the impression that the far shore of the lake lapped against the base of a double towered West-side skyscraper. Under the gaze of this perforated cliff, T-shirted men hauled metal boats past reedy islands, girlfriends photographed each other laughing among the oars, immobile children bulged in blue life jackets.

"Look," said Robert, not quite able to express how astonishingly typical it all seemed.

"I want to go on the lake," said Thomas.

"Not today," said Robert's father.

"But I want to," he screamed, tears instantly beading his eyelids.

"Let's go for a run," said Robert's father, grabbing the stroller and sprinting down an avenue of bronze statues, Thomas's protests gradually replaced by cries of "Faster!"

By the time they caught up with him, Robert's father was bent double over the handles of the stroller, getting his breath back.

"The selection committee must have been based in Edinburgh," he gasped, nodding at the giant statues of Robert Burns and Walter Scott, stooped beneath the weight of their genius. A little further on a much smaller sprightly Shakespeare sported a period costume.

The Churchill Hotel where they were staying had no room service, and so Robert's father went out to buy a kettle and some "basic provisions." When he got back, Robert could smell the fresh whiskey on his breath.

"Jesus," said his father, fishing a box out of his shopping bag, "you go out to buy a kettle and you come back with nothing less than a Travel Smart Hot Beverage Maker."

Like Linda's and Mom's unconstrained tushes, phrases seemed to feel entitled to take up as much room as they could. Robert watched his father unloading tea and coffee and a bottle of whiskey from a brown paper bag. The bottle had already been drunk from.

"Look at these filthy curtains," said his father, seeing Robert calculating the proportion of the bottle that was already empty. "The reason why the rest of New York is breathing lovely clean air is that we've got these special pollution filters in our room sucking all the dirt out of the atmosphere. Sally said that the decoration in this place 'grows on you'—that's exactly what I'm worried about. Try not to touch any of the surfaces."

Robert, who had been excited to be staying in any hotel at all, started to look skeptically at his surroundings. A Chinese carpet in mouse's underbelly pink, with a medallioned pictogram at the center, gave way to the greasy French provincial upholstery of the sofa and armchair. Above the sofa, against the buttercup walls, an Indian tapestry of women dancing rigidly by a well, with some cows in the foreground, stood opposite a big painting of two ballerinas, one in a lemon yellow and the other in a rose-pink tutu. The bath was as cratered as the moon. The chrome had grayed on the taps and the enamel was stained. If you didn't really need a bath before getting in it, you certainly would afterward. The view from his parents' room, where Thomas was bouncing up and down on the bed shouting, "Look at me! I'm an astronaut!" gave onto a rusty air-conditioning system that throbbed a few feet beneath the ill-fitting window. From the drawing room, where he was going to sleep on the sofa bed with Thomas—or, knowing Thomas, where his father was going to sleep after Thomas had taken over his mother's bed—there was a perfect view of the Sheetrock that covered the neighboring skyscraper.

"It's like living in a quarry," said his father, splashing a couple of inches of whiskey into a glass. He strode over to the window and pulled down the gray plastic blind. The pole holding the blind crashed down onto the drawing room's air-conditioning unit with a hollow clang.

"Bloody hell," he said.

Robert's mother burst out laughing. "It's only for a few nights," she said. "Let's go out to dinner. Thomas isn't going to get back to sleep for ages. He had three hours on the plane. What about you, darling?" she asked Robert.

"I want to motor on. Can I have a Coca-Cola?"

"No," said his mother, "you're quite excited enough already."

"Apple and cinnamon flavor," muttered Robert's father as he continued to unpack the shopping. "I couldn't find any oats that taste of oats or apples that taste of apples, only oats that taste of apples. And cinnamon, of course, to blend with the tooth-paste. A less sober man might end up brushing his teeth with oats, or having a bowl of toothpaste for breakfast—without noticing. It's enough to drive you mad. If there aren't any additives, they boast about that too. I saw a packet of chamomile tea that said 'caffeine free.' Why would chamomile have any caffeine in it?" He took out the last package.

"Morning Thunder," said Robert's mother. "Isn't Thomas enough morning thunder already?"

"That's your trouble, darling, you think Thomas can substitute for everything: tea, coffee, work, social life . . ." He let the list hurtle on in silence, and then quickly buried the remark in more general commentary. "Morning Thunder is very literary, it just has added quotations." He cleared his throat and read out loud, "*Born often under another sky, placed in the middle of an always moving scene, himself driven by an irresistible torrent, which draws all about him, the American has no time to tie himself to anything, he grows accustomed only to change, and ends by regarding it as the natural state of man. He feels the need of it, more he loves it; for the instability, instead of meaning disaster to him, seems to give birth only to miracles all about him."*—Alexis de Tocqueville."

"So you see," he said, ruffling Robert's hair, "wanting to 'motor on' is in perfect keeping with the mood of this country, at least in 1840, or whatever."

Thomas clambered onto a table whose protective circle of glass was about a foot less wide than the table itself, leaving the mulberry polyester tablecloth exposed at the edges.

"Let's go out to a restaurant," said Robert's mother, lifting him gently into her arms.

Robert felt the sense of almost violent silence in the lift, made up of the things that his parents were not saying to each other, but also caused by the aroma of mental illness surrounding the knobbly headed lift operator who informed them with pride, rather than the apologies Robert felt they deserved, that the lift had been installed in 1926. Robert liked some things to be old—dinosaurs, for instance, or planets—but he liked his lifts brand new. The family's longing to escape the red velveteen cage was explosive. While the madman jerked a brass lever back and forth, the lift lurched around in the vicinity of the ground floor and finally came to rest only an inch or two below the lobby.

In the fading light, they walked over glittering pavements, steam surging from corner drains, and giant grills replacing the paving stones for feverishly long stretches. Robert refused to give in to the cowardice of avoiding them altogether, but he walked on them reluctantly, trying to make himself lighter. Gravity had never seemed so grave.

"Why do the pavements glitter?" he asked.

"God knows," said his father. "It's probably the added iron, or the crushed quotations. Or maybe they've just had the caffeine sucked right out of them."

Apart from a few yellowing newspaper articles displayed in the window, and a handwritten sign saying GOD BLESS OUR TROOPS, Venus Pizza gave no hint of the disgusting food that was being prepared indoors. The ingredients of the salads and pizzas seemed to fit in with the unreflecting expansion which Robert had been noticing since Heathrow. A list would start out reasonably enough with feta and tomato, and then roll over the border into pineapple and Swiss cheese. Smoked chicken burst in on what had seemed to be a seafood party, and "all the above" were served with french fries and onion rings.

"Everything is 'mouthwatering,'" said Robert. "What does that mean? That you need a huge glass of water to wash away the taste?"

His mother burst out laughing.

"It's more like a police report on what they found in someone's dustbin than a dish," his father complained. "The suspect was obviously a tropical-fruit freak with a hearty love of Brie and shellfish," he muttered in an American accent.

"I thought french fries were called freedom fries now," said Robert.

"It's cheaper to write 'God Bless Our Troops' than reprint a hundred menus," said his father. "Thank goodness Spain joined the coalition of the willing, otherwise we'd be saying things like, 'Mine's a Supreme Court omelette with some freedom fries on the side.' English muffins will probably survive the purge, but I wouldn't go around asking for Turkish coffee after the way they behaved. I'm sorry," Robert's father sank back into the booth, "I had such a love affair with America, I suppose I feel jilted by its current incarnation. Of course it's a vast and complex society, and I have great faith in its powers of self-correction. But where are they? What happened to rioting? Satire? Skepticism?"

"Hi!" The waitress wore a badge saying KAREN. "Have you guys made a menu selection? Oh," she sighed, looking at Thomas, "you are gorgeous."

Robert was mesmerized by the strange hollow friendliness of her manner. He wanted to set her free from the obligation to be cheerful. He could tell she really wanted to go home.

His mother smiled at her and said, "Could we have a Vesuvio without the pineapple chunks or the smoked turkey or . . ." She started laughing helplessly. "I'm sorry . . ."

"Mummy!" said Robert, starting to laugh as well.

Thomas scrunched up his eyes and rocked back and forth, not wanting to be left out. "I mean," he said, "it's incredible."

"Maybe we should approach this from the other direction," said Robert's father. "Could we have a pizza with tomato, anchovy, and black olives?"

"Like the pizzas in Les Lecques," said Robert.

"We'll see," said his father.

Karen tried to master her bewilderment at the poverty of the ingredients.

"You want mozzarella, right?"

"No thanks."

"How about a drizzle of basil oil?"

"No drizzle, thank you."

"Okay," she said, hardened by their stubbornness.

Robert slid across the Formica table and rested his head sideways on the pillow of his folded arms. He felt he had been trapped all day in an argument with his body: confined on the plane when he was ready to run around, and running around now when he should have been in bed. In the corner, a television with the sound turned down enough to be inaudible but too little to be silent, radiated diagonally into the room. Robert had never seen a baseball game before, but he had seen films in which the human spirit triumphed over adversity on a baseball field. He thought he could remember one in which some gangsters tried to make a sincere baseball star deliberately lose a game, but at the last moment, just when he was about to throw the whole thing away and the groans of disappointment from the crowd seemed to express the whole unsatisfactoriness of a world in which there was nothing left to believe in, he went into a trance and remembered when he had first hit a ball a long way, into the middle of a wheat field in the middle of America. He couldn't betray that amazing slow-motion sky-bound feeling from his childhood, and he couldn't betray his mother who always wore an apron and told him not to lie, and so he hit the ball right out of the stadium, and the gangsters looked a bit like Karen when she took the pizza order, only much angrier, but his girlfriend looked proud of him, even though the gangsters were standing on either side of her, because she was basically like his mother, with much more expensive peach-colored clothes, and the crowd went crazy because there was something to believe in again. And then there was a car chase and the gangsters, whose reflexes were not honed by a lifetime in sports and whose bad character turned into bad driving on a crucial bend, crashed their car and exploded.

In the game on television the gangsters seemed to be having much more success and the ball hardly got hit at all. Every few minutes advertisements interrupted the play and then the words WORLD SERIES in huge gold letters spun out of nowhere and glinted on the screen.

"Where's our wine?" said his father.

"Your wine," Robert's mother corrected him.

He saw his father clench his jaw and swallow a remark. When Karen arrived with the bottle of red wine, his father started drinking decisively, as if the remark he had not made was stuck in his throat. Karen gave Robert and Thomas huge glasses of ice stained with cranberry juice. Robert sipped his drink listlessly. The day had been unbearably long. Not just the pressurized biscuit-colored staleness of the flight, but the Immigration formalities as well. His father, who had joked that he was going to describe himself as an "international tourist" on the grounds that that was how President Bush pronounced "international terrorist," managed to resist the temptation. He was nevertheless taken into a side room by a black female immigration officer after having his passport stamped.

"She couldn't understand why an English lawyer was born in France," he explained in the taxi. "She clasped her head and said, 'I'm just trying to get a concept of your life, Mr. Melrose.' I told her I was trying to do the same thing and that if I ever wrote an autobiography I'd send her a copy."

"Oh," said Robert's mother, "so that's why we waited an extra half hour."

"Well, you know, when people hate officialdom, they either become craven or facetious."

"Try craven next time, it's quicker."

When the pizzas finally arrived Robert saw that they were hopeless. As thick as nappies, they hadn't been adjusted to the 90 percent reduction in ingredients. Robert scraped all the tomato and anchovy and olives into one corner and made two mouthfuls of miniature pizza. It was not at all like the delicious, thin, slightly burned pizza in Les Lecques but somehow, because he had thought it might be, he had opened a trap door into the summers he used to have and would never have again.

"What's wrong?" asked his mother.

"I just want a pizza like the ones in Les Lecques." He was assailed by injustice and despair. He really didn't want to cry.

"Oh, darling, I so understand," she said, touching his hand. "I know it seems far-fetched in this mad restaurant, but we're going to have a lovely time in America."

"Why is Bobby crying?" asked Thomas.

"He's upset."

"But I don't want him to cry," said Thomas. "I don't want him to!" he screamed, and started crying himself.

"Fucking hell," said Robert's father. "I knew we should have gone to Ramsgate."

On the way back to the hotel, Thomas fell asleep in his stroller.

"Let's cut to the chase," said Robert's father, "and not pretend we're going to sleep with each other. You take both of the boys into the bedroom and I'll take the sofa bed."

"Fine," said Robert's mother, "if that's what you want."

"There's no need to introduce exciting words like 'want.' It's what I'm realistically anticipating."

Robert fell asleep immediately, but woke up again when the red digits on the bedside clock said 2:11. His mother and Thomas were still asleep but he could hear a muffled sound from the drawing room. He found his father on the floor in front of the television.

"I put my back out unfolding that fucking sofa bed," he said, doing push-ups with his hips still pressed to the carpet.

The bottle of whiskey was on the glass table, three-quarters empty next to a ravaged sheet of Codis painkillers.

"I'm sorry about the Venus pizza," said his father. "After going there, and shopping at Carnegie Foods, and watching a few hours of this delinquent network television, I've come to the conclusion that we should probably fast during our holiday here. Factory farming doesn't stop in the slaughterhouse, it stops in our bloodstreams, after the Henry Ford food missiles have hurtled out of their cages into our open mouths and dissolved their growth hormones and their genetically modified feed into our increasingly wobbly bodies. Even when the food isn't 'fast,' the bill is instantaneous, dumping an idle eater back on the snack-crowded streets. In the end, we're on the same conveyor belt as the featherless, electrocuted chickens."

Robert found his father vaguely frightening, with his blood-shot eyes and the sweat stains on his shirt, twisting the corkscrew of his own talk. Robert knew that he wasn't being communicated with, but allowed to listen to his father practicing speeches. All this time while he had been asleep, his father had been pacing up and down a mental courtroom, prosecuting.

"I liked the park," said Robert.

"The park's nice," his father conceded, "but the rest of the country is just people in huge cars wondering what to eat next. When we hire a car you'll see that it's really a mobile dining room, with little tables all over the place and cup holders. It's a nation of hungry children with real guns. If you're not blown up by a bomb, you're blown up by a Vesuvius pizza. It's absolutely terrifying."

"Please stop," said Robert

"I'm sorry. I just feel . . ." His father suddenly seemed lost. "I just can't sleep. The park is great. The city is breathtakingly beautiful. It's just me."

"Is whiskey going to be part of the fast?"

"Unfortunately," said his father, imitating the mischievous way that Thomas liked to say that word, 'the whiskey is something *very* pure and can't reasonably be included in the war against corruption."

"Oh," said Robert.

"Or war *on* corruption, as they would say here. War on terror; war on crime; war on drugs. I suppose if you're a pacifist here you have to have a war on war, or nobody would notice."

"Daddy," Robert warned him.

"I'm sorry, I'm sorry." He grabbed the remote control. "Let's turn off this mind-shattering rubbish and read a story."

"Excellent," said Robert, jumping onto the sofa bed. He felt he was pretending to be more cheerful than he was, a little bit like Karen. Perhaps it was infectious, or something in the food supply.

14

"Oh, Patrick, why weren't we told that the lovely life we had was going to end?" said Aunt Nancy, turning the pages of the photograph album.

"Weren't you told that?" asked Patrick. "How maddening. But then again, it didn't end for the people who might have told you. Your mother just ruined it by trusting your stepfather."

"Do you know the worst thing about that—I'm going to use the word 'evil' . . ."

"Popular word these days," murmured Patrick.

". . . man?" Nancy continued, only briefly closing her eyelids to refuse admittance to Patrick's distracting remark. "He used to grope me in the back of Mummy's car while she was at home dying of cancer. He had Parkinson's by then, so he had a shaky grip, if you know what I'm saying. After Mummy died, he actually asked me to marry him. Can you believe that? I just laughed, but sometimes I think I should have accepted. He only lasted two more years, and I might have been spared the sight of the little nephew's removal men carrying my dressing table out of my bedroom, while I lay in bed, on the morning of Jean's death.

I said to the brutes in blue overalls, 'What are you doing? Those are my hairbrushes.' 'We were told to take everything,' they grunted, and then they threw me out of bed, so they could load that on the van as well."

"It might have been even more traumatic to marry someone you loathed and found physically disgusting," said Patrick.

"Oh, look," said Nancy, turning a page of the album, "here's Fairley, where we spent the beginning of the war, while Mummy was still stuck in France. It was the most divine house on Long Island. Do you know that Uncle Bill had a one-hundred-and-fifty-acre garden; I'm not talking about woods and fields, there were plenty of those as well. Nowadays people think they're God almighty if they have a ten-acre garden on Long Island. There was *the* most beautiful pink marble throne in the middle of the topiary garden where we used to play grandmother's footsteps. It used to belong to the Emperor of Byzantium . . ." she sighed. "All lost, all the beautiful things."

"The thing about things is that they just keep getting lost," said Patrick. "The emperor lost his throne before Uncle Bill lost his garden furniture."

"Well, at least Uncle Bill's children got to sell Fairley," Nancy flared up. "They didn't have it stolen."

"Listen, I'm the first to sympathize. After what Margot did, we're the most financially withered branch of the family," said Patrick. "How long were you separated from your mother?" he asked, as if to introduce a lighter note.

"Four years."

"Four years!"

"Well, we went to America two years before the war started. Mummy stayed in Europe trying to get the really good things out of France and England and Italy, and she only made it to America two years after the Germans invaded. She and Jean escaped via Portugal and when they arrived I remember that her shoe trunk had fallen overboard from the fishing boat they hired to get them across to New York. I thought that if you could get away from the Germans and only lose a trunk with nothing in it but shoes, you weren't having such a bad war."

"But how did you feel about not seeing her all that time?"

"Well, you know, I had the oddest conversation with Eleanor a couple of years before she had her stroke. She told me that when Mummy and Jean arrived at Fairley, she rowed out to the middle of the lake and refused to talk to them because she was so angry that Mummy had abandoned us for four years. I was shocked because I couldn't remember anything about it. I mean, that would have been a big deal in our young lives. But all I remember is Mummy's shoes getting lost."

"I guess everybody remembers what's important to them," said Patrick.

"She told me that she hated Mummy," said Nancy. "I mean, I didn't know that was *genetically* possible."

"Her genes probably just stood by horrified," said Patrick. "The story Eleanor always told me was that she hated your mother for sacking the two people she loved and depended on: her father and her nanny."

"I tied myself to the car when Nanny was being driven away," said Nancy competitively.

"Well, there you have it—didn't you feel a little gene-defying twinge . . ."

"No! I blamed Jean. He was the one who persuaded Mummy that we were too old to have a nanny."

"And your father?"

"Well, Mummy said that she just couldn't afford to keep him anymore. Every week he would drive her crazy with some new extravagance. In the run up to Ascot, for instance, he didn't just buy a racehorse, he bought a stable of racehorses. Do you know what I'm saying?"

"Those were the days," said Patrick. "I'd love to be in a position to be irritated by Mary buying a couple of dozen racehorses, rather than getting in a blind panic when Thomas needs a new pair of shoes."

"You're exaggerating."

"It's the only extravagance I can still afford."

The telephone rang, drawing Nancy into a study next to her library, and leaving Patrick on the soft sofa dented by the weight of the red leather album, with 1940 stamped in gold on its spine.

The image of Eleanor rowing out to the middle of the lake and refusing to talk to anyone, fused in Patrick's imagination with her present condition, bedridden and cut off from the rest of the world.

The day after she had settled into her thickly carpeted, over-heated, nursing tomb in Kensington, Patrick was rung by the director.

"Your mother would like to see you straight away. She thinks she's going to die today."

"Is there any reason to believe she's right?"

"There's no medical reason as such, but she is very insistent."

Patrick hauled himself out of his chambers and went over to see Eleanor. He found her crying from the unspeakable frustration of having something so important to say. After half an hour, she finally gave birth to, "Die today," delivered with all the stunned wonder of recent motherhood. After that, hardly a day passed without a death promise emerging from half an hour's gibbering, weeping struggle.

When Patrick complained to Kathleen, the perky Irish nurse in charge of Eleanor's floor, she clasped his forearm and hooted, "She'll probably outlive us all. Take Dr. MacDougal on the next floor. When he was seventy, he married a lady half his age—she was a lovely lady, so friendly. Well, the next year, it was quite tragic really, he got the Alzheimer's and moved in here. She was ever so devoted, came to see him every day. Anyway, if she didn't get breast cancer the following year. She was dead three years after marrying him, and he's still upstairs, *going strong.*"

After a final hoot of laughter, she left him standing alone in the airless corridor next to the locked dispensary.

What depressed him even more than the inaccuracy of Margot's predictions was the doggedness of her self-deception and her spiritual vanity. The idea that she had any special insight into the exact time of her death was typical of the daydreams which ruled her life. It was only in June, after she had fallen over and broken her hip, that she began to take a more realistic attitude about the degree of control she could have over her death.

Patrick went to visit her in the Chelsea and Westminster hospital after her fall.

Eleanor had been given morphine for breakfast, but her restlessness was unsubdued. The desperate need to get out of bed, which had produced several falls, bruising her right temple purple black, leaving her nose swollen and red, staining her right eyelid yellow, and eventually fracturing her hip, made her, even now, reach for the bar on the side of her Evans Nesbit Jubilee bed and try to pull herself up with those flabby white arms bruised by fresh puncture marks Patrick could not help envying. A few clear phrases reared up like Pacific islands from a mumbling moaning ocean of meaningless syllables.

"I have a rendezvous," she said, making a renewed surge toward the end of the bed.

"I'm sure whoever you have to meet will come here," said Patrick, "knowing that you can't move."

"Yes," she said, collapsing back on the bloodstained pillows for a moment, but lurching forward again and wailing, "I have a rendezvous."

She was not strong enough to stay up for long, and soon resumed a slow writhing motion on the bed, and the long haul through another stretch of murmurous, urgent nonsense. And then "No longer" appeared, not attached to anything else. She ran her hands down her face in exasperation, looking as if she wanted to cry but was being let down by her body in that respect as well.

At last she managed it.

"I want you to kill me," she said, gripping his hand surprisingly hard.

"I'd love to help," said Patrick, "but unfortunately it's against the law."

"No longer," shouted Eleanor.

"We're doing all we can," he said vaguely.

Looking for solace in practicality, Patrick tried to give his mother a sip of pineapple juice from the plastic glass on her bedside table. He eased his hand under the top pillow and lifted her head, tipping the juice gently toward her peeling lips. He felt himself being transformed by the tenderness of the act. He had never treated anyone so carefully except his own children. The flow of generations was reversed and he found himself holding his useless, treacherous, confused mother with exquisite anxiety. How to lift her head, how to make sure she didn't choke. He watched her roll the sip of juice around her mouth, an alarmed and disconnected look on her face, and he willed her to succeed while she tried to remind her throat how to swallow.

Poor Eleanor, poor little Eleanor, she wasn't well at all, she needed help, she needed protection. There was no obstacle, no interruption to his desire to help her. He was amazed to see his argumentative, disappointed mind overwhelmed by a physical act. He leaned over further and kissed her on the forehead.

A nurse came in and saw the glass in Patrick's hand.

"Did you give her some of the Thicken Up?" she asked.

"Some what?"

"Thicken Up," she said, tapping a tin of that name.

"I don't think my mother wants to thicken up," said Patrick. "You haven't got a tin called 'Waste Away,' have you?"

The nurse looked shocked, but Eleanor smiled.

"Aste way," she echoed.

"She had a very good breakfast this morning," the nurse persevered.

"Orce," said Eleanor.

"Forced?" Patrick suggested.

She turned her wild-eyed face toward him and said, "Yes."

"When you get back to the nursing home, you can stop eating if you want to," said Patrick. "You'll have more control over your fate."

"Yes," she whispered, smiling.

She seemed to relax for the first time. And so did Patrick. He was going to guard his mother from having more horrible life imposed on her. Here at last was a filial role he could throw himself into.

Patrick looked at Nancy's other photograph albums, over a hundred identical red leather volumes dated from 1919 to 2001, ranged in the shelves directly in front of him. The rest of the room was lined with decorative blocks of leather books and, lower down, glossy books on the art of decoration. Even the two doors, one into the hall and the other into the study where Nancy was talking on the phone, did not interrupt the library theme. Their backs were crowded with the spines of false books resting on trompe l'oeil shelves perfectly aligned with the real shelves, so that when the doors were closed the room generated an impressive claustrophobia. The blast of resentment and nostalgia coming from Nancy, undiminished since he last saw her eight years before, made Patrick all the more determined not to live in the has-been world enshrined in the wall of albums—let alone in the might-have-been realm where Nancy's imagination burned even more ferociously. There seemed little point in trying to give her a bracing lecture on the value of staying contemporary when she wouldn't even stick to the past as it was, but preferred a version cleansed of the injustice which had been done to her nearly forty years earlier. The afterglow of plutocracy was no more alluring to him than a pile of dirty dishes after a dinner party. Something had died, and its death was tied in with the tenderness he had felt for Eleanor when he helped her drink that glass of pineapple juice in hospital.

Seeing his aunt made him marvel again at how different she was from her sister. And yet their attitudes of extreme worldliness and extreme unworldliness had a common origin in a sense of maternal betrayal and financial disappointment. The blame had been reattributed to her stepfather by Nancy, while Eleanor had tried to unload the sense of betrayal onto Patrick. Unsuccessfully, he now liked to think, although after only a few hours with his aunt he felt like a recovering alcoholic who has been given a cocktail shaker for his birthday.

The tall clear windows looked onto a broad lawn sloping down to an ornamental pond and spanned by a wooden Japanese bridge. From where he sat he could see Thomas trying to hang over the side of the bridge, gently restrained by Mary, while he pointed at the exotic waterfowl rippling across the bright coin of water. Or perhaps there were Koi carp giving depth to the Japanese theme. Or some samurai armor gleaming in the mud. It was dangerous to underestimate Nancy's decorative thoroughness. Robert was writing in his diary in the little pond-side pagoda.

Several shelves of unreadable classics creaked open and Nancy strode back into the room.

"That was our rich cousin," she said, as if invigorated by contact with money.

"Which one?"

"Henry. He says you're going to his island next week."

"That's right," said Patrick. "We're just paw whi-te trash throwin' ourself on the cha-ri-tee of our American kin."

"He wanted to know if your children were well behaved. I told him they hadn't broken anything yet. "How long have they been there?" he asked.

"When I said you arrived about two hours ago, he said, "Oh, for God sake's, Nancy, what kind of a sample is that? I'm ringing back tomorrow for a full report." I guess not everybody has the world's most important collection of Meissen figurines."

"I don't suppose he will either, after Thomas has been to stay."

"Don't say that!" said Nancy. "Now you're making me nervous."

"I didn't know Henry had become so pompous. I haven't seen him in at least twenty years; it was really very hospitable of him to let us come. As a teenager he belonged to that familiar type, the complacent rebel. I suppose the rebel was defeated by the army of Meissen figurines. Who can blame him for surrendering? Imagine the gleaming hordes of porcelain milkmaids clearing the brow of the hill and flooding the bowl of the valley, and poor Henry with only a rolled-up portfolio statement to beat them off."

"You get awfully carried away by your imagination," said Nancy.

"Sorry," said Patrick. "I haven't been in court for three weeks. The speeches pile up . . ."

"Well, your ancient aunt is going to have a rest now. We're going to Walter's and Beth's for tea, and I'd better be on top form for that. Don't let the children walk on the grass barefoot, or go into the woods at all. I'm afraid this part of Connecticut is a Lyme disease hot spot, and the ticks are just dreadful this year. The gardener tries to keep the poison ivy out of the garden, but he can't control the woods. Lyme disease is just horrible. It's recurring and if it goes untreated it can destroy your life. There's a little boy who lives in the village here and he's really not at all well. He has psychotic fits and things. Beth just takes the antibiotics around the clock. She 'self-medicates.' She says it's safer to assume you're always in danger."

"Grounds for perpetual war," said Patrick. *"Tout ce qu'il y a de plus chic."*

"Well, if you want to put it that way."

"I think I do. Not necessarily to her face."

"Necessarily *not* to her face," Nancy flared up. "She's one of my oldest friends and besides, she's the most powerful of the Park Avenue women, and it's not a good idea to cross her."

"I wouldn't dream of it," said Patrick.

After Nancy had left, Patrick walked over to the drinks tray and, so as not to leave a dirty glass, drank several gulps of bourbon from a bottle of Maker's Mark. He sank back into an armchair and stared out of the window. The impenetrable New England countryside looked pretty enough, but was in fact packed with more dangers than a Cambodian swamp. Mary already had several pamphlets on Lyme disease—named after a Connecticut county only a few miles away—and so there was no need to rush out and tell the family.

"It's safer to assume you're always in danger." Some verbal tick made him want to say, "It's safer to assume you're safe unless you're in danger," but he was quickly won over by the plausibility of paranoia. In any case, he now felt in danger all the time. Danger of liver collapse, marital breakdown, terminal fear. Nobody ever died of a feeling, he would say to himself, not believing a word of it, as he sweated his way through the feeling that he was dying of fear. People died of feelings all the time, once they had gone through the formality of materializing them into bullets and bottles and tumors. Someone who was organized like him, with utterly chaotic foundations, a quite strongly developed intellect, and almost nothing in between, desperately needed to develop the middle ground. Without it, he split into a vigilant day mind, a bird of prey hovering over a landscape, and a helpless night mind, a jellyfish splattered on the deck of a ship. "The Eagle and the Jellyfish," a fable Aesop just couldn't be bothered to write. He guffawed with abrupt, slightly deranged laughter and got up to take another gulp of bourbon from the bottle. Yes, the middle ground was now occupied by a lake of alcohol. The first drink centered him for about twenty minutes and then the rest brought his night mind rushing over the landscape like the dark blade of an eclipse.

The whole thing, he knew, was a humiliating Oedipal drama. Despite the superficial revolution in his relations with Eleanor, a local victory of compassion over loathing, the underlying impact she had made on his life remained undisturbed. His fundamental sense of being was a kind of free fall, a limitless dread, a claustrophobic agoraphobia. Doubtless there was something universal about fear. His sons, despite their lavish treatment from Mary, had moments of fear, but these were temporary afflictions, whereas Patrick felt that fear was the ground he stood on, or the groundlessness he fell into, and he couldn't help connecting this conviction with his mother's absolute inability to concentrate on another human being. He had to remind himself that the defining characteristic of Eleanor's life was her incompetence. She wanted to have a child and became a lousy mother; she wanted to write children's stories and became a lousy writer; she wanted to be a philanthropist and gave all her money to a self-serving charlatan. Now she wanted to die and she couldn't do that either. She could only communicate with people who presented themselves as the portals to some bombastic generalization, like "humanity" or "salvation," something the mewling, puking Patrick must have been unable to do. One of the troubles with being an infant was the difficulty of distinguishing incompetence from malice, and this difficulty sometimes returned to him in the drunken middle of the night. It was now beginning to invade his view of Mary as well.

Mary had been a devoted mother to Robert but after the absorption of the first year she had resurfaced as a wife, if only because she wanted another child. With Thomas, perhaps because she knew that he was her last child, she seemed to be trapped in a Madonna and Child force field, preserving a precinct of purity, including her own rediscovered virginity. Patrick was in the unenviable role of Joseph in this enduring, unendurable Bethlehem. Mary had completely withdrawn her attention from him and the more he requested it the more he appeared in the light of an imposturous rival to his younger son. He had turned elsewhere, to Julia, and once that had collapsed, to the oblivious embrace of alcohol. He must stop. At his age he either had to join the resistance or become a collaborator with death. There was no room to play with self-destruction once the juvenile illusion of indestructibility had evaporated.

Oh dear, he'd made rather too much progress with the Maker's Mark. The logical thing to do was to take this bottle upstairs and pour the rest of it into the depleted bottle of bourbon hidden in his rucksack, and then nip into town to buy another one for Nancy's drinks table. He would, of course, have to make convincing inroads into the new bottle so that it resembled the old bottle before he had almost finished it. Practically anything was less complicated than being a successful alcoholic. Bombing third world countries—now, there was an occupation for a man of leisure. "It's all right for some," he muttered, weaving his way across the room. He was arguably just a teeny weeny bit too drunk for this time of day. His thoughts were cracking up, going staccato, getting over trumped just as he was about to pick up the trick.

Check: family in the garden. Check: silence in the hall. Run up the stairs, close the door, get the rucksack, decant the bourbon—all over his hand. Hide the empty on top of cupboard. Car keys. Down and out. Tell family? Yes. No. Yes. No! Get in car. Ding ding ding. Fucking American car safety ding ding. Safer to assume sudden violent death. Police no please no police, p-l-e-a-s-e. Slip away over crunchy nutritious gravel. Cruise control, out of control. Suggestible suggestions. Jump the tracks, get out of the syllable cruncher and into, into the sunlit death trap countryside. Better pave the whole thing over. Angry posses of ordinary citizens with chain saws and concrete mixers. "We've lived in fear for long enough! We've got a right to protect our families! It says in the Bible, 'The wild places shall be made tame. And the people shall have dominion over the ticks.'"

He was drifting along in his silvery blue Buick Le Sabre, screaming in a hillbilly accent. He couldn't stop. He couldn't stop anything. He couldn't stop the car, he couldn't stop drinking, he couldn't stop the Koncrete Klux Klan. A bright red STOP sign slipped by as he merged quietly with the main road into town. He parked next to the Vino Veritas liquor store. The car had somehow locked itself, just to be on the safe side. Ding ding ding. Keys still in the ignition. He arched backward trying to ease the dull pain in his lower back. Eroded vertebrae? Swollen kidneys? "We have to think our way out of the box of our habitual dichotomies," he purred, in the smug tones of a self-help tape. "It's not an *either* vertebrae *or* kidneys situation, it's a *both* kidneys *and* vertebrae situation. Think outside the box! Be creative!"

And here, straight ahead of him, across the railway tracks, down among the playing fields, was another *both and* situation. Both the exuberant sentimentality of American family life unfolding among the brightly colored tubes and slides and swings of a playground, with its soft wood-chip landing sites and, on a large area of grass beyond the chain-link fence, two pot-bellied policemen training an Alsatian to tear apart any sick fucks who thought to disturb the peace and prosperity of New Milton. One policeman held the dog by the collar, the other stood at the far end of the green with a huge padded arm guard. The Alsatian streaked across the grass, leaped onto the padded arm, and shook his head savagely from side to side, his growling just audible through the humid air, pierced by the cries of children and the sonic solicitude of safety-conscious cars. Did the children feel safer, or just feel that it was safer to assume they were always in danger? A Botero-shaped family munching soft buns at a round-cornered picnic table looked on as the first policeman hurried across the green and tried to detach the keen young Alsatian from his colleague's arm. The second policeman was by now floundering on the grass trying to persuade the dog that he was not a sick fuck but one of the good guys.

Vino Veritas had three sizes of Maker's Mark. Not sure which one he was supposed to replace, Patrick bought all three.

"Better be safe than sorry," he explained to the salesman.

"You'd better believe it," said the salesman with a fervor that catapulted Patrick back into the parking lot.

He was already in another phase of drunkenness. Sweatier, sadder, slower. He needed *both* another drink *and* a huge amount of coffee, so that he could stand up at Walter and Beth's, or indeed anywhere. He was in fact certain, he might as well admit it, that the smallest bottle of Maker's Mark was not the one he had to replace. He hadn't been able to resist buying the baby bottle to complete the family. Ding ding ding. He unpeeled the red faux wax cap and uncorked the bottle. As the bourbon slipped down his throat, he pictured a flaming beam crashing through the floors and ceilings of a building, spreading fire and wreckage. What a relief.

The Better Latte Than Never coffee shop lived up to the maddening promise of its name. Patrick sailed past the invitation to a skinny caramel grande vanilla frapuccino in a transparent plastic cup jam-packed with mouthwatering ice and strawberry-flavored whipped cream, and ordered some black coffee. He moved along the assembly line.

"Have a great one!" said Pete, a heavy-jawed blond beast in an apron, sliding the coffee across the counter.

Old enough to remember the arrival of "Have a nice day," Patrick could only look with alarm on the hyperinflation of "Have a great one." Where would this Weimar of bullying cheerfulness end? "You have a profound and meaningful day now," he simpered under his breath as he tottered across the room with his giant mug. "Have a blissful one," he snapped as he sat at a table. "You all make sure you have an all-body orgasm," he whispered in a Southern accent, "and make it last." Because you deserve it. Because you owe it to yourself. Because you're a unique and special person. In the end, there was only so much you could expect from a cup of coffee and an uneatable muffin. If only Pete had confined himself to realistic achievements. "Have a cold shower," or "Try not to crash your car."

He was back in the inflammatory, deranged drunkenness he had lost in the hot parking lot. Yes yes yes. After a few gallons of coffee there'd be no stopping him. Across the room, a voluptuous medical student in a pink cardigan and faded jeans was working on her computer. Her mobile phone was on the slate ledge of the Heat and Glow fireplace, next to the Walkman and the complicated drink. She sat on her chair with her knees raised and her legs wide open as if she had just given birth to her Hewlett Packard; *The Pathology of Disease* squashing some loose notes on the edge of the table. He must have her, on a must have basis. She was so relaxed in her body. He stared at her and she looked back at him with a calm even gaze. She smiled. It was absolutely terrifying how perfect she was. He looked away and smiled bashfully at his kneecap. He couldn't bear her being friendly. It made him want to cry. She was practically a doctor, she could probably completely save him. His sons would miss him at first, but they'd get over it. Anyway, they could come and stay. She was obviously an incredibly warm and loving person.

The Oedipal vortex had him caught like a dead leaf in its compulsory spin, wanting one consolation after another. Some languages kept the ideas of desire and privation apart, but English forced them into the naked intimacy of a single syllable: want. Wanting love to ease the want of love. The war on want which made one want more. Whiskey was no better at looking after him than his mother had been, or his wife had become, or the pink cardigan would be if he lurched across the room, fell to his knees, and begged her for mercy. Why did he want to do that? Where was the Eagle now? Why wasn't he coolly registering the feeling of attraction and reabsorbing it into a sense of his present state of mind, or beyond that, into the simple fact of being alive? Why rush naively toward the objects of his thoughts, when he could stay at their source? He closed his eyes and slumped in his chair.

So, here he was in the magnificence of the inner realm, no longer chasing after pink cardigans and amber bottles, but watching thoughts flick open like so many fans in a hot crowded room. He was no longer jumping into the painted scenes, but noticing the flicking, noticing the heat, noticing that drunkenness gave a certain predominance to images in his otherwise predominantly verbal mind, noticing that the conclusion he was looking for was not blackout and orgasm, but knowledge and insight. The trouble was that even when the object of pursuit changed, the anguish of pursuit remained. He found himself hurtling toward a vacuum rather than hurtling away from it. Big deal. In the end he was better off galloping after the syrupy mirage of a hot fuck. He opened his eyes. She was gone. Want in both directions. Directions delusions anyway. A universe of want. Infinite melancholy.

The scraping chair. Late. Family. Tea. Try not to think. Think: don't think. Madness. Ding ding ding. Cruise control, out of control. Please stop thinking. Who's asking? Who's being asked?

When he drew up to the house, The Others were arranged around Nancy's car in a tableau of reproach and irritation.

"You wouldn't believe what happened to me in New Milton," he said, wondering what he would say if anybody asked.

"We were about to leave without you," said Nancy. "Beth can't stand people being late; they just drop right off her guest list."

"A slobbering thought," said Patrick. "I mean sobering thought," he corrected himself. Neither version was heard above the sound of crunching gravel and slamming doors. He climbed into the back of Nancy's car and slumped next to Thomas, wishing he had the baby bottle of Maker's Mark to nurse him through tea. During the journey he dozed superficially until he felt the car slow down and come to a halt. When he clambered out he found himself surrounded by unpunctuated woodland. The Berkshire Hills rolled off in every direction, like a heavy swell in a green and yellow ocean, with Walter and Beth's white clapboard ark cresting the nearest wave. He felt seasick and land bound at the same time.

"Unbelievable," he muttered.

"I know," said Nancy. "They pretty much own the view."

The tea party unfolded for Patrick in an unreliable middle distance. One moment he felt as glazed over as an aquarium on television, the next he was drowning. There were maids in uniform with eyeball aching white shoes. A small Hispanic butler. Sweet brown cinnamony iced tea. Park Avenue gossip. People laughing about something Henry Kissinger had said at dinner on Thursday.

Then the garden tour began. Walter went ahead, sometimes unlocking his arm from Nancy's in order to clip an impertinent shoot with the secateurs he held in his suede gloved hand. He certainly wouldn't be doing any gardening if it hadn't been done already. He bore the same relation to the gardening as a mayor to the housing development on which he cuts the inaugural ribbon. Beth followed with Mary and the children. She was persistently modest about the garden and sometimes downright dissatisfied. When she came to a topiary deer that stood on the edge of a flowerbed, she said, "I hate it! It looks like a kangaroo. I pour vinegar on it to try to kill it off. The climate here is impossible: we're up to our waists in snow until the middle of May, and two weeks later we're living in Vietnam."

Patrick dragged behind the rest of the party, trying to pretend he was in a horticultural trance, leaning over to stare blindly at a nameless flower, hoping he looked like the shade of Andrew Marvell rather than a stale drunk who dreaded being drawn into conversation. The vast lawn turned into a box maze, a topiary zoo (from which the doomed kangaroo was excluded), and finally a lime grove.

"Look Dada! A *sanglier!*" said Thomas, pointing to a curly-haired, heavy-snouted bronze boar, with legs that looked too delicate to bear the weight of its pendulous belly and massive tusked head.

"Yes, darling," said Patrick.

Wild boar had always been French for Patrick and he was heartbroken that they were French for Thomas as well. How could he have retained that word over the whole year? Was he thinking of the wild boar at Saint Nazaire trotting across the garden to eat the fallen figs, or snuffling among the vines at night, looking for ripe grapes? No he wasn't. *Sanglier* was just a word for the animal in the statue. He had already turned his back on it and was running down the lime grove pretending to be an airplane. Patrick's heartbreak was all his own, and even that was hollow. He no longer felt a corrosive nostalgia for Saint Nazaire, its loss just clarified the real failure: that he couldn't be the sort of father he wanted to be, a man who had transcended his ancestral muddle and offered his children unhaunted love. He had made it out of what he thought of as Zone One, where a parent was doomed to make his child experience what he had hated most about his life, but he was still stuck in Zone Two, where the painstaking avoidance of Zone One blinded him to fresh mistakes. In Zone Two giving was based on what the giver lacked. Nothing was more exhausting than this deficiency-driven, overcompensating zeal. He dreamed of Zone Three. He sensed that it was there, just over the hill, like the rumor of a fertile valley. Perhaps his present chaos was the final rejection of an unsustainable way of being. He must stop drinking, not tomorrow but later this afternoon when the next opportunity arose.

Strangely excited by this glint of hope, Patrick continued to hang back. The tour drifted on. A stone Diana stood at the far end of the grove, eternally hunting the bronze boar at the other end. Behind the house, a springy chip-wood path meandered through an improved wood. Patches of light shivered on the denuded ground between the broad trunks of oaks and beeches. Beyond the wood they passed a hangar where huge fans, consuming enough electricity to run a small village, kept agapanthus warm in the winter. Next to the hangar was a henhouse somewhat larger than Patrick's London flat, and so strangely undefiled that he couldn't help wondering if these were genetically modified hens who had been crossed with cucumbers to stop them from defecating. Beth walked over the fresh sawdust, under the red heat lamps, and discovered three speckled brown eggs in the laying boxes. Every plate of scrambled eggs must cost her several thousand dollars. The truth was that he hated the very rich, especially since he was never going to be one of them. They were all too often only the shrill pea in the whistle of their possessions. Without the editorial influence of the word "afford," their desires rambled on like unstoppable bores, relentless and whimsical at the same time. They could give the appearance of generosity to all sorts of emotional meanness—"Do borrow the fourth house we never get around to using. We won't be there ourselves, but Carmen and Alfonso will look after you. No, really, it's no trouble at all, and besides, it's about time we got our money's worth out of those two. We pay them a fortune and they never do a stroke of work."

"What are you muttering about?" said Nancy, who was clearly annoyed that Patrick had underperformed as an admiring guest.

"Oh, nothing," said Patrick.

"Isn't this henhouse divine?" she prompted him.

"It would be a privilege to live here," said Patrick, catching up abruptly with his social duties.

When the garden tour ended, with a gift of eggs, the visit ended as well. On the way back to Nancy's, Patrick was confronted by his decision not to go on drinking. It was all very well to decide not to drink when he had no choice, but in a few minutes he would be able to climb into the Buick's private liquor store. What did it matter if he started stopping tomorrow? He knew that it somehow mattered completely. If he went on now he would be hungover tomorrow morning and the whole day would begin with a poisonous legacy. But more than that, he wanted to cultivate the faint hope he had felt in the garden. If he stopped tomorrow it would be from an excess of shame, a nastier and less reliable motivation. What, on the other hand, was Zone Three? His mind was occluded by tension; he couldn't reconstruct the hope.

Back in Nancy's library, he stared out of the window feeling that he was being stared at in turn by the bottle of bourbon he had replaced on the drinks tray. It would be so much neater to bring it down to the level the empty one had started at. Just as he was about to give in, Nancy came into the room and sank with a theatrical sigh into the armchair opposite him.

"I feel we haven't really talked about Eleanor," she said. "I think I'm frightened of asking because I was so shocked when I last saw her."

"You heard about the fall?"

"No!"

"She broke her hip and went into hospital. When I went to see her she started asking me to kill her. She hasn't stopped asking me since. Every time I go . . ."

"Oh, come on," said Nancy, "I really don't think that's fair! I mean, it's all too Greek. There must be some special Furies for children who kill their parents."

"Yeah," said Patrick. "Wormwood Scrubs."

"Oh, God," said Nancy, twisting in her chair. "It's so complicated. I mean, I know I wouldn't want to go on living if I couldn't speak, or move, or read, or watch a movie."

"I have no doubt that helping her to die would be the most loving thing to do."

"Well, I don't want you to misinterpret me, but maybe we should rent an ambulance and drive her to Holland."

"Arriving in Holland isn't in itself fatal," said Patrick.

"Oh, please, let's not talk about it anymore. I find it too upsetting. I really couldn't bear it if I ended up like that."

"Do you want a drink?" asked Patrick.

"Oh, no. I don't drink," said Nancy. "Didn't you know? I watched it destroy Daddy's life. But do help yourself if you want one."

Patrick imagined one of his children saying, "I watched it destroy Daddy's life." He noticed that he was leaning forward in his chair.

"I might help myself by not having one," he said, sinking back and closing his eyes.

15

Mary could hardly believe that Patrick and Robert were in one thinly carpeted motel room and she and Thomas were in another, with plastic wraps on the plastic glasses, and Sanitized For Your Protection sashes on the plastic loo seats, and a machine down the corridor whose shuddering ejaculations of ice reminded her unwillingly of the state of her marriage. She could hear the steady hum of the freeway thickening in the early morning. It was the perfect sound track to the quick, slick flow of her anxiety. At about four in the morning a phrase had started clicking like a metronome she was too tired to reach out and stop: "Interstate-inner state, interstate-inner state." Sleeplessness was the breeding ground of these sardonic harmonies; ice machine-marriage; interstate-inner state. It was enough to drive you mad. Or was it enough to stop you from going mad? Making connections. She could hardly believe that her family was hemorrhaging more money in order to have a horrible time in one of America's migratory nowheres. So much road and so few places, so much friendliness and so little intimacy, so much flavor and so little taste. She longed to get the children back home to

London, away from the thin rush of America and back to the density of their ordinary lives.

Patrick had kept up the tradition of getting them thrown out of somewhere rather lovely quite a long time before the end of the holidays; Saint Nazaire last year, Henry's island this year. Of course she was delighted that he had stopped drinking, but the effect in the first week was to make him behave like other people when they were blind drunk: explosive, irascible, despairing. All the boils were being lanced at once, the kidney dishes overflowing. Henry was certainly a nightmare, but he was also some sort of relation and, above all, a host who was providing a playground for the children, with its own harbor and beaches and sailing boats and motorboats and, to Thomas's undying amazement, its own petrol pump.

"I mean, it's unbelievable, Henry has his own petrol pump!" Thomas said several times a day, opening his palms and shaking his head. Robert was in a statistical frenzy of acres and bedrooms, totting up the immensity of Henry's domain, but both boys were mainly having a wonderful time dashing briefly into the freezing water and going out in Henry's speedboats, riding the wake behind the big ferries that served the public islands.

The only thing that went wrong was everything else. During the first lunch Henry asked Mary to remove Thomas from the dining room when his monologue on the moral necessity of increasing Israel's nuclear-strike capacity was interrupted by Thomas's impersonation of a petrol pump.

"The Syrians are filling their pants right now and they're right to be . . ." Henry was saying gleefully.

"Bvvvv," said Thomas. "Bvvvv . . ."

"I'm sure you're familiar with the phrase, 'Children should be seen and not heard,'" said Henry.

"Who isn't?" said Mary.

"I've always thought it was too liberal," said Henry, craning his neck out of his shirt to emphasize his *bon mot*.

"You'd rather not see him either?" said Mary, suddenly furi-ous. She picked Thomas up and carried him out of the room rapidly, Henry's unmolested monologue resuming its flow behind her.

"When Admiral Yamamoto had finished his attack on Pearl Harbor, he had the wisdom to be more apprehensive than tri-umphant. "Gentlemen," he said, "we have roused a sleeping Dragon." It is that thought that should be uppermost in the minds of the world's international terrorists and their state sponsors. With an arsenal of tactical nuclear weapons, not just a deterrent nuclear shield, Israel will send a clear message to the region that it stands shoulder to shoulder . . ."

She burst onto the lawn picturing Henry as one of those unknotted balloons Thomas liked to watch swirling flatulently around the room until it suddenly flopped to the ground in wrinkled exhaustion.

"I'm letting go of a balloon, Mama," said Thomas, spinning his hand in tight circles.

"How did you know I was thinking about a balloon?" said Mary.

"I did know that," said Thomas, tilting his head to one side and smiling.

These borderless moments happened often enough for Mary to get used to them, but she couldn't quite shake off her surprise at how precise they were.

By silent agreement the two of them walked away from the house to the little rocky beach at the foot of the lawn. Mary sat down on a small patch of silvery white sand among rocks fes-tooned with beaded black seaweed.

"Will you look after me for a long time?" asked Thomas.

"Yes, darling."

"Until I'm fourteen?"

"As long as you want me to," she said. "As long as I can . . . ," she added. He had asked her the other day if she was going to die and she had said, "Yes, but not for a long time, I hope." His discovery of her mortality blew away the dust which had dimmed the menace of it in her own mind and made it glare at her again with all its root horror restored. She loathed death for making her let him down. Why couldn't he play a little longer? Why couldn't he feel safe a little longer? She had recovered her balance to some extent, attributing his interest in death to the transition from infancy to childhood, but also wondering if Patrick's impatience with that transition was making it happen sooner than necessary. Robert had been through the same sort of crisis when he was five; Thomas was only three.

Thomas sat down on her lap and sucked his thumb, fingering the smooth label of his raggie with the other hand. He was minutes away from sleep. Mary sat back on her heels and made herself calm. She could do things for Thomas that she couldn't do for herself or anyone else, not even Robert. Thomas needed her for his protection, that was obvious enough, but she needed him for her sense of virtue. When she felt gloomy he made her want to be cheerful, when she was drained he made her find new wells of energy, when she was exasperated she searched for a deeper patience. She sat there as still as the rocks around her and waited while he dropped off.

However hot the day became, the sea here was a refrigerator throwing off a skeptical little breeze. She liked the feeling that Maine was basically inhospitable, that it would soon shake out its summer visitors, like a dog on a beach. In the chink between two winters the Northern light sparkled hungrily on the sea. She imagined it stretched out like a gaunt El Greco saint. The thought made her want to paint again. She wanted to make love again. She wanted to think again, if she was going to start making lists, but somehow she had lost her independence. Her being was fused with Thomas's. She was like someone whose clothes had been stolen while she was having a swim, and now she didn't know how to get out of this tiring beautiful pool.

After Thomas had been asleep for five minutes she was able to move to a more comfortable position. She sat against the bank at the bottom of the lawn and placed him lengthwise between her legs, as if he was still being born, still the wrong way round. She formed a canopy with his raggie to protect him from the sun, and leaned back and closed her eyes and tried to rest, but her thoughts looped back tightly enough onto Kettle's remote style of mothering and the part it played in producing her own fanatical availability. She thought of her nanny, her kind, dedicated nanny, solving one little problem after the next, inhabiting a nursery world without sex or art or intoxicants or conversation, just practical kindness and food. Of course looking after a child made her feel like the nanny who had looked after her when she was a child. And of course it made her determined to be unlike Kettle who had failed to look after her. Personality seemed to her at once absurd and compulsive: she remained trapped inside it even when she could see through it. Her thoughts on mothers and mothering twisted around, following the thread of a knot they couldn't untie.

For some reason sitting by this black sea with its slightly chill breeze made her feel she could see everything very clearly. Thomas was asleep and nobody else knew exactly where she was. For the first time in months nobody knew how to make any demands on her and in that sudden absence of pressure she could appreciate the family's tropical atmosphere of unresolved dependency; Eleanor like a sick child pleading with Patrick to "make it stop"; Thomas like a referee pushing his parents apart if Patrick ever tried to get close to her indifferent body; Robert keeping his diary, keeping his distance. She was at the eye of the storm, with her need to be needed making her appear more self-sufficient than she really was. In reality she couldn't survive on the glory of satisfying other people's unreasonable demands. Her passion for self-sacrifice sometimes made her feel like a prisoner who meekly digs the trench for her own execution.

Patrick needed a revolution against the tyranny of dependency, but she needed one against the tyranny of self-sacrifice. Although she was overstretched and monopolized, an appeal to her best instincts only drove her farther into the trap. The protests which might be expected to come from Robert's sibling rivalry came instead from the relatively unstable Patrick. It was bad luck that she had become disgusted by the slightest sign of need in Patrick at a time when he had Thomas as well as Eleanor to stimulate his own sense of helplessness. Patrick accused her of overindulging Thomas, but if Thomas was ready to do without certain maternal comforts, Patrick must be even readier. Perhaps he was no longer ripe but rotten. Perhaps a psychic gangrene had set in and it was the smell of corruption that revolted her.

That evening she excused herself from dinner and stayed with Thomas, leaving Patrick and Robert to face the roused dragon of Henry's table talk on their own. Even before dinner, as she sat on the faded-pink cushions of the window seat, the panes of the bay window around her bleeding and glittering in the sea-reflected evening light, with the children behaving beautifully and Patrick smiling over a glass of mineral water, she knew she couldn't stand more than a few minutes of Henry's address to the nation. He was on a whirlwind tour of foreign policy, heading east from Israel, through the Stans and the formers, and on his way to the people's republics. She had a dreadful feeling that he intended to get to North Korea before bedtime. No doubt he had a cunning plan to nuke North Korea before it nuked South Korea and Japan. She didn't want to hear it.

After his bath, Thomas wanted to climb into her bed and she didn't have the heart to refuse him. They snuggled up together reading *Wind in the Willows*. Thomas fell asleep as Rat and Mole started to drift down the river after their picnic. When Patrick came into the room she realized that she had also dropped off with the book on her lap and her reading glasses still on.

"I so nearly had a fight with Henry," said Patrick, striding into the room with his clenched fists still looking for a destination.

"Oh dear, what was it this evening?" she asked.

Patrick was always saying that their erotic, conversational, and social lives were over, that they were just parental bureaucrats. Well, here she was, shattered and abruptly woken, but ready for a lively conversation.

"North Korea."

"I knew it."

"You always know everything. No wonder you felt you could miss dinner."

Everything she said was wrong. No matter what she did, Patrick felt abandoned. She tried again.

"I mean, I just had a feeling before dinner that North Korea would be next."

"That's what Henry thinks: North Korea is next. You should form a coalition."

"Did you argue with him, or are you going to have to argue with me instead?"

"We relied heavily on the democratic miracle of agreeing to disagree. Henry hates free speech but, partly as a result of that, he isn't free to say so. He banged on about how lucky we were not to live in a country where you could be shot for holding the wrong opinions."

"He wants to shoot you."

"Exactly."

"Great. That'll make our holiday more fun."

"More fun? Don't you have to be having fun in the first place to have more fun?"

"I think the children are having fun."

"Oh, well, that's all that matters," said Patrick with rigid piety. "I did hint to Henry," he continued, pacing up and down at the end of the bed, "that I felt the present administration's foreign policy was made up of projection. That America is the rogue state with a fundamentalist president, and several thousand times the weapons of mass destruction of all other nations combined; et cetera, et cetera."

"How did that go down?" Mary wanted to keep him going, keep the aggression political.

"Incredulous laughter. A lot of neck craning. False smiles. Reminded me of 'a certain event which played no small part in our lives over here.' I said that 9/11 was one of the most shocking things in history, but that its exploitation, what I'd like to call 9/12, was just as shocking in its own way. The tracer bullet was the use of the word 'war' on the following day. War is an activity between nation states. A word the British government spent thirty years carefully avoiding in its struggle with the IRA. Why give the standing of a nation state to a few hundred homicidal maniacs, unless you're going to use them as the pretext to make war with some real nation states? Henry said, "I think that's a distinction that would be lost on Joe Six-Pack. We had a war to sell to the American public.' That was the trouble with our conversation—my accusations are his assumptions, selling war to the American public, testing new weapons, stimulating the military-industrial complex, using public money to demolish a country which the cabinet's pet corporations benefit from rebuilding, and so forth. He loves it all, so he can't be caught making hollow apologies."

"How was Robert?"

"An excellent junior counsel," said Patrick. "He made the no proven links point and played pretty skillfully with the idea of 'innocent lives.' He asked Henry whether innocence was exclusively American. Again, the trouble is that for Henry the answer is really 'Yes,' so it's hard to get him on the run. He didn't bother to pretend much, except about free speech."

"How did he answer Robert?"

"Oh, he just said that he could see that I'd 'trained' him. He obviously thought we were the tag team from hell. The thing that ruffled him was my last bombing mission in which I said that a really 'developed' nation, as opposed to a merely powerful one, might bother to imagine the impact of two percent of the world's population consuming fifty percent of its resources, of the rapid extinction of every species of non-American culture, and so forth. I got a little bit carried away and also said that the death of Nature was a high price to pay for adding the few last curlicues of convenience to the lives of the very rich."

"It's amazing he didn't throw us out," said Mary.

"Don't worry, I'll try again tomorrow. I'll get him in the end. I can see now what upsets him. Politics is an exciting game, but money is sacred."

She could tell that Patrick was serious. His sense of tension was so extreme that he had to destroy something, and this time it wasn't going to be himself.

"Do you mind not getting us thrown out for a couple of days? I've only just finished unpacking." She tried to sound breezy.

"And you're comfortably installed with your lover as usual," said Patrick.

"God, for a man who claims not to suffer from jealousy . . ."

"I don't suffer from jealousy, I suffer from rage. It's more fundamental. Loss produces anger first, possessiveness afterward."

"Before the rage, there's anxiety," said Mary, feeling she knew what she was talking about. "Anyway, I think you move through all three, even if one is usually dominant. It's not like shopping, you can't just opt for rage."

"You'd be surprised."

"I know you prefer anger because you think it's less humiliating."

"I don't prefer anger," shouted Patrick, "but I get it anyway."

"I mean prefer it to the neighboring emotions."

Thomas, disturbed by Patrick's shouting, shifted in the bed and muttered to himself inaudibly.

"You're straying from the point," said Patrick, more quietly. "As usual we can't sleep together because you're in bed with our three-year-old son."

"We can sleep together," sighed Mary, "I'll move him over to the side."

"I want to make love to a woman, not a sighing heap of guilt and resignation," hissed Patrick, in an ineffective whisper.

Thomas sat up blearily.

"No, Dada, you stop talking nonsense!" he shouted. "And Mama, stop upsetting Dada!"

He collapsed back on the pillow and fell asleep again, his work done. A silence fell over the room, which Patrick was the first to interrupt.

"I wasn't talking nonsense . . . ," he began.

"Oh, for God's sake," said Mary. "You don't have to win an argument with him as well. Can't you hear what he's saying? He wants us to stop arguing, not for you to start arguing with him."

"Sure," said Patrick in his suddenly bored way. "I'll go to his bed, although I don't know why I call it 'his' bed. I might as well stop pretending and call it mine."

"You don't have to . . ."

"No—I do have to," said Patrick, and ducked out of the room.

He had abandoned her abruptly, but failed to transfer his sense of abandonment to her. She felt relieved, angry, guilty, mournful. The cloudscape of her emotional life was so rolling and rapid that she couldn't help marveling at, sometimes envying, people who were "out of touch with their feelings." How did they do it? Right now she wouldn't mind knowing.

Her bedroom had a terrace built above the bay window of the drawing room where she had been sitting before dinner. She walked up to the French windows and imagined herself throwing them open, contemplating the stars, having an epiphany.

It wasn't going to happen. Her body had started its landslide toward sleep. She took one last glance out of the window and wished she hadn't. A thin streak of cloud was crossing the moon in a way that reminded her of the elision in *Un Chien Andalou*, between the same image and a razor blade slicing open an eyeball. Her vision was the end of vision. Was she blinded by something she couldn't see, or blinded by seeing something she couldn't bear to look at? She was too tired to work anything out. Her thoughts were just threats, sleep just the rubble of wakefulness.

She got into bed and was covered by a thin layer of broken rest. Soon afterward, she was disturbed by hearing Patrick slink back into the room. She could feel him staring at her to see if she was awake. She gave nothing away. He eventually settled on the other side of Thomas, who lay in the middle like the sword placed between the unmarried in a medieval bed. Why couldn't she reach out to Patrick? Why couldn't she make a nest of pillows for Thomas on one side of the bed and stay with Patrick on the other? She had no charity left for Patrick. In fact, for the first time in her marriage she could picture herself and the children living alone in the flat while Patrick was off somewhere, anywhere, being miserable.

The next day she was shocked by her coldness, but she soon got used to it. She had always known it was there, the alternative to the warmth which struck everyone as so typical. Now she took it up like a hermit moving into a cave. She resisted Patrick's rashes of nervous charm without effort. It was too tiring to move back and forth to the jumpy rhythm of his moods. She might as well stay where she was. He was going to ruin their holiday, but first he wanted to make her agree that fighting with Henry was a sign of his splendid integrity rather than his uncontrollable irritation. She refused. By that evening it was clear that Patrick's agreement to disagree with Henry was in peril.

"It's going to be tough to make conversation if you don't stop attacking everything I say," said plain-speaking Henry. "Let's stick to talking family."

"That proven formula for goodwill and unity," said Patrick with one of his short barking laughs.

"You're as bad as Yasser Arafat," said Henry. "You think peace and defeat are the same thing. I'm just trying to extend some hospitality here. You don't have to accept it, if you've got an ideological problem with that." Henry chuckled at the word "ideological," which for him was as inherently comic as the word "bottom" to an exuberant four-year-old.

"That's right," said Patrick, "we don't."

"But we'd like to," said Mary quickly.

"Speak for yourself," said Patrick.

"I am," she said, "and unlike you I'm also trying to speak for the children."

"Are you? Only this morning Thomas was saying that Henry is 'a very funny man' and, as you know, Robert's nickname for him is 'Hitler.' I doubt you're even speaking for yourself after you were thrown out of lunch yesterday."

That had been that. They left the next morning. She expected Patrick to be stubborn and proud and destructive, but she hadn't yet forgiven him for including the children in his final explosive charge.

The ice machine in the motel corridor produced another juddering emission of cubes on the other side of their thin hotel room wall. The interstate's mosquito whine had given way to a hornet drone. Thomas stirred beside her and then, with his usual prompt transition to full desire, he sat up and said, "I want you to read me a story." She obediently picked up the copy of *The Wind in the Willows*, which they had started reading in Maine.

"Do you remember where we were?" asked Mary.

"Ratty was saying to Molie that he was a plain pig," said Thomas, rounding his eyes in amazement. "But, actually, he's a rat."

"That's right," laughed Mary. Rat and Mole were on their way back to River Bank in the gathering darkness of a December afternoon. Mole had just smelled the traces of his old home and was overwhelmed by longing and nostalgia. Rat had pressed on to River Bank, his own home, assuming Mole would want to go there as well. Then Mole broke down and told Rat about his homesickness. Mary reread the sentence they had finished with the night before.

"The Rat stared straight in front of him, saying nothing, only patting Mole gently on the shoulder. After a time he muttered gloomily, 'I see it all now! What a pig I've been! A pig—that's me! Just a pig—a plain pig!'"

"I mean . . . ," Thomas began.

There was a knock on the door. Mary put the book down and asked who it was.

"Bobby!" said Thomas. "I knew it was you because—well, because it is you!"

Robert sat down on the bed with his shoulders slumped, ignoring his brother's reasoning.

"I hate this place," he said.

"I know," said Mary, "but we'll move on this morning."

"Again," groaned Robert. "We've been to three motels since The Prosecuting Attorney got us thrown off that brilliant island. We might as well get a mobile home."

"I'm going to ring Sally after breakfast and ask her if we could go to Long Island a few days earlier than planned."

"I don't want to go to Long Island, I want to go home," said Robert.

"Molie smells his home and he wants it," said Thomas, leaning forward to support his brother's case.

They agreed that if they couldn't go straight to Long Island, they would tell Patrick they wanted to go back to England.

"No more magic of the open road," said Robert. "Please."

When she rang Sally there was no answer in Long Island. Eventually she found her in New York.

"We had to come back to the city because our water tank burst and flooded the apartment downstairs. Our neighbors are suing us, so we're suing the plumbers, who only put the tank in last year. The plumbers are suing the tank company for defective design. And the residents are suing the building, even though they're all on vacation, because the water was cut off for two days instead of two hours, which caused them a lot of mental stress in Tuscany and Nantucket."

"Gosh," said Mary. "What's wrong with mopping up and getting a new water tank?"

"That is *so* English," said Sally, delighted by Mary's quaint stoicism.

Mary explained at breakfast that there wasn't really room in the New York apartment, but Sally said they were welcome to all squeeze in somehow.

"I don't want to squeeze in," said Robert, "I want to fly out."

"We're on an airplane now," said Thomas, thrusting his arms out like wings, "and Alabala is in the cockpit!"

"Uh-oh," said Robert, "we'd better catch the next flight."

"He's on the next flight as well," said Thomas, as surprised as anyone by Alabala's resourcefulness.

"How did he manage that?" said Robert.

Thomas glanced sideways for a moment to look for the explanation.

"He used his ejector seat," he said, making an ejector-seat noise, "and then Felan stopped the next plane and Alabala got on!"

"There's the little matter of our unrefundable tickets," said Patrick.

"We could have bought new ones with the money we've spent in these disgusting motels," said Robert.

"You've taught him to argue too well," said Mary.

"There's no one to argue with, is there?" said Patrick. "I think we're all sick of America by now."

16

After her fall, Eleanor's ceaseless pleas for death had forced Patrick to look into the legalities of euthanasia and assisted suicide. Once again, as with his own disinheritance, he became the legal servant of his mother's repulsive demands. Superficially, there was something more attractive about getting rid of Eleanor than there had been about losing Saint Nazaire, but then the obscenity of what he was being asked to do would break through the stockade of practicalities with Jacobean vigor. Even if a nursing home was not the usual setting for a revenger's tragedy, he felt the perils of usurping God's monopoly on vengeance just as keenly as he would have in the catacombs of an Italian castle. He tried to pull himself together, to examine his motives scrupulously. The dead were not dogged enough to make ghosts without the guilt of the living. His mother was like a rock fall blocking a mountain pass. Perhaps he could clear her out of the way, but if his intentions were murderous, her ghost would haunt the pass forever.

He decided to have nothing to do with organizing her death. Asking him to help her die was the last and nastiest trick of a woman who had always insisted, from the moment he was born, that she was the one who needed cheering up. And then he would visit Eleanor again and see that the cruelest thing he could do was to leave her exactly where she was. He tried to remain angry so he could forbid himself to help, but compassion tortured him as well. The compassion was far harder to bear and he came to think of his vengefulness as a relatively frivolous state of mind.

"Go on, do yourself a favor, get homicidal," he muttered to himself as he dialed the number of the Voluntary Euthanasia Society.

Before going to America, he kept his research secret. He didn't tell Mary because they never discussed anything important without having a row. He didn't tell Julia because his affair with her was in the final stages of its decay. In any case, secrecy was essential in a country where helping someone to die could be punished with fourteen years imprisonment. He read articles in the papers about nurses sent to jail for generous injections. The Voluntary Euthanasia Society, despite its promising name, was unable to help. It was a campaigning organization trying to change the legislation. Patrick could remember reading about Arthur Koestler and his wife using the plastic bags provided by Exit to asphyxiate themselves in their house in Montpelier Square. The lady who answered the phone at the Voluntary Euthanasia Society had no knowledge of an organization called Exit. She couldn't even comment on most of his questions, because her advice might be construed as suicide "counseling," an offense under the same statute that punished assisting and aiding. She hadn't heard of an organization called Dignitas either and couldn't tell him how to get in touch with it. The Everlasting was not the only one to have "fixed his canon against self-slaughter," Patrick couldn't help thinking as the fruitless conversation dragged to a close. Directory inquiries, careless of the legal consequences, gave him the number of Dignitas a few minutes later.

He rang Switzerland, his pulse racing. The calm voice which answered the phone in German turned out to speak English as well, and promised to send some information. When Patrick pressed him on the legal points, he said that it was not a matter of euthanasia, administered by the doctor, but of assisted suicide administered by the patient. The barbiturate would be prescribed if a Swiss doctor was convinced that it was warranted and that the suicide was entirely voluntary. If Patrick wanted to make progress while he waited for the membership forms to arrive, he should get a letter of consent from Eleanor and a doctor's report on her condition. Patrick pointed out that his mother could no longer write and he doubted that she could give herself an injection either.

"Can she sign?"

"Just."

"Can she swallow?"

"Just."

"So, maybe we can help."

Patrick felt a surge of excitement after his telephone call to Switzerland. Signing and swallowing, those were the keys to the kingdom, the code for the missile launch. There wasn't much time before Eleanor lost them. He dreaded the precious barbiturate dribbling uselessly down her shining chin. As to her signature, it now formed an alpine silhouette reminiscent of Thomas's earliest stabs at writing. Patrick paced up and down the drawing room of his flat. He was "working at home," and had waited for Robert to go to school and for Mary to take Thomas to Holland Park before carrying on with his secret research. Now the whole flat was his to bounce around; there was nobody to be efficient for, nobody to be friendly to. Just as well, since he couldn't stop pacing, couldn't stop repeating, "Sign and swallow, sign and swallow," like a chained parrot in the corner of an overstuffed room. He felt increasingly tense, having to pause and breathe out slowly, to expel the feeling that he was about to faint. There was a sinister, knife-grinding quality to his excitement. He was going to give Eleanor exactly what she wanted. But should he be wanting it quite so much as well?

He recognized the signature of his murderous longings and felt duly troubled. What seemed new, but then admitted that it had been there all along, was his own desire for a glass of barbiturate. "To cease upon the midnight with no pain"—rearranged a little, it might almost be the chemical name for that final drink: Sismidnopin.

"Oh, my God! You've got a bottle of Sismidnopin! Can I have some?" he suddenly squealed as he reached the end of the corridor and spun around to pace back again. His thoughts were all over the place, or rather they were in one place dragging everything toward them. He imagined a modest little protest march, starting out in Hampstead with a few ethical types trying to ban unnecessary suffering, and then swelling rapidly as it flowed down to Swiss Cottage, until soon every shop was closed and every restaurant empty and all the trains stood still and the petrol pumps were unattended, and the whole population of London was flowing toward Whitehall and Trafalgar Square and Parliament Square, cursing unnecessary suffering and screaming for Sismidnopin.

"Why should a dog, a cat have death," he wailed front stage, "and she . . ." He forced himself to stop. "Oh, shut up," he said, collapsing on a sofa.

"I'm just trying to help my old mum," he cajoled himself in a new voice. "She's a bit past her sell-by date, to be honest. Not enjoying life as much as she used to. Can't even watch the old goggle box. Eyes gone. No use reading to her, just gets her agitated. Every little thing frightens her, even her own happy memories. Terrible situation really."

Who was talking? Who was he talking to? He felt taken over.

He breathed out slowly. He was feeling way too tense. He was going to give himself a heart attack, finishing off the wrong person by mistake. He could see that he was breaking into fragments because the simplicity of his situation—son asked to kill mother—was unbearable; and the simplicity of her situation—person dreads every second of her existence—was more unbearable still. He tried to stay with it, to think about what didn't bear thinking about: Eleanor's experience. He felt her writhing on the bed, begging for death. He suddenly burst into tears, all his evasions exhausted.

The rivalry between revenge and compassion ended during that morning in his flat, and he was left with a more straightforward longing for everyone in his family to be free, including his mother. He decided to press ahead with getting a medical report before his trip to America. There was little point in applying to the nursing home's doctor, whose entire mission was to keep patients alive despite their craving for a lethal injection. Dr. Fenelon was Patrick's family doctor, but he had not taken care of Eleanor before. He was a sympathetic and intelligent man whose Catholicism had not yet stood in the way of useful prescriptions and rapid specialist appointments. Patrick was used to thinking of him as grown up and was bewildered to hear him speak of his ethics classes at Ampleforth, as if he had allowed a priest to spray his teenage sketch of the world with an Infallible fixative.

"I still believe that suicide is a sin," said Dr. Fenelon, "but I no longer believe that people who want to commit suicide are being tempted by the Devil, because we now know that they're suffering from a disease called depression."

"Listen," said Patrick, trying to recover as unobtrusively as possible from finding the Devil on the guest list, "when you can't move, can't speak, can't read, and know that you're losing control of your mind, depression is not a disease, it's the only reasonable response. It's cheerfulness that would require a glandular dysfunction, or a supernatural force to explain it."

"When people are depressed, we give them antidepressants," Dr. Fenelon persevered.

"She's already on them. It's true that they gave a certain enthusiasm to her loathing of life. It was only after she started taking them that she asked me to kill her."

"It can be a great privilege to work with the dying," Dr. Fenelon began.

"I don't think she's going to start working with the dying," Patrick interrupted. "She can't even stand up. If you mean that it's a great privilege for you, I have to say that I'm more concerned about her quality of life than yours."

"I mean," said the doctor, with more equanimity than Patrick's sarcasm might have deserved, "that suffering can have a transfiguring effect. One sees people, after an enormous struggle, breaking through to a kind of peacefulness they've never known before."

"There has to be some sense of self to experience the peacefulness—that's precisely what my mother is losing."

Dr. Fenelon sat back in his buttoned leather chair with a sympathetic nod, exposing the crucifix he kept on the shelf behind him. Patrick had often noticed it before, but it now seemed to be mocking him with its brilliant inversion of glory and suffering, making the thing it was natural to be disgusted by into the central meaning of life, not just the mundane meaning of forcing a person to reflect more deeply, but the entirely mysterious meaning of the world being redeemed from sin because Jesus got on the wrong side of the law two thousand years ago. What did it mean that the world had been redeemed from sin? It obviously didn't mean that there was any less sin. And how was Christ's nasty, kinky execution supposed to be responsible for this redemption, which, as far as Patrick could tell, hadn't taken place? Until then he had only been dazzled by the irrelevance of Christianity in his own life, but now he found himself loathing it for threatening to cheat Eleanor of a punctual death. After some more schoolboy reminiscences, Dr. Fenelon agreed to compile a report on Eleanor's condition. What use was made of it was none of his affair, he assured himself, and made an appointment to meet Patrick at the nursing home two days later.

Patrick went to tell his mother the good news and prepare her for the doctor's visit.

"I want . . ." she howled, and then half an hour later, "Swiss . . . land."

Patrick braced himself for his impatience with his mother's impatience.

"Everything is going as fast as possible," he answered smoothly.

"You . . . ook . . . like . . . my . . . son," Eleanor managed eventually.

"There's a simple explanation for that," said Patrick. "I am your son."

"No!" said Eleanor, sure of her ground at last.

Patrick left with the even more pressing sense that Eleanor would soon be too senile to consent.

When he took Dr. Fenelon into Eleanor's fetid room the next day, she was in a state of hysterical cheerfulness that Patrick had never seen before but immediately understood. She thought that she had to be on best behavior, to win the doctor over, to show him that she was a good girl who deserved a favor. She stared at him adoringly. He was her liberator, her angel of death. Dr. Fenelon asked Patrick to stay, to help him understand Eleanor's incoherent speech. He was impressed by the good quality of her reflexes, the absence of bedsores and the general condition of her skin. Patrick looked away from the white wrinkled expanse of her belly, feeling that he really shouldn't be allowed to see so much of his mother, and certainly didn't want to. He was driven mad by her eagerness. Why couldn't she manifest the misery he had spent the last week laboring to put into words? She never tired of letting him down. He imagined the unbearably upbeat report that Dr. Fenelon would be dictating on his return to the surgery. That evening he composed a letter of consent but he couldn't face seeing his mother again straight away. In any case, Fenelon's report wouldn't arrive before the family left on their American holiday and so Patrick resolved to let the whole thing drop until his return.

In America he tried not to think about a situation he could make no progress with, but he knew that the secret of his macabre project was alienating him from the rest of his family. After sobering up, he clung to his somewhat drunken vision of "Zone Three" in Walter and Beth's garden. Whenever he tried to define Zone Three, he could only think of it as a generosity that was not based on compensation or duty. Even though he could not quite describe it, he clung to this fragile intuition of what it might mean to be well.

It was only on the plane back to England that he finally told Mary what was going on. Thomas was asleep and Robert was watching a movie. At first Mary said nothing beyond sympathizing with the trouble Patrick had been through. She didn't know whether to voice her suspicion that Patrick had been so busy examining his own motives that he might not have looked carefully enough at Eleanor's. Wanting to die was one of the most commonplace things about life, but dying was something else. Eleanor's demands for help were not an offer to clear herself out of the way, but the only way she had left to keep herself at the center of her family's attention. And did she really understand that she would have to do the killing herself? Mary felt sure that Eleanor was imagining an infinitely wise doctor with a gaze as deep as a mountain lake, leaning over to give her a fatal goodnight kiss, not a tumbler of bitter barbiturates she had to hoist to her own lips. Eleanor was the most childish person Mary knew, including Thomas.

"She won't do it," she finally said to Patrick. "She won't swallow. You'll have to get some special air ambulance, and take her to see the Swiss doctors, and get the prescription, and then she won't do it."

"If she makes me take her to Switzerland for nothing, I'll kill her," said Patrick.

"I'm sure that would suit her perfectly," said Mary. "She wants death taken out of her hands, not put into them."

"Whatever," said Patrick with an impatient sigh. "But I have to treat her as if she really meant the only thing she ever manages to say."

"I'm sure she's sincere about wanting to die," said Mary. "I'm just not sure she's up to it."

From within the hub of his headphones, Robert sensed that his parents were having a heated conversation. He took off his headset and asked them what they were talking about.

"Just about Granny—how we can help her," said Mary.

Robert put his headphones back on. As far as he was concerned Eleanor was just someone who was not yet dead. His parents no longer took him or Thomas to see her because they said it was too disturbing. It was an effort for him to remember, ages ago, being close to her, and it wasn't an effort that seemed worth making. Sometimes, in the presence of his other grandmother, his indifference to Eleanor was taken by surprise, and in contrast to the tight little knot of Kettle's selfishness, he would remember Eleanor's softness and the great aching bruise of her good intentions. Then he would forget how unfair it was that Eleanor had cheated them of Saint Nazaire and feel how unfair it was for Eleanor being Eleanor—not just her dire circumstances, but being who she was. In the end it was unfair on everyone being who they were because they couldn't be anyone else. It wasn't even that he wanted to be anybody else, it was just a horrible thought that he couldn't be, in an emergency. He took off his headphones again, as if they were the thing that was limiting him. The comedy about the talking dog who became president of the United States wasn't that good anyway. Robert switched channels to the map. It showed their plane hovering near the Irish coast, south of Cork. Then it expanded to show London and Paris and the Bay of Biscay. The next scale included Casablanca and Djibouti and Warsaw. How long was this informational feast going to go on? Where were they in relation to the moon? The only thing anybody wanted to know finally came up: fifty-two minutes to arrival. They were flying through seven fat hours, pumped full of darkening time zones. Speed; height; temperature; local time in New York; local time in London. They told you everything, except the local time on the plane. Watches just couldn't keep up with those warped, enriched minutes. They ought to flip their dials around and say NOW until they could get back on the ground and start counting distinctly again.

He longed to get back on the ground as well, back home to London. Losing Saint Nazaire had made London into his total home. He had heard about children who pretended they had been adopted and that their real parents were much more glamorous than the dreary people they lived with. He had done something similar with Saint Nazaire, pretending it was his real home. After the shock of losing it, he had gradually relaxed into the knowledge that he really belonged among the sodden billboards and giant plane trees of his native city. Compared to the density of New York, London's backward glance at the countryside and the rambling privacy of its streets seemed to be the opposite of what a city was for, and yet he longed to get back to the greasy black mud of the parks, the rained-out playgrounds and paddocks of dead leaves, the glance at his scratchy school uniform in the hall mirror, the clunk of the car door on the way to school. Nothing seemed more exotic than the depth of those feelings.

A stewardess told Mary she must wake Thomas for the landing. Thomas woke up and Mary gave him a bottle of milk. Halfway through, he unplugged the bottle and said, "Alabala is in the cockpit!" His eyes rounded as he looked up at his brother, "He's going to land the plane!"

"Oh-oh," said Robert, "we're in trouble."

"The captain says, "No, Alabala, you are *not* allowed to land the plane," said Thomas thumping his thigh, "but Felan is allowed to land the plane."

"Is Felan in there, too?"

"Yes he is. He's the co-pilot."

"Really? And who's the pilot?"

"Scott Tracy."

"So this is an International Rescue plane?"

"Yes. We have to rescue a pentatenton."

"What's a pentatenton?"

"Well, it's a hedgehog actually, and it's fallen in the river!"

"In the Thames?"

"Yes! And it doesn't know how to swim, so Gordon Tracy has to rescue it with Thunderbird 4."

Thomas thrust out his hand and moved the submarine through the muddy waters of the Thames.

Robert hummed the theme tune from *Thunderbirds*, drumming on the armrest between them.

"Perhaps you could get her to sign the letter of consent," said Patrick.

"Okay," said Mary.

"At least we can assemble all the elements . . ."

"What elements?" asked Robert.

"Never mind," said Mary. "Look, we're about to land," she said, trying to infuse the glinting fields, congested roads, and small crowds of reddish houses with an excitement they were unlikely to generate on their own.

On the day of their arrival, the Dignitas membership form and Dr. Fenelon's report emerged from the heap of letters in the hall. Sprawled exhausted on the black sofa Patrick read through the Dignitas brochures.

"All the people in the cases they quote have agonizing terminal diseases or can only move one eyelid," he commented. "I'm
worried she may just not be ill enough."

"Let's get everything together and see what they think about
her case," said Mary.

Patrick gave her the letter of consent he had written before
leaving for America and she set off with it to the nursing home.
In the upper corridor the cleaners had wedged open the doors to
air the rooms. Through the doorway Eleanor looked quite calm,
until she detected another presence entering the room and stared
with a kind of furious blankness in the direction of the new-
comer. When Mary announced who she was, Eleanor grabbed
the side rail of her barred bed and tried to heave herself up,
making desperate mumbling sounds. Mary felt that she had
interrupted Eleanor's communion with some other realm in
which things were not quite as bad as they were on planet Earth.
She suddenly felt that both ends of life were absolutely terrifying, with a quite frightening stretch in between. No wonder people did what they could to escape.

There was no point in asking Eleanor how she was, no point
in trying to make conversation, and so Mary plunged in with a
summary of what had been going on with the rest of them.
Eleanor seemed horrified to be placed within the coordinates of
her family. Mary quickly moved on to the purpose of her visit,
suggesting that she read the letter out loud.

"If you feel it's what you want to say, you can sign it," she
said.

Eleanor nodded.

Mary got up and closed the door, glancing down the corridor to check that there were no nurses on their way. She pulled
her chair close to Eleanor's bed and placed her chin over the
handrail, holding the letter on Eleanor's side of the bars. She
began to read with surprising nervousness.

I have had several strokes over the last few years, each one leaving me more shattered than the last. I can hardly move and I can hardly speak. I am bedridden and incontinent. I feel uninterrupted anguish and terror and frustration at my own immobility and uselessness. There is no prospect of improvement, only of drifting into dementia, the thing I dread most. I can already feel my faculties betraying me. I do not look on death with fear but with longing. There is no other liberation from the daily torture of my existence. Please help me if you can.

Yours sincerely,

"Do you think that's fair?" asked Mary, trying not to cry.

"No . . . es," said Eleanor with great difficulty.

"I mean a fair description."

"Es."

They gripped each other's hands for a while, saying nothing. Eleanor looked at her with a kind of dry-eyed hunger.

"Do you want to sign it?"

"Sign," said Eleanor, swallowing hard.

When Mary broke out into the streets, along with her sense of physical relief at getting away from the smell of urine and boiled cabbage, and the waiting room atmosphere in which death was the delayed train, she felt grateful that there had been a moment of communication with Eleanor. In that gripped hand she had felt not just an appeal but a determination that made her wonder if she was right to doubt Eleanor's preparedness to commit suicide. And yet there was something fundamentally lost about Eleanor, a sense that she had neither engaged in the mundane realm of family and friendship and politics and property, nor had she engaged with the realm of contemplation and spiritual fulfillment; she had simply sacrificed one to the other. If she belonged to the tribe who always heard the siren call of the choice they were about to lose, she was bound to feel an absolute need to stay alive once suicide had been perfectly organized for her. Salvation would always be elsewhere. Suddenly it would be more spiritual to stay alive—to learn patience, remain in the refining fires of suffering, whatever. More dreadful life would be imposed on her and it would inevitably seem more spiritual to die—to be reunited with the source, stop being a burden, meet Jesus at the end of a tunnel, whatever. The spiritual, because she had never committed herself to it any more effectively than to the rest of life, was subject to endless metamorphosis without losing its theoretical centrality.

When Mary got home, Thomas ran out into the hall to greet her. He wrapped his arms around her thigh with some difficulty, due to the Hoberman sphere, a multicolored collapsible dodecahedron frame, which he had allowed to close around his neck and wore as a spiky helmet. His hands were clad in a pair of socks and he was holding a battery-operated propeller fan of fairy lights acquired on a visit to the Chinese State Circus on Blackheath.

"We're on Earth, aren't we, Mama?"

"Most of us," said Mary, thinking of the look she had glimpsed on Eleanor's face through the open door of her room.

"Yes, I did know that," said Thomas wisely. "Except astronauts who are in outer space. And they just float about because there's no gravity!"

"Did she sign?" said Patrick, appearing in the doorway.

"Yes," said Mary, handing him the letter.

Patrick sent the letter and membership form and doctor's report to Switzerland and waited for a couple of days before ringing to find out if his mother's application was likely to be successful.

"In this case I think we will be able to help," was the answer he received. He stubbornly refused to get involved with his emotions, letting panic and elation and solemnity lean on the doorbell while he only glanced at them from behind closed curtains, pretending not to be at home. He was helped by the storm of practical demands which enveloped the family during the next week. Mary told Eleanor the news and was answered with a radiant smile. Patrick arranged a flight for the following Thursday. The nursing home was told that Eleanor was moving, without being told where. A consultation was booked with a doctor in Zurich.

"We could all go on Wednesday to say goodbye," said Patrick.

"Not Thomas," said Mary. "It's been too long since he's seen her and the last time he made it very clear that he was upset. Robert can still remember her when she was well."

None of Mary's close friends could look after Thomas on Wednesday afternoon and she was finally forced to ask her mother.

"Of course, I'll do anything I can to help," said Kettle, feeling that if ever there was a time to make all the right noises, it was now. "Why don't you drop him off at lunchtime? Amparo can make him some lovely fish fingers and you can all come to tea after you've said goodbye to poor old Eleanor."

When Wednesday came around Mary brought Thomas to the door of her mother's flat.

"Your mother is not here," said Amparo.

"Oh," said Mary, surprised and at the same time wondering why she was surprised.

"She go out to buy the cakes for tea."

"But she'll be back soon . . ."

"She has lunch with a friend and then she come back, but don't you worry, I look after the little boy."

Amparo reached out her child-greedy, ingratiating hands. Thomas had only met her once before and Mary handed him over with some reluctance but above all with a sense of terminal boredom. Never again, she would never ask her mother to help again. The decision seemed as irrevocable and overdue as a slab of cliff falling into the sea. She smiled at Amparo and handed over Thomas, not reassuring him too much in case it made him think there was something troubling about his situation.

The thing to do is the thing to do, thought Thomas, heading toward the disconnected bell beside the fireplace in the drawing room. He liked to stand on the small chair and press the bell and then let in whoever came to the fireplace door. By the time Amparo had said goodbye to Mary and caught up with him, he was welcoming a visitor.

"It's Badger!" he said.

"Who is this Badger?" said Amparo with precautionary alarm.

"Mr. Badger is not in the habit of smoking cigarettes," said Thomas, "because they make him grow bigger and smaller. So he smokes cigars!"

"Oh, no, my darling, you must not smoke," said Amparo. "It's very bad for you."

Thomas climbed onto the small chair and pressed the bell again.

"Listen," he said, "there's somebody at the door."

He leaped down and ran around the table. "I'm running to open the door," he explained, coming back to the fireplace.

"Be careful," said Amparo.

"It's Lady Penelope," said Thomas. "You be Lady Penelope!"

"Would you like to help me with the hoovering?" asked Amparo.

"Yes, m'lady," said Thomas in his Parker voice. "You'll find a thermos of hot chocolate in your hatbox." He howled with pleasure and flung himself on the cushions of the sofa.

"Oh, my God, I just tidy this," wailed Amparo.

"Build me a house," said Thomas, pulling the cushions onto the floor. "Build me a house!" he shouted when she started to put them back. He lowered his head and frowned severely. "Look, Amparo, this is my grumpy face."

Amparo caved in to his desire for a house and Thomas crawled into the space between two cushions and underneath the roof of a third.

"Unfortunately," he remarked once he had settled into position, "Beatrix Potter died a long time ago."

"Oh, I'm sorry, darling," said Amparo.

Thomas hoped that his parents would live for a very long time. He wanted them to be immortalized. That was a word he had learned in his *Childrens' Book of Greek Myths*. Ariadne was immortalized when she was turned into a star by Dionysus. Immortalized meant that she lived forever—except that she was a star. He didn't want his parents to turn into stars. What would be the point of that? Just twinkling away.

"Just twinkling away," he said skeptically.

"Oh, my God, you come with Amparo to the bathroom."

He couldn't understand why Amparo stood him by the loo and tried to pull his trousers down.

"I don't want to do peepee," he said flatly and started to walk away. The truth was that Amparo was quite difficult to have a conversation with. She didn't seem to understand anything. He decided to go on an expedition. She trailed behind him, wittering on.

"No, Amparo," he said, turning on her, "leave me alone!"

"I can't leave you, darling. You have to have an adult with you."

"No! I!" said Thomas, "You are frustrating me!"

Amparo bent double with laughter. "Oh, my God," she said. "You know so many words."

"I have to talk, otherwise my mouth gets clogged up with bits and pieces of words," said Thomas.

"How old are you now, darling?"

"I'm three," said Thomas. "How old did you think I was?"

"I thought you were at least five, you're such a grown-up boy."

"Hum," said Thomas.

He saw that there was no prospect of shaking her off and so he decided to treat her the way his parents treated him when they wanted to bring him under control.

"Shall I tell you an Alabala story?" he said.

They were back in the drawing room. He sat Amparo down on an armchair and climbed into his cushion cave.

"Once upon a time," he began, "Alabala was in California and he was driving along with his Mummy and there was an earthquake!"

"I hope this story has a happy ending," said Amparo.

"No!" said Thomas. "You don't interrupt me!" He sighed and began again. "And the ground opened up and California fell into the sea, which was not very convenient, as you can imagine. And there was a huge tidal wave, and Alabala said to his Mummy, "We can surf to Australia!" And so they did, and Alabala was allowed to drive the car." He searched the ceiling for inspiration and then added with all the naturalness of suddenly remembering. "When they arrived on the beach in Australia, Alan Razor was there giving a concert!"

"Who is Alan Razor?" asked Amparo, completely lost.

"He's a composer," said Thomas. "He has helicopters and violins and trumpets and drills, and Alabala played in the concert."

"What did he play?"

"Well, he played a hoover, actually."

When Kettle returned from her lunch, she found Amparo clutching her sides, thinking she was helpless with laughter at the thought of a hoover being played at a concert, but in fact hysterical at having her idea of what children should be like disrupted by being with Thomas.

"Oh, dear," she panted, "he's really an amazing little boy."

While the two women struggled not to look after him, Thomas was at last able to have some time to himself. He decided that he never wanted to be an adult. He didn't like the look of adults. Anyway, if he became an adult what would happen to his parents? They would become old, like Eleanor and Kettle.

The intercom buzzed and Thomas leaped to his feet.

"I'll answer it!" he said.

"It's too high up," said Kettle.

"But I want to!"

Kettle ignored him and pressed the intercom to let the others into the building. Thomas screamed in the background.

"What was that screaming about?" asked Mary when she arrived in the flat.

"Granny wouldn't let me press the button," said Thomas.

"It's not a child's toy," said Kettle.

"No, but he's a child playing," said Mary. "Why not let him play with the intercom?"

Kettle thought of rising above her daughter's argumentative style, but decided against it.

"I can't do anything right," she said, "so we might as well assume I'm wrong—then there won't be any need to point it out. I've only just come in, so I'm afraid tea isn't ready. I rushed home from a lunch that I couldn't get out of."

"Yes," laughed Mary. "We saw you gazing through the shop windows when we were trying to park the car. Don't worry, I won't ask you to help with the children again."

"I'll make the tea, if you like," said Amparo, offering Kettle the opportunity to stay with her family.

"It's all right," snapped Kettle. "I'm still capable of making a pot of tea."

"Am I being childish?" said Thomas, approaching his father.

"No," said Patrick. "You're being a child. Only grown-ups can be childish, and my God, we take advantage of the fact."

"I see," said Thomas, nodding wisely.

Robert was slumped in an armchair, feeling despondent. He'd had enough of both his grandmothers to last him a lifetime.

Kettle tottered back in, laying the tray down with a groan of relief.

"So, how was your mother?" she asked Patrick.

"She only spoke two words," he answered.

"Did they make any sense?"

"Perfect sense: 'Do nothing.'"

"You mean she doesn't want to . . . to go to Switzerland?" asked Kettle, emphasizing a code she knew the children were excluded from.

"That's right," said Patrick.

"That's a bit of a muddle," said Kettle.

Mary felt the effort she was putting into avoiding her favorite word: "disappointment."

"It's something we're all entitled to feel ambivalent about," said Patrick. "Mary saw it all along. I suppose she was less invested in the results, or just clearer. Anyhow, I intend to take this last instruction very seriously indeed. I will do nothing."

"Do nothing!?" said Thomas. "I mean, how do you do nothing? Because if you *do* nothing, you do something!"

Patrick burst out laughing. He picked up Thomas and put him on his knee and kissed the top of his head.

"I shan't be visiting her again," said Patrick. "Not out of spite, but out of gratitude. She's made us a gift and it would be ungracious not to accept it."

"A gift?" said Kettle. "Aren't you reading rather too much into those two words?"

"What else is there to do but read too much into things?" said Patrick breezily. "What a poor, thin, dull world we'd live in if we didn't. Besides, is it possible? There's always more meaning than we can lay our hands on."

Kettle was transfixed by several kinds of indignation at once, but Thomas filled the silence by jumping off his father's knee and shouting, "Do nothing! Do nothing!" as he circled the table laden with cakes and tea.